In a Moment

CAROLINE
FINNERTY

POOLBEG

Published 2013
by Poolbeg Press Ltd
123 Grange Hill, Baldoyle
Dublin 13, Ireland
E-mail: poolbeg@poolbeg.com
www.poolbeg.com

© Caroline Finnerty 2012

Copyright for typesetting, layout, design, ebook
© Poolbeg Press Ltd

1

A catalogue record for this book is available from the British Library.

ISBN 978-1-84223-530-0

Typeset by Patricia Hope in Sabon
Printed by CPI Group (UK) Ltd

www.poolbeg.com

About the author

Caroline Finnerty lives in County Kildare with her husband Simon, daughter Lila, twins Tom and Bea, and their two dogs. *In a Moment* is her first novel.

Acknowledgements

Firstly a huge thank you to Paula Campbell in Poolbeg for the phone call that made my dreams come true. Paula, I will say it again – I don't know how you do it! I am delighted to come on board with you and all the team.

Also thank you to Gaye Shortland for your amazing eye, your encouraging words and also your enthusiasm for the characters, which means a lot to me. I look forward to working together on future books.

To Simon, thank you for taking the children off at weekends to give me time to write. I can't think of anyone else I would rather share this life with. I love our little family. xx

Thank you to Mam and Dad – everyone should have parents like you. Thank you for everything throughout the years and all that you still do for me now. I couldn't even begin to mention how much I appreciate this. Mam – this book would not have happened without your unwavering belief in me and your constant encouragement. Dad – thank you for instilling a love of books from a young age.

To Dee Finnerty for your help on all kinds of things, from being a spare pair of hands for the twins, to your knowledge of all things photography-related and of weird computer glitches.

For my parents-in-law Mary and Neil for all that you do for us, from child-minding to dinner-making, but above all for your support.

To the staff on St Peter's Ward in Our Lady's Children's Hospital, Crumlin for taking such good care of my babies.

Thanks also to Elaine and Darren for the play-dates when you already have your hands full.

To Daisy Cummins for your advice.

To my wonderful friends for the chats, fun and laughter.

And, of course, thank you, reader, for choosing this book from all the great titles that are out there. I really do appreciate it. I hope you enjoy reading it and I would love to hear from you on my website www.carolinefinnerty.ie or on www.facebook.com/carolinefinnertywriter.

With much love, Caroline xxx

For Simon, Lila, Tom & Bea,
my beautiful family
xxxx

Prologue

She felt her knees buckle beneath her and she reached out to grab onto the post of the staircase. She used it to guide herself downwards so that she was sitting on the bottom step. Just as she thought she might be starting to heal, taking tentative steps forward, this had come and knocked her off balance again. She wasn't expecting it – it was like a below-the-belt punch coming at her, leaving her reeling in its wake. She needed to see his face, as if somehow by looking at him it would confirm that he had been a real person. She ran upstairs and into her bedroom. Pulling out the drawer of her bedside table, she reached for his photo.

Part I

1

Winter, 2010

The lift doors separated and Adam White stepped out into the bright reception of Parker & Associates. As he walked across the high-glaze cream travertine tiles he was almost overpowered by the scent emanating from the two extravagant conical vases standing on either side of the reception desk. They were brimming with fresh metre-high arrangements of snapdragons, burnt-orange birds of paradise and fuchsia-toned orchids. The area was minimally furnished with only a simple Scandinavian-style bench, which was more for show than functionality.

Parker & Associates was a young firm of business analysts located just off the Grand Canal on the south side of Dublin City. Their ultra-modern headquarters took over the entire top floor of the building and consisted of floor-to-ceiling glazed offices surrounding a central roof garden. Depending on which end of the office you went to, the view extended all the way up to Howth Head on the north side of the city or down to Killiney Hill on the south side.

By the time Adam had grabbed himself a coffee, sat at his desk and switched on his PC, his rising in the small hours of the morning seemed like eons ago. He rubbed his eyes for the umpteenth time. He felt fuzzy with tiredness, he found it hard even to think straight, his reactions were slow and his whole body felt heavy as if he was lugging two huge suitcases on either side of him whenever he walked. As he tried to concentrate on a spreadsheet on the screen in front of him, the rows seemed to merge together.

Although it was eight thirty, it was very early by Parker's standards and the office was still largely empty. On any given day the majority of people wouldn't arrive in until nine at the earliest but normally on Friday people didn't show their faces until much later after the ritual of Thursday-night drinks. Fridays were a write-off as far as work was concerned; it was generally accepted that you did only the bare minimum to get by and then spent Monday to Thursday making up for it. The company prided itself on its 'relaxed and casual' culture. The open-plan office was decorated with leafy, tropical foliage and beanbags were interspersed randomly to help soften the corporate feel. Croissants and pastries were delivered fresh from the local bakery every morning and there were always baskets scattered arbitrarily around the place, brimming with sweets and chocolate. Employees were also welcome to help themselves to the fully stocked fridge which was laden with ice-cream and soft drinks. It was lamented by all who worked there that once you joined Parker & Associates, there was no avoiding gaining the 'Parker-stone'.

A while later Adam's colleagues started arriving in. He greeted them and watched as one by one they dropped their bags at their desks before heading straight to the staff room for a pecan-nut pie, the only pastry deemed suitable for the hangover of Fridays.

* * *

Emma made her way with slow footsteps down the grey vinyled corridor. As she walked, she couldn't help but think what a contagious shade of grey it was; it wasn't the soft dove-grey of a cashmere sweater or the inky grey of a storm cloud before it burst – it was that awful shade of grey that sucked the life out of you just from merely looking at it. As she rounded the corner, she could hear the high-pitched screeches coming from behind the canteen door. Well, 'canteen' was probably stretching it – it was a room barely six metres square. The floor was covered with worn lino and it was sparsely furnished with a Formica table, six red shiny plastic-backed chairs, a cork noticeboard and a dire fridge where, no matter how many group emails were sent warning users to discard their foods after their best-before date, no one ever seemed to lay claim to the mouldy ham.

You could almost tell the day of the week it was by the roars that filtered out into the corridor. Fridays were full of raucous laughter; Mondays were a more sombre, almost silent affair.

Emma pushed open the door and glanced around at the usual posse of girls sitting at the table scattered with takeaway sandwich-wrappers and foil crisp-bags. The roars from two seconds earlier disappeared almost like someone had twisted a volume-switch on the whole room. Nothing new there, she thought to herself. She was used to having this effect on people recently. The stench from some rice-and-ham dish that Dan from IT was reheating in the microwave almost made her gag.

"Hiya, Emma. Busy?" Helen the receptionist chimed, in an overly cheery voice.

"Y'know yourself, kept going."

Helen nodded. "Tell me about it."

What would you know about being busy unless it's trying to stick your gel nail back on and answer the phone at the same time?

"That won't keep you going!" Helen nodded to the teabag that Emma was taking out of the jar above the microwave.

"I'm not hungry just now, I'll grab something later."

Emma knew her tone sounded defensive, but she felt self-conscious in front of the group about her lack of lunch – but she just couldn't stomach anything right now. She turned away from Helen and her cronies and as soon as the kettle had boiled she busied herself by pouring boiling water onto her teabag.

Helen turned back around to her gang and proceeded to moan about how her bridesmaid had put on weight since the last dress fitting and that now she would have to get the dress altered for her. Her audience tutted in sympathy and agreed that her friend had some cheek to gain a few pounds. One of them even added that if she were a real friend she would *at least* offer to do the cabbage-soup diet to fit back into the dress. Emma wasn't included in the conversation, nor did she want to be.

Emma worked on the creative team for A1 Adverts but A1 Adverts was not your typical glamorous advertising agency residing in beautiful glazed offices with a sea view and bountiful budgets. Rather A1 specialised in bright and zingy 'can't get it out of your head' type adverts for their clients. A1's specialty was the discount market; they didn't do the high-end adverts that won awards. How she would love to work on campaigns such as those! A1's customers were discount furniture stores, tile shops, budget airlines and basically anyone in the business of discount retailing in Ireland. All their adverts were the same: flashing bubble-text on a neon-coloured background and always backed with shouty voices. In fairness to A1 Adverts, it was a model that worked; they were cheaper than their competitors and they were tailored to that end of the market. But it was a long, long way from the glossy editorials with their subtle imaging that she had spent so much time analysing in college. Emma was a 'campaign developer' – in other words, she had to come up with new ideas for their clients' adverts.

She went back, sat at her desk and sighed wearily as she

scrolled down to the next red-flagged email from her overflowing inbox. No matter how hard she tried, she never seemed to be able to get on top of the work that was piling up around her. At the moment she was working on a pitch for a company called Sofa World which had asked Dublin's top advertising agencies to come up with a tag line for their Christmas campaign. Oh, she was a long way from Chanel adverts starring Keira Knightley! It was very late for launching a Christmas campaign. A1 suspected Sofa World had rejected other advertisers' efforts before turning to them at the last minute.

Moments later, Emma's boss Maureen Hanley popped her head around the screen of her cubicle. Her frizzy hair was tied back with a scrunchy in a manner that made Emma wonder if the woman even possessed a hairbrush.

"Hi, Emma – can you come in for a chat in five?"

Emma felt herself redden as if Maureen could read her mind about what she had just been thinking. "Sure."

"Don't worry, it's nothing major," Maureen added, obviously noticing Emma's red face.

Emma hated her high colouring; it always betrayed her innermost feelings. At the drop of a hat her cheeks would go red for almost any reason: embarrassment, frustration, alcohol, spicy food, and God forbid she should try to tell a lie. Emma just had to accept it was part and parcel of the raw deal of having fair skin.

She watched as Maureen walked back to her office in her black pencil-leg trousers that didn't quite meet her court shoes and revealed her white cotton socks. On top she wore a brown tweed blazer buttoned entirely up to the top so that it was puckered across her large bust; she'd had that blazer ever since Emma had started working there seven years ago and Emma imagined she had probably had it at least seven years before that. Maureen was a harmless enough sort of woman – well, as much as a boss can be harmless. She had never married; she'd been too busy sacrificing her life for A1 Adverts. The woman lived and breathed A1, so Emma suspected that the only reason she wanted a meeting was probably because she wanted her to jump up and down about the chance to pitch to Sofa World. But Emma would not be doing any jumping.

Five minutes later Emma grabbed her A4 refill pad so she could scribble down any ideas that would be thrown at her and walked back down the life-sucking, grey-vinyled corridor towards Maureen's office. She knocked on her door and let herself in. Maureen looked up from her computer, almost in confusion.

Don't tell me she doesn't remember asking me to come in five minutes ago?

"Oh yes, of course, Emma – come in and sit down." She let out a heavy sigh as she set about clearing bundles of paper and mugs with coffee stains running down the sides off the messy desk in front of her.

Emma did as she was told and sat opposite her.

Emma cut to the chase. "Did you see the email from Sofa World?"

"What?" Maureen was distracted. "Oh yes, I saw that. You might draft something up and send it on and we can sit down then and have a look, yes?"

Emma was taken aback. What did Maureen want her for if not that?

"Well, Emma . . ." Maureen paused.

Well, Maureen. Emma felt she should say something but Maureen's tone told her it wasn't her place to speak.

"Well . . . God, Emma I'm not sure how to broach this . . ." She breathed in deeply through her nostrils, so that they flared slightly. "Well, it's just I've noticed you've been putting in a lot of hours here lately. Some of the times on your emails have me worried – eleven p.m., midnight – there was even one at two a.m. last week! Now don't get me wrong, I'm all too happy for people to show their commitment to A1 Adverts but well . . ." She hesitated. "Just with everything going on, I'm a bit worried about you, that's all." She was starting to get flustered. "What I'm trying to say is – and I'm not doing a very good job of it – I know you're a good worker, I've never had a problem with your work. I just want you to make sure you're looking after yourself? That's all."

Emma was stunned; she wasn't used to such public displays of concern from Maureen. She instantly felt the heat creep into her cheeks. *I don't want to talk about this.*

"I'm okay, Maureen," she said coolly so that Maureen would know it wasn't a discussion she wished to get into.

"Well, that's good then," Maureen added nervously. "It's just, you're not long back and well . . . well, I think you should ease yourself in a bit, that's all."

Emma shifted in her seat and the discomfort between the two was palpable.

"Okay, so you'll send me on your proposal for Sofa World then?" Maureen said in an obvious decision to change the subject.

"I'll have something for you by Monday afternoon," Emma replied curtly.

"Great, so."

"Right, if that's all?"

Maureen gestured to the door, indicating Emma was free to go. Emma stood up to leave. She wanted to get the hell out of there. She wasn't a person who liked discussing her feelings at the best of times, least of all with her boss.

She went back and sat at her desk and the more she thought about the conversation she'd just had, the more she felt rage building inside her. Why were people so nosy, always trying to push it with her to see if they could be the one to make her crack and fall apart into a mess? It was nobody's business what time she worked until. If she was skiving off, they'd be on her back – she couldn't win! She was used to Helen and the rest of them pushing her buttons, trying their best to see if they could be the one to elicit a reaction. But Maureen? She had expected more from her boss. They had always had a perfectly healthy standoffish relationship, so what the hell was Maureen doing trying to change the playing field?

Jesus, what had got into the woman? Surely she was too old for the menopause?

2

Come three o'clock and as the hangovers began to ease, Parker's entire workforce were already planning where they would head later on that night and at five to five they began to pack up to leave.

Adam was just heading for the lift when Ronan from Accounts joined him.

"Are you coming for one?"

"Nah, I should probably be heading home." Adam was hesitant. Not that it would make any difference, he thought bitterly to himself. She barely spoke to him anyway.

"C'mon for one!"

"I'd better not – maybe next time, yeah?"

"Are you sure?"

"Yeah."

"No worries."

They took the lift down.

"See you Monday, so," said Ronan.

"Have a good one!"

Ronan joined some of the others and Adam stood watching as

they walked over to McCormack's bar, carefree and untroubled. How he wished he could join them – he would rather be going anywhere else but home.

He took his bike from the shelter and headed for Rathmines. He pedalled slowly and allowed the cool evening air to fill his lungs, feeling his chest rise in fullness before falling again. He felt his thigh muscles work hard as he pedalled up the steep incline before turning left over Harold's Cross Bridge. His cycle to and from work was the only time of day he had with his thoughts to himself. It was his time when he got to think about everything that had happened and try and make sense of it all. It was still so fresh. He only had to look at himself to see angry reminders criss-crossing his skin. Usually when he cycled he racked his head trying to remember the exact sequence of events but his brain would only allow him to go so far.

When he reached their house, he pushed open the wrought-iron gate and wheeled his bike up the path. He could see the lights were all off downstairs. He fumbled with his keys in the lock for a few moments before he was finally able to get into his house. Today's post sat waiting for him on the mat inside the door. He stooped to pick it up. The envelopes told him it was nothing more interesting than bills, junk mail and a bank statement. He placed them unopened on the hall table. He shouted out to see if Emma was home but no voice answered his call. He hardly knew why he did that as he knew she wouldn't answer anyway. He went into the kitchen and took a cool beer out of the fridge. He pulled off the metal top and gulped it back.

* * *

Emma's head hadn't been up to much for the rest of the day. She'd tried her best to think of some winning tag lines for the Sofa World campaign but she didn't have much luck.

The office began to empty out after four with everyone

heading off to various parts of the country for the weekend and by seven she was alone in the open-plan office. She preferred it that way; she could concentrate better without the constant drone of voices. She tried putting some words onto her notepad but nothing was coming. Eventually, after nine, she admitted defeat and knew that stupid tag lines for springy sofas would be swimming around in her head all weekend long.

In keeping with their low-cost strategy, A1's offices were located on Rosses Street, in a dingy part of Dublin City, which was long overdue rejuvenation. It was a notorious area for muggers, so she made her way hurriedly down towards the quays. She watched as hordes of teenagers, hen and stag parties, already bladdered, made their way towards the city's current hot-spots, gearing themselves up for a heavy night of drinking.

She didn't want to go home just yet so she decided to keep walking and headed down towards Dawson Street. The narrow paths were crowded with gangs of smokers standing outside so she turned onto a cobble-locked side-street where crowds were sitting along the outdoor terraces under café-bar awnings, protected from the cold evening air by patio heaters. By immersing herself amongst these people, she didn't feel so alone.

She wandered aimlessly for a while until she felt her stomach growl and she suddenly realised she was hungry. After skipping lunch, she had forgotten to eat anything for the rest of the day. She looked at her watch and it was nearly eleven o'clock so she hailed a taxi and headed home to Rathmines. She climbed into the back, stated her destination and sank into the leatherette upholstery. She sat listening to the constant buzzing and conversation over and back on the radio between the base station and the different drivers. The driver made half-hearted chit-chat with her – well, he talked and she made occasional sounds of agreement, which seemed to be enough for him to keep rambling on. By the time they turned onto Rathmines Road, she could feel her stomach begin twisting into its familiar knot and, as the car pulled up outside her home, Emma felt her heart lurch. She took her time to locate her money in her wallet before paying him and slamming the door shut.

At least the lights were off.

With trepidation and slow steps she walked up the driveway to her home. No matter how hard she tried and how successfully she carried it off at work, once she was on her own doorstep, she couldn't push the reality of her life out of her head any more.

3

Emma put on her heavy wool coat over her work suit and gloves and wrapped her thick-knit scarf twice around her neck. The day was cool and crisp and as she left the office block and walked briskly towards St Stephen's Green she watched her breath turn white on the air in front of her. Although it was lunchtime, the weak sunlight still hadn't managed to melt the morning's frost. She made her way to the bench where she had arranged to meet Zoe.

Zoe and Emma had been friends since they had met at Irish dancing classes at the age of eight. The two of them would be thrown into class every Saturday morning and Emma (who had zero co-ordination and could never keep up with all the steps) and Zoe (who was too busy being the class clown to learn how to do a reel) became firm friends. They were the weakest link of their class so were usually left to their own devices, playing together at the back of the hall.

They had attended the same primary school but were in different classes so would only get to meet at break-times in the school-yard. It wasn't until secondary school that they managed to persuade their teachers to put them into the same class and it was then that their friendship flourished. Where Emma was a serious soul, Zoe was a messer. Anne Fitzpatrick had lit many holy candles and said many novenas over the years in worry about Zoe's influence on her daughter, but still Emma would get yet another letter home for talking or for sniggering at a note that Zoe had passed to her in class.

Emma used to have a great circle of friends. They had all met in secondary school, gravitating towards each other because they were neither the popular girls nor the geeks. They had managed to stay close even when they all had gone to universities and colleges scattered all over the country. Throughout their twenties they would meet for dinner once a week and have a great natter over a few bottles of wine about what they were up to in their lives: about who had just got a promotion, who was getting married, who was being tormented by having to watch their ex getting loved up by his new girlfriend. They would spend hours chatting until they were the last ones left in the restaurant. But that had all gone by the wayside now and one by one the visits had become less frequent until they had petered out altogether. She knew it was probably the deadly combination of looking at a broken woman – when they looked at her she was a reminder of how cruel life could be – that and the fact she was hardly 'Exuberant Emma' these days. The last few months had been the litmus test for most of her friendships and in the end it was only her best friend Zoe still left flying the flag solo for the former group of schoolfriends.

A few minutes later, a panting Zoe wearing a cream baker-boy cap on top of her sleek black bob came running up.

"Sorry I'm late – I got called into a design meeting. Fucking directors wondering how thin we can make the fabric before the dress becomes completely see-through! Bloody tight-arses!"

"No worries. I've only just arrived myself."

Zoe had studied fashion design in college and now worked in the rag-trade for a company that ripped off catwalk designs and sold them on to low-cost retailers. It was a job that allowed her a limited amount of creativity but not nearly the amount that a person like her needed. It was constantly drilled into her that she needed to be more commercially astute; she needed to be aware of fabric costs and whether she could substitute a particular fabric for a cheaper one instead. Did she really need to use six buttons down the front of a cardigan or would they get away with five? She hated having to be so cost-conscious and she would argue that the cardigan would "look shit" with five buttons but, inevitably, her bosses would win out.

"So how're you doing today?" Zoe asked, her face showing her concern.

"Same as all the other days."

"Stupid question, isn't it?"

Emma smiled. "I know, but what else can you say?"

"True."

"So how was the date with 'The Accountant'?" Emma asked, changing the subject. It was great just to switch off and get a break from her thoughts and get caught up in Zoe's world instead.

"Disastrous. The man is potentially deranged."

"Why?"

"What kind of man bores a girl to tears about the size of his diversified stock portfolio? The only question he asked about me was whether I was worried about my pension provision! Do I look like the kind of girl losing sleep over a pension? *Then* he nearly lost his life when I ordered a cocktail! He checked the menu to see the price and then he kept on exclaiming 'Nine euro, *nine euro* for one of them!' He tried to talk me out of it by saying that they wouldn't use full measures and that maybe I should just get a vodka and Coke!"

Emma had to laugh.

"Oh, it gets worse, Emma – when the bill arrived he totted up who had eaten what and made me pay the extra because I had ordered the bloody cocktail!"

"He did not!" Emma said in horror.

"Oh yes! You see what I have to deal with? This is what is left on the Dublin dating scene!"

Zoe had spent her twenties, and now her early thirties too, plunging from one disastrous relationship to the next. She had stories that made Emma, who had been in a relationship for almost her entire twenties, wince with wide-eyed disbelief at the dating game. The Accountant had been a blind date set up for Zoe by her cousin but, as she said, she had to wonder which was the blind one – herself or her cousin?

Emma's theory was that Zoe's inability to take life seriously stemmed from the fact that her father had walked out on her mother when she was only four years old. Her mother had gone on a year later to have a nervous breakdown when she learned that her ex-husband's new girlfriend was now pregnant with his baby. It was all too much for her to take and she ended up spending three months in the psychiatric unit in St Anne's Hospital. Zoe had been shipped off to her grandmother who at the age of seventy-five wasn't able to devote the attention to her that a spirited five-year-old required. This had resulted in Zoe being passed around to various aunties and friends of her mother's until her mother was well enough to care for her again. To this day, Zoe always had that fear of people leaving her and Emma believed that humour was Zoe's internal defence mechanism. She could imagine the five-year-old Zoe acting the joker just to put a smile on her mother's face and believing that if she could stop her mother from feeling sad, then perhaps she wouldn't need to go back into hospital.

After Zoe filled her in on her escapades, Emma checked her watch and it was just gone two.

"Jesus – where does the time go? It's gone two. I'd better head back before Maureen starts trying to track me down."

"Shit, I'd better run too – I'll mail you tomorrow."

They walked back through the park together and hugged warmly before heading off to their respective office blocks.

4

Behind the spare-bedroom door, Emma lay wide awake; sleep had forsaken her in the early hours of the morning. She listened to the sounds of the house breathing at night, the rattling pipe in the attic, cars whirring past on the road outside. She was plagued by her own thoughts; they kept on swirling over and over, sloshing around inside her head, spinning like a top until she could no longer keep up with them. She could hear the sound of contented slumber brimming from the bedroom next door. *Well for some, being able to sleep,* she thought bitterly.

She lay there looking around the familiar room. Its high ceilings were adorned with the original cornicing and the sash windows still retained the folding wooden shutters. It had been one of the main reasons that they had fallen in love with the house: to think that over one hundred years ago someone had chosen to decorate the house in this way and the features remained to this day! They had spent so long agonising over the shade of grey for this room; they had tried at least ten different samples before eventually settling on a shade called 'Elephant's Breath', but now the grey walls just made the room feel cold.

She must have drifted back to sleep at some stage because she woke to find her alarm blaring beside her. She never slept through her alarm; she was normally awake before it even had time to sound. She jolted upright and tried to silence the bleeping. It took her a few seconds to register what day it was and, when she realised she didn't have to get up for work, she eased herself back down onto the pillows again for a few moments. But it was already after eight and she knew she would need to hurry on if she wanted to be gone before Adam got up. She wondered where she would go today. Emma didn't like weekends; the constant feeling of trying to avoid her own husband wore her out. At least when he was in work, she didn't come into contact with him. But at the weekends the day was stretched out ahead of her in an endless field of time that would have to be killed and she felt weary even thinking about it. But she had no choice; it had to be done.

She had a quick shower and got dressed in black leggings, black leather riding boots and a black and white silk tunic with a butterfly print. It was almost nine when she finally sat into her car, wondering where she was going to go. It was too early to call in on anyone; most of her friends had a life and would be enjoying their Saturday morning lie-ins. And she was *sick* of shopping centres. Normally these were her usual port of call but at this stage she had seen all the clothes in every shop. She decided to go to Dee's coffee shop on Gregory Street, which was the only café that would be open at this hour. That would kill time until ten o'clock and then she would call in to her parents. Ten was a safe time; if she went too early they would start to worry.

She cut a lonely figure in Dee's. She was obviously their first customer of the day and the wiry dark-haired girl working there resented actually having to be functional at that time on a Saturday morning. The radio was blaring something that sounded like an eastern European Eurovision entry backed by a techno beat. Emma ordered a black coffee and sat down at a small circular laminated table in the corner, out of the way. Out of the way of what she wasn't sure because there wasn't a soul in the place – but that was how she felt, almost like she wanted to hide away from the world. She stirred the spoon around in circular movements so that the coffee swirled around inside the mug. She took a few sips but it tasted smoky and scalded. She took out her notebook and tried to come up with tag lines for the Sofa World campaign. She scribbled down a few words – 'snugly', 'comfort' – but nothing was jumping out at her, every sofa retailer was using the same straplines. She wanted to create a warm-feeling advert, especially as it was targeted at the Christmas market. Frustrated at her efforts, she shut her notebook again.

After a while she looked at her watch, it was almost ten. She could call in to her parents now, without too much suspicion. She knew that they would be up at this stage; they didn't have that hectic a social life that they'd need a lie-in. She finished the last of her coffee and moved her chair back with such force that it caused the waitress to jump up from where she had been perched on a stool, sleeping with her head resting on her folded arms.

* * *

When she arrived into their driveway, she opened the creaking, rusty gate that had been there since before she was born. Rounding the corner to the back door, she met her dad pottering around the back yard with two pieces of pipe in his hands.

"Hi there, Dad!" She forced herself to sound cheery but it didn't ring true in her voice.

"Emma, love! How're you keeping?" He sounded surprised but thrilled to see her.

"Not bad, Dad, thanks. How're you?"

24

"Aragh, you know yourself. You're over early?"

It wasn't a statement, it was a question.

"Yeah, I was passing out this way anyway so I said I'd drop in for a cuppa."

"Well, it's great to see you. Your mother's inside – go on in and get yourself a cup of tea and I'll be in shortly."

She let herself into the house and found her mother standing over the cooker, busy frying sausages and rashers.

"Hi, Mam!"

"Emma, darling! Come in, come in, love, here, sit down here." She flustered around the place, acting like Emma was a very important visitor. She started scattering magazines and newspapers off chairs and clearing bundles of clothes from the table. "Here, sit here, love. Here you are now." She patted the armchair.

Emma did as she was told, happy to let her mam make a fuss of her. Even though she was the eldest daughter, her mam still treated her like she was her baby.

"Will you have a fry, love? I've one on for your dad and your brother. He's still in bed – it was after four when he got in last night – I was listening out for him. Twenty-five years of age and he still has no sense, that fella!"

"Okay, if you're cooking for everyone I'll have just a small one so."

"Well now, love, you're looking a bit frail to me. Do you know, I was just looking at you there when you came through the door and you look like you've lost even more weight."

"I'm fine, Mam," she said curtly. Her mother was always harping on about her weight and it irritated the hell out of her.

"But you're a bag of bones, love! Look at your collarbone, jutting out, and your cheekbones – you look almost, well – almost malnourished!"

Emma automatically put her hand to her collarbone.

"Jesus, Mam, will you give me a break!"

"Well, I'm just saying every time I see you you're thinner than the last time – a few sausages will do you all the good in the world!"

Oh yeah, a few sausages will solve everything.

"I said I'd have a fry, didn't I?"

Her mother looked at her, hurt by her harsh tone.

"Sorry, Mam," she said contritely.

"No problem, dear."

"So, any news?"

"Well, I got new shrubs in the garden centre, that's what your father's doing now. He's going to plant them in the rockery – you know, there beside the laurel bush at the front of the house."

Emma tried to feign interest. "Oh really?"

"Yes, it'll look lovely when it's all done. Then I met your Auntie Wendy afterwards and we went for coffee. I had a slice of apple tart with cream but Wendy's on a diet so she wouldn't have cream on her rhubarb crumble. I said, Wendy, if you're going to have the crumble you might as well have the cream but she wouldn't hear any of it!"

Emma groaned inwardly. She could imagine her mother giving her younger sister Wendy the same lecture about not eating.

While the fry hissed in the pan, Anne moved away from the cooker, placed two mugs of tea on the table and sat down opposite her daughter. They sat in silence for a few moments.

"So how's Adam?" Anne Fitzpatrick broached cautiously.

Emma felt herself tense up at the mere mention of his name. "He's fine." The words felt prickly and awkward coming from her throat.

"Oh love, it's not easy, God love you. I pray for you both every night. It's going to take a while but time is a great healer." Her hands fluttered anxiously towards her throat and she began to fidget with her gold cross.

If one more person says that to me, I won't be accountable for my actions.

Time wasn't helping. She knew her mam meant well. When she considered things calmly, everyone *meant* well.

Her mother stood up from her chair and walked over to where her daughter was sitting and wrapped her in a warm hug. Emma was glad she couldn't see her face because she was afraid what might happen if she looked her in the eye. She wished she could stay in her mother's arms forever where things like this didn't happen. Even though a year had passed, some days it all seemed so fresh, the hurt so raw, that every day she felt like she was reliving it all over again. Time wasn't helping.

5

When Emma got home from her parents' house that evening, she was relieved to find that Adam had gone out. She went up to the spare room and drew the curtains. She kicked off her boots and flopped onto the bed. As she lay there her hand automatically reached out and she found herself opening the drawer beneath her bedside table and taking out the book which fell open at the pages where the photo had been slotted in the last time. Even though she knew it wasn't going to do her any good, she couldn't help herself. It was a compulsion; she needed to see his face. She held the photograph firm in her hands and just stared at it like she had done so many times since. She pored over the face, her finger tracing the outline in a well-worn gesture. The smile beaming back at her made her feel like someone had twisted her heart with both their hands and then wrung it out again, leaving it void.

The longer she stared, the more her eyes were starting to play tricks on her and the photo didn't look right. She held it away from herself and stared hard at it to see if that helped but it still looked wrong. She began to panic. She forced herself to try and recall the face as she remembered it but it wouldn't come to mind. She told herself to stay calm, she tried to breathe in but it wouldn't come. *Please, please, please let me remember.* She noticed that the pillow under her cheek felt damp and she realised that fat tears were running down the side of her face, dropping onto the brushed-cotton pillowcase beneath her. She chastised herself. *What am I doing thinking about these things?* It was futile. Crying wouldn't change anything.

She heard the key twist in the lock downstairs and started. She listened as his boots thudded across the wooden floorboards of their hallway, making their way across the kitchen tiles. They then walked back down the hallway, *thud, thud, thud,* and made their way upstairs, getting ever closer until the thuds were right outside her door. The continuously present feeling of dread that haunted her every waking moment intensified until she could feel it rising up from her stomach and burning the inside of her throat.

The door opened inwards and his head appeared around it.

* * *

Adam had noticed her coat hanging on the stand and her keys on the hall table. As he climbed the stairs he saw a soft light coming from underneath her bedroom door. He knocked softly. No answer. He took a deep breath and pushed it back. His wife was lying in her usual position on her side under the glow of her lamp. He noticed that the photograph lay beside her. It caught him off guard, a wobble that he wasn't expecting. He had to stop a moment to catch his breath and swallow back hard.

"Hi there . . . How are you doing today?"

"Hi," she said back, tilting her face at an awkward angle because she couldn't quite make eye contact with her husband.

Her voice was unsteady and he knew by her face that she had been crying. He watched her eyes move towards his rolled-up shirt sleeves until they fixed upon the pinky-red keloid scar that ran vertically down the inside of his left forearm – a lumpy mass of knitted skin, still raw. It only stopped where his wrist met the soft flesh of his palm. His eyes automatically followed Emma's and he rolled down his sleeves self-consciously.

"Are you hungry? I'm going to get a takeaway." He tried to divert her attention from his arm but his voice sounded shaky and was a tell-tale sign of his desperation.

She shook her head. No words uttered.

"Right." The silence filled the space between them. "Okay, well, I'll be downstairs if you want me, yeah?" *Jesus, this is bad.*

He turned and left the room, pulling the door behind him, thus effectively sealing them into their separate quarters of the house. He made his way downstairs and, storming into the kitchen, jerked open the fridge and reached for a can of Heineken. He put it up to his lips and gulped a large mouthful back before swallowing hard. He wiped a dribble from the edge of his mouth. *Fuck dinner*, he was no longer hungry. Things were getting worse, if that was possible. He had believed that by now the pain of the last year should be starting to ease for her – but no.

He went into the living room and threw himself wearily onto the sofa. He flicked through the channels and eventually stopped on a *Top Gear* re-run. Sometime later he nodded off in the armchair, still with the remote in his hand, but no sooner had he drifted off than he was jolted awake again. It felt as though he had been asleep only for minutes. His neck was stiff – he stretched it out. The dream had been back again.

He forced himself to recall exactly what had happened. He could always remember the start of it – it always started off the same way. He was driving along with one hand on his grey-leather steering wheel and the other hand resting on the gearstick. The sun was always strong, almost white with brightness. He knew it was chilly because the frost had covered the evergreen trees in its velvety white coat and there were patches of ice here and there on the road. But this time there was more, he had remembered more. There was a house too: a two-storey white-washed farmhouse with old-style wrought-iron gates marking the start of the path leading to the red front door. He remembered a bend in the road and a crossroads beyond. He needed to remember more but somehow his body managed to wake him up at just this point each time.

It was really starting to get to him now; the dreams were becoming too frequent. They were getting in under his skin and leaving him with an uneasy aftertaste each time, a constant reminder from which he couldn't escape.

He went up to bed a while later, tip-toeing past Emma's bedroom door. He lay in bed alone, desperately wishing she was beside him. He needed her. He longed for the closeness of holding her; it had been so long since they had even touched. He needed to tell her about the dreams. They needed to talk but when he had called into her room earlier on, he had been a coward as usual. Confrontation had never been his strong point – in fact, that had been Emma's forte. If there was something to be said, she wasn't one for beating around the bush, but now it was as if she didn't care enough to fight for what they had. One of them was going to have to do something to get things back on track between them and it sure as hell wasn't going to be Emma.

6

Emma poured herself a glass of red wine, allowing it to fill up the glass almost to the top. Taking a sip, she instantly started to relax. She had arranged to meet Zoe for a drink in Taylor's Bar. As per usual Zoe was late but for once Emma wasn't looking at her watch – in fact, it was nice to sit and people-watch while sipping her glass of wine in a dark, wooden-clad alcove.

After a little while a blur could be seen making its way down towards her at the back of the bar.

"Here, pour me some of that, I'm parched," Zoe said, out of breath, while she took her coat off.

Emma filled Zoe's glass and Zoe grabbed it from her and knocked it back like water.

"Sorry I'm late – I won't even bore you with the reason," she said. "Let's just say, who knew that some shades of cream could be cheaper than others?"

Emma laughed. They chatted easily about work and other things before Zoe broached the awkward question.

"So how's Adam? Are things any better?" she asked softly.

Emma could feel herself bristle at the mere mention of his name.

"Well, we're still not really talking," she said quietly.

"Still? I hoped things might have improved a little?"

Emma shook her head. "It's not easy, Zoe – whenever I look at him I feel like shouting at him, lashing out at him."

"But it wasn't his fault, Emma."

"I know but what if he hadn't gone or if he had done something differently? I can't help it, that's all I can think about."

"You shouldn't think about things like that, it won't change anything."

"Easier said than done."

"But the 'what ifs?' will just consume you – they'll eat you up!"

"I know all this," Emma said wearily. "I know . . ." She paused. "I'm just so angry – so angry. I want him to feel like I do. To hurt like I do. How is he just able to move on like that, as if nothing has happened and life still goes on?"

"But why don't you try talking to him about your feelings?" Zoe kept her tone gentle, as she always did, though at times she felt weary to the point of exasperation – they had been over this ground so many times.

"I can't," Emma whispered, shifting uncomfortably under her friend's gaze.

"I don't think he has forgotten, Emma – he's just coping the only way he knows how to – everyone reacts differently."

"I can't help it, Zoe, I really can't. I'm trying so hard but the rage builds up inside me and it just takes over." She started to cry. "I'm sorry."

"Don't be sorry. God, don't be sorry at all. Here –" Zoe took a tissue from a packet inside her bag and passed it to Emma. "You know I'm here for you, you know that, don't you?" She put her arm around Emma's shoulders and hugged her hard.

"Sometimes the pain is so awful and Adam is just like this looming reminder of everything that has been taken away from me."

"It's only natural, after all you've been through. It is so unfair and nothing you can do will change it. I can only imagine how you're feeling."

When they left Taylor's bar, they walked home together. Reaching Emma's gate, they stood there chatting for a few moments under the street-lamp.

"Talk to him, Emma."

"I'll try," she said half-heartedly and Zoe knew she wouldn't.

7

Summer, 2000

Adam and Emma had first met in San Francisco. It was the year of the millennium and they had both come over on J1 student working visas. It seemed that the entire student population of Ireland had decamped to California that summer, spreading themselves out across infamous cities such as San Diego, Los Angeles and Santa Cruz.

Emma had come over with two of her friends and, after searching the city high and low, they had found a bijou apartment on the top floor of a three-storey slatted wooden house right on Union Square in the heart of the city. The rent was a bit on the steep side but it was their first time living away from home and they had wanted to do it properly. They had been saving up for this trip for the last year, using the money they earned from their part-time jobs. They wanted to experience real city living – the buzzing streets, being able to walk everywhere, having myriad shops and cafés on their doorstep – so they had overlooked the astronomical rent and signed the lease.

Before they even came over, Emma and her friends had jobs

lined up in a call centre that handled the customer-service operations for several large corporations. The company was going through a period of rapid expansion. It could not keep up with the volume of new business coming its way and the disposable workforce of students was perfect to meet their needs.

They had been working there for a month when Adam joined. He had come over with a large crowd of the lads from college. Rather than waste money that could be used for beer on renting an apartment, they had gone for the cheaper option and were staying in a live-in hostel in the Tenderloin district. Every day when they stepped outside the hostel they were met with the stench of urine rising up off the street in the heat and they had to step over drunks and homeless people to get outside their door. The four of them had squashed into a double room, so small that the door couldn't be opened fully because there wasn't enough room between the wall and the ends of the bed. They had to squeeze through a small gap to get in and out. Their room was next door to a guy called Mike who had been living in the hostel since the sixties and was growing a small garden-centre worth of marijuana in his room – sometimes he had to sit outside in the hall in a canvas deckchair because he couldn't move for the amount of plants in the place. But the novelty of the free grass soon wore thin when they realised that they and their room permanently smelt of weed. When all the money that they had come over with was spent and they finally had to face up to the fact that they needed to get jobs, they had heard about this call-centre that was in desperate need of more bodies, so that had been their first port of call. The human resources manager, who was coming under pressure from the directors to get more bodies to fill the short-term requirements of their clients, decided to overlook the fact that they all smelt of grass and no one was more surprised than they were to find themselves hired that same day.

On his first day they had paired Adam up with Emma. She was to be his 'buddy' but within five minutes Emma had already shown him everything he needed to know about the job. They had clicked straight away. She told him that all they had to do was follow a flowchart which had every conceivable answer built into a script so you could do it with your eyes closed.

Adam was intrigued by this willowy girl, with skin so pale that it was almost translucent, showing a network of bluey-green veins underneath. Her white-blonde hair was long with small springy curls and she had a fine, delicate bone structure. Only for her striking height, she would have almost seemed fragile. When she smiled her whole face was illuminated and her eyes lit up. The more he got to know her, the more he liked her cool and calm demeanour. She was so different to the usual girls he went for, with their fake-tanned midriffs permanently on show, voluminous hair extensions and gel-nails. Emma was classy, the antithesis of the other girls, and for some reason he couldn't help but be drawn to her. She was all he could think about and the more he got to know her, the more he found himself needing to know.

When Emma was finished training him in, he had pretended to their team-leader that he was still a bit unsure of how the whole thing worked and would feel more confident if he knew that his 'buddy' was nearby. Their team-leader had given him a despairing look and had made a mental note to speak with HR about the calibre of the candidates they were taking on recently. Reluctantly she had put him sitting at the desk beside Emma's.

By choice the students worked late most evenings. There were no supervisors on duty so they got paid time-and-a-half and would sit around drinking cans. So that they wouldn't be disturbed, they would push a button on their phone to divert incoming calls back to the end of the queue again. Then they would clock off around nine and head to whatever bar was running a dollar-a-beer promotion that night. Adam and Emma would always spend the whole night talking together, with everyone else blending into the periphery. Their focus was on each other but he was still too afraid to make a move on her. He knew she wouldn't be one for his usual charms.

Emma couldn't wait to get into work every day to see Adam; she had never enjoyed a job so much. They spent all day talking around their partition and taking the mick out of customers on the other end of the phone. Of course it helped that he was good-looking: six foot one and broad-chested, with messy dark hair. He had a cheeky smile and white even teeth but he always had girls fawning all over him and she didn't want to be just another one of his conquests. Her friends had told her that he looked at her in 'that' way but she wasn't sure. They were very different people. He was a complete alpha-male, always the centre of attention, whereas she was quieter and was more comfortable with one-on-ones than large groups.

One evening as they were walking home together after work, they had stood for a moment on the steps outside Emma's front door, looking at life busying on around them. They watched Crazy Vinnie, an amputee who had lost both of his legs in Vietnam but managed to get around the place by putting his trunk on a skateboard and pushing himself along with his hands. He got his kicks from shouting at people in the street and then laughing at them as they screamed when they turned around to see him whizzing past them on his skateboard.

They stayed talking for hours, only sitting down on the

steps when it was dusk, and even though they were both starting to get chilly, neither one wanted to move. Eventually Adam knew he needed to seize the moment. It was now or never, so with a wildly beating heart he had leant across mid-conversation and kissed Emma with firm lips, showing the strength of his feelings for her. She had kissed him back with the same intensity, all the passion that had been building for months between them finally released.

Things had moved pretty quickly after that evening. They spent all their time together. They would go for picnics in the park, cycle across the Golden Gate Bridge to Sausalito or spend a leisurely few hours just having brunch. Adam would stay at hers most nights. They would lie beside each other, bodies entwined, talking all night long. She had braved the live-in hostel in the Tenderloin once but once was enough.

The rest of the summer passed wrapped up in each other until the inevitable time came when they had to go home. After three months, they had fallen in love not just with each other but with this city too. They felt as though they had become like San Franciscans themselves; they now belonged in this pulsing city with its micro-climate and the fog over the bay every morning, where artists, homeless war veterans and careerists hurrying along to the financial district all co-existed to bring the city to life. They felt different to the tourists who swarmed around Pier 49, queuing to get a boat out to Alcatraz; now tourists asked *them* for directions. They both knew that the combination of coming from opposite ends of Dublin city, him a southsider and her from the north side, and the pressures of their studies meant they wouldn't have the luxury of so much time together back home.

So when the summer of fun was over, they had sadly said goodbye to the city that had brought them together and wondered how their relationship would survive against the backdrop of the reality of their lives at home. They had made a pact that they would do everything in their power to make it work and to the amazement of their friends and families, who assumed it was just another holiday romance, that was what they had done.

8

As Zoe walked home after meeting Emma she thought over the conversation they'd just had. It was painful to watch her friend. She seemed so lost. She was going through the motions and getting on with her life but there was still a deep sadness in her eyes. Even when she smiled, it wasn't a real smile – there was still an unmistakable pain lurking behind it. Zoe could understand why Emma felt the need to lash out; life had been very cruel to her. People reacted in different ways and she supposed that Adam must be a painful reminder to Emma of all that had happened. He mirrored her grief and it was impossible to be around him without dredging up all the hurt again. Zoe hoped that in time it would pass because, although Emma didn't realise it, she needed Adam.

As she strolled down the well-lit street, suddenly a car pulled up a little way ahead of her, jolting her out of her thoughts. She watched as the driver threw something out from the window which landed onto the footpath ahead of her. As quickly as it had stopped, the car screeched off again. She ran up the path to see what it was and she was completely shocked to discover it was a puppy. He lay whimpering on the footpath.

"Hey!" she roared after the car. "Come back here!"

A jeep pulled up on the footpath beside her moments later and a man hopped out.

"Did you see that?" she asked in disbelief.

"I tried to get the registration but they were gone too quick," he said.

Zoe bent down to the puppy who was now crying in distress. His brown eyes pleaded with her to help. He was so tiny; he was definitely no more than a few weeks old. She bundled him up into her arms.

"Oh God – we have to help him."

"There's a vet down on Charles Street – they're probably still open," the man said. "Here, get in!"

Zoe looked at the man for a second; for all she knew he could be a serial killer.

"Sorry, I should introduce myself – I'm Steve." He held out his hand to shake hers. His blue eyes seemed kind and trustworthy.

"Zoe." She shook his hand tentatively. She climbed up into his battered jeep. Putting the puppy on her lap, she listened to him crying while Steve drove towards the vet.

When they got there, they both jumped out quickly and ran into the surgery where they explained breathlessly to the nurse what had happened. Gingerly the nurse whose name was Carla, took the pup from Zoe's arms.

"Unfortunately we're seeing a lot more of this type of behaviour. Some people blame the recession for the rise in animal cruelty but there's no excuse for that!" She shook her head at them.

"God, that is awful – people are sick!" Steve said.

"I'll bring him in to the vet straightaway. He has most likely broken something from the fall. He's still quite young to be apart from his mother as well so we'll give him a good check-up, poor little mite."

"Will he be okay?"

"It's too early to say but we'll do our best for him – poor fella. If you want to leave me one of your numbers, I'll give you a call and let you know how he is."

"Oh, thank you," Zoe scribbled her number on a piece of paper.

"Now – I hate having to do this but I do need to know who is going to cover the bill?"

"Oh God, of course – sorry, I wasn't thinking," Steve said quickly. "I'll take care of it."

They both went outside and stood in the yard.

"I can't believe the bastards did that to a poor defenceless animal – I'm sorry, I shouldn't use language like that but that's how I feel about them."

Zoe shook her head in disbelieving agreement.

"Here, look, there's a little café around the corner," he said. "Do you – well, do you want to go for a coffee – I need something to settle my nerves after that."

Zoe looked at her watch and tried to think of an excuse. Yes, he had helped her get the puppy to a vet but he was a complete stranger she had literally met on the street. Plus she really wasn't in the mood for this – she was upset after seeing Emma, she was worried about her.

"Well, I –"

"C'mon, I could do with something to calm me down." His smile was broad and easy.

"Okay . . ." she said hesitantly. "Well, I suppose I could go for a quick one . . ."

"Great!"

They walked into the café and took seats. The waitress brought them over the evening menu. Zoe shook her head but was appalled when, instead of ordering coffee, Steve proceeded to order a steak and chips.

"Sorry, you don't mind, do you? I'm starving – it's been a long day."

"No, work away." She forced a smile. It would be at least an hour now before she could leave. All she wanted to do this evening was just to go home, have a nice soak in the bath and then sit on the couch in her PJs with a glass of wine.

"You might as well order something – no point looking at me stuffing my gob." He smiled at her.

"Sure," she said through gritted teeth as she scanned the menu. "Okay . . . lasagne, please."

The waitress took the menus and left.

Zoe's thoughts flipped back to the puppy. "That was awful, wasn't it? To do that to a poor little creature like that!"

"What kind of people throw a dog out of a car window? Jesus, there's plenty of animal shelters around!"

"I hope to God he'll be okay. What a crappy introduction to the world!"

He nodded in agreement. "I've had dogs all my life. The best pet you'll ever have – loyal to the last. I grew up on a farm."

He looked like the farming type, Zoe thought to herself. He was wearing a green wax jacket over a maroon-coloured sweater and navy cords. He stood out amongst all the office types seated around them in the café.

"I always wanted a dog when I was growing up," Zoe said.

"You *never* had a dog?" he asked, incredulous.

She had to smile at his surprise. "My mother could barely take care of me – let alone a dog."

"I see," he said quietly. "So, Zoe, what do you do with yourself – when you're not rescuing injured puppies?"

"I work in fashion design."

"Wow – now that's impressive!"

"Not really, we just rip off catwalk designs and sell them on to the high street – it's pretty mundane actually."

"It sounds exciting to me!"

"Believe me, it really isn't."

"Now I can't tell you what I do – my job is so boring in comparison."

"Go on!"

"I'm warning you, it's not very glamorous!"

"Tell me!"

"I work for myself actually. I have a small food company. I make bread, cheeses, pâtés, jams, chutneys, that kind of stuff. All organic, of course – then I travel the country selling them at Farmers' Markets."

"Wow, that's pretty cool!"

"Why?"

"Making your own produce and selling it – it must be great seeing people buying something you have made."

"Are you into food?"

"I love food – I just don't have the patience for cooking it."

"Well, I should give you some of my pâté. I'm told it's good."

Zoe could tell that, although he didn't think his job was glamorous, he was still very passionate about it.

"Well, I'd love to try it." She was really starting to warm to him now. His open nature made him very appealing.

When they were finished eating, Steve offered to drop her home. Somewhat hesitantly she agreed. He seemed like a nice guy.

They chatted away easily on the trip home and when they pulled up outside Zoe's apartment block, they stayed talking until eventually Steve said he'd better get on the road because he had to be up early to bake bread for the market in the morning.

"Can I leave you my number – you might give me a call as soon as you get an update from the surgery on the little fella?"

"Oh yeah – of course I will."

"Great, thanks for that. Well, Zoe, goodnight – and it was lovely to meet you even if the circumstances weren't the best."

"And you too."

"Goodnight, Zoe."

"Goodnight, Steve."

She walked off towards the foyer of her apartment block, wondering if she would ever see him again.

9

Adam woke up saturated again. Beads of sweat were coursing down his forehead, neck and back but he still felt chilly. He took a deep breath. The frost-covered hedgerows, the sunlight so low in the sky that it was glinting in through the car window, his grey-leather steering wheel, the farmhouse with the red door. The bend in the road. The crossroads. *Why couldn't he remember more?* The dream constantly haunted him during the night hours as if mocking his attempts at sleeping. He needed to do something. *Anything*. He lay there in the darkness listening to the traffic going up and down the road, the sound of footsteps on the pavement outside, a dog barking somewhere in the distance.

* * *

Adam moved noisily around the kitchen, tidying up things that had gathered on the worktops. He roughly lined up glass bottles for recycling so that they clattered together, threatening to smash. He opened the fridge and took packages of food past their sell-by date off the shelves and fired them into the bin. He had got up early, having spent most of the night lying awake in the aftermath of the dream. *Bloody stupid fucking nightmare! Why the fuck will it not leave me alone?*

The lack of sleep was really starting to get to him. The dreams were now occurring almost every night and even the heavy slumber of alcohol couldn't ward them off; drink only allowed him to forget temporarily. When he was awake, he constantly felt detached from the world that surrounded him. When he was in work he found it difficult to concentrate; if he tried to focus on a task his mind could often just go blank. His brain didn't even have the energy to daydream. He was constantly feeling foggy and was afraid that one of these days he might just keel over onto his keyboard in work and fall into a deep sleep. The thoughts kept swirling around and about his head. *What if he hadn't gone? What if . . .?* He was bloody sick of '*what ifs?*' He tried to suppress them because they weren't going to help him but like all bad thoughts that invade in the middle of the night, they were always the hardest to push away. It was gone to the stage that he was like a small child who was too scared to go to bed, scared of the nightmares that lay waiting for him in his sleep.

Although it was the weekend, Adam almost wished he could go to work – anything that would distract him from the misery of his home life. No matter how hard he tried and how successfully he carried it off at work, once he was within the four walls of his own home, he couldn't push the reality of his life out of his head any more.

He had heard Emma creep out of the house after eight, like she did every weekend. She hadn't even bothered to come into the kitchen and say she was going, he thought angrily, though she must have heard him.

He heard the electronic buzz of their doorbell, jolting him out of his thoughts. It had better not be the goddamn Jehovah's Witnesses again, he thought as he stormed out towards the front door. If it was them, he swore he would take their end-of-the-world-inferno pile of crap and stuff it down their own throats instead. In fact, on second thoughts, he hoped it *was* the Jehovah's Witnesses; it would do him good to take his anger out on someone. He pulled their heavy front door back with force and was almost disappointed to see the diminutive figure of his mother standing there with her back to him.

"Mam?" he exclaimed in surprise as his mother, who was dressed in a camel-coloured mohair coat that was swamping her petite frame, turned around to face him. When he was a child she had taught him that whenever you rang the bell you should always face away from the door and you should only turn around when it was opened. It never made any sense to him even now but Ita White obviously still adhered to her teaching.

"Hi there, love."

"I wasn't expecting you, come in."

"Surely your own mother doesn't need an invitation to drop by?"

"No, of course you don't – sorry, Mam. Come in."

He showed her into the living room and cleared off a space for her on the sofa.

"Will you have a cup of tea?" he asked.

"I won't, thanks, dear – it's only a quick visit to see how you both are."

He sat down next to her.

"Where's Emma?" She peered around the room as if Emma might magically appear from behind the couch or jump down from the bookshelves.

"She's gone out."

"Oh, I see." Silence. "Again?"

Adam nodded.

"Look, I don't want to speak out of turn but . . . is everything all right?"

"Of course it is. Why?" Adam tried to keep his voice level but he knew he didn't sound very convincing.

"Well, it's just that I haven't seen Emma in ages. Every time I call she's gone out and you haven't been over to the house together since . . . well, since . . ." She started to get flustered. "I'm just a bit concerned, that's all."

"We're working through it, Mam."

"Really, Adam?"

He couldn't lie to his own mother so he just said nothing. He couldn't meet her eyes.

She reached across and took her son's hand in hers and stroked it like she would a child's. When Adam looked at her, her eyes were brimming with tears and her face etched with worry.

The silence stretched itself out between them. Tension mounted in Adam as he steeled himself for the questions to come.

Then suddenly she relinquished his hand and stood up.

"Look, I'd better go . . . your father will be wondering where I got to. You look after yourself, love, won't you?"

"Of course I will, Mam." Adam tried to disguise his relief but it showed in his voice.

"And you know where I am if you need a chat? Any time of the day or night – y'know that, don't you, love?"

"I know, Mam. Thanks for calling in."

"All right, love. Tell Emma I was asking for her."

"I will," he replied even though they both knew it was a blatant lie.

10

Zoe couldn't sleep that night worrying about the poor dog and thinking about the strange evening she'd had. One minute she was walking down the road on her way home after meeting Emma and the next she was in the vet's with a strange man with an injured puppy and then they were having dinner. Life was bizarre.

The next morning she waited for news from the surgery. She was still upset at the thought of the fate of the poor puppy, only a few weeks old and already suffering at the hands of humans. Some people had no heart. Finally she got the call she had been waiting for all morning.

"Zoe – hi, it's Carla from Southside Surgery."

"Oh hi, Carla – how is he doing?"

"Well, the poor little guy had a broken leg from the fall and he's quite malnourished but he's responding well and we would expect him to make a full recovery."

"Oh thank God – I didn't sleep a wink worrying about him!"

"Well, he's in good hands here. He's a little dote actually. We're all mad about him."

"What are you going to do with him when he's better?" Zoe asked.

"How do you mean?"

"Well, are you going to find a home for him?"

"Well, unfortunately we have no control over that. We'll give the animal shelters a call – hopefully they'll be able to take him – but they are inundated with strays at the moment."

"Hopefully? But – but, what if they're not – you're not going to put him down are you?" She was horrified.

"I'm sorry, Zoe, it's not my call."

"Right." Zoe swallowed. She hung up feeling desperate. The poor little guy, his worries were only just beginning. If she didn't live in an apartment she would keep him herself.

She checked in her notebook and found Steve's number where he had scribbled it down. Even his handwriting seemed friendly and confident.

"Hello?" he answered cheerily.

"Hi, Steve – it's Zoe – the girl you met last night – we rescued the puppy?"

"Ah, Zoe – how are you? Have you any news on the poor little creature?"

She could hear the windy noise of the outdoors in the background. "He's going to be okay – he's broken his leg and he's quite malnourished but the nurse, Carla, said he is doing well. She said he's a gorgeous little thing."

"Well, thank God for that, I was worried sick about him. I hate seeing an animal in pain like that."

"But, Steve –"

"What?"

"Well, if the animal shelters can't take him because of overcrowding, they might have to put him down!"

"Jesus – that's awful."

"I'd take him myself but I live in an apartment and he looks like he could be a big dog but I'm going to ask around everyone I know to see if they would give him a home. I couldn't bear the thought of him being put to sleep. Maybe you could put the word out as well?"

"We can't let that happen to him! I'll ask around the farmers at the market – surely one of them would take him in."

"Oh, I hope so! I'm going to put fliers up on the way home too. Okay, well, let me know how it goes. It's my mission now to help him."

"You're a good sort, Zoe."

She was taken aback with the surprise compliment. "Thanks! So are you!"

When she got off the phone to Steve, she felt marginally better. Surely between the two of them they could find a home for the puppy, especially him with all his farming contacts – he would have to know someone out there who would take him in. She sent an email around to all her friends to let them know and she designed some posters to put in the local supermarket and shops to look for a home for him.

When she came in from work that evening, she had got changed into her tracksuit and Ugg boots and was just putting her feet up when the buzzer on her apartment door went. She looked through the peephole and saw Steve's face smiling back at her. *Oh God*, what the hell was he doing calling to her apartment? He'd better not be a psycho – she'd enough drama in her life now without having to deal with a lunatic nut-bar that thought it was okay to call on her because they had rescued a dog together. She cursed herself for being so stupid – what had she been doing going for dinner with a complete stranger anyway?

She pulled back the door, making sure the security chain was kept on.

"Steve?" she said cautiously.

"Surprise!" Steve was grinning from ear to ear.

She looked down and he was holding the rescued puppy in his arms.

"Sorry for calling unexpectedly but I wanted to surprise you. Say hello to my new dog!"

"Your new dog!"

"Well, after you told me that he could end up in a dog pound or worse, I couldn't let that happen to him. And, sure, I've been meaning to get a dog for a while now anyway – I've loads of space. And then this little guy happens to come along. Sure, I couldn't not take him!"

"Oh that's wonderful news, I'm so happy he's found a home!" Zoe said as she undid the security chain and opened the door. "Do you want to come in?" In fairness he seemed like a harmless sort.

"Sure, I've loads of fields around the house for him to roam in and he can keep me company driving around the country," Steve said as he stepped inside.

He was dressed the same way as the last time, wearing his wax jacket again, but this time with a navy sweater and beige cords. The look suited him – she could imagine him standing behind his table at the markets, selling his produce.

He followed Zoe into the kitchen and sat himself on one of the highchairs at her breakfast bar.

"He looks better already." Zoe stroked the chocolate-brown fur of the dog. His front left leg was bandaged up but other than that he looked quite content where he was snuggled in Steve's arms. "What breed do you think he is?"

"Well, I definitely think there's a bit of a Labrador in him – especially around his face, but God only knows what else."

"He's gorgeous!"

"Well, what are we going to call him?"

"We?"

"Sure – as his honorary mother, I thought you should be involved in the naming ceremony."

"Well, I think he should have a proper name – not Lucky or Patch, a real name."

"I completely agree – how about Dave?"

"*Dave?* Where on earth did you come up with that from?"

"He looks like a Dave, don't you think?"

Zoe looked at the sleeping puppy. "Mmmh, I actually think you're right. It suits him. Hello, Dave!" She cooed to the sleeping puppy. "He is so cute – I just love him!"

"Well, you know you can have visitation rights whenever you want."

Zoe laughed. "That's good to know!"

11

Today was the day that Arthur Pilkington, the managing director of Sofa World and his senior management team were coming into the offices of A1 Adverts to listen to Emma pitch for their business. Somehow she had managed to converge all the words that had been swimming around in her head for the last few weeks and put them together into what she hoped would be a winning presentation. She had tried to put her heart and soul into it like she did for every one of A1's clients but this time she just couldn't get enthusiastic about the pitch at all. Maureen had asked her if she was sure she was okay to do the presentation, saying that she had no problem stepping in herself, but Emma was determined to do it. She had gone through the pitch with Maureen already and she had given her the thumbs-up, so she supposed it was as good as it ever was going to be.

She had a black coffee in hand as she read and re-read the presentation. She visualised in her head the level of her intonation and pitch. She tried to cover all the angles that Arthur might pick to come at her with questions: budgets, target markets, efficacy of TV ads over radio. She was making sure that she had every detail engrained on her brain. She would be prepared.

Five minutes before they were due to start, Maureen popped her head over her desk partition.

"All set?"

"Uh-huh, think so."

"As I said before, I have no problem stepping in – are you sure you're okay to do this?"

"I'm fine," Emma replied through gritted teeth.

"Okay, well, deep breaths then – I've every confidence in you, Emma."

Emma walked into the board room with her shoulders squared. She was wearing her favourite red-suede stiletto heels and grey-tweed pencil-skirt with matching jacket. That was a trick she always used: she knew if she felt good about her appearance it would give her that extra edge of confidence. She took a deep breath and greeted the rotund Arthur Pilkington and his team with a warm smile and a firm handshake and introduced herself and Maureen to the group. Her calm, collected, composed exterior belied her racing heart.

Maureen initiated some general chit-chat for a few minutes about how times were hard for businesses at the moment, while Emma nodded sympathetically. Soon, though, all eyes were on her as they waited for her to start. She stood up and turned on the projector. Her heart was beating nineteen to the dozen, so loud she was sure everyone in the room could hear it.

"Gentlemen, thank you so much for coming here today and for giving A1 Adverts the opportunity to pitch for your business. We appreciate in these cost-conscious times that now more than ever customers need to see value for their money, or as the Americans say 'bang for their buck'."

She knew it was weak but the men laughed and she was grateful.

"So we are going to present to you now what A1 Adverts can do for Sofa World and how we can work together to ensure Sofa World is the number-one sofa-store of choice in the Irish furniture market."

Maureen flashed her an encouraging smile.

"We've looked at how all Sofa World sofas are designed by a team of in-house designers but the main competitive advantage you have over other sofa retailers is the fact that these designs are so competitive on price. Quality at the right price. So without further ado I would like to introduce you to the concept we believe sums up the core values of the Sofa World Christmas campaign."

She could hear an intake of breath from Arthur Pilkington as he waited with bated breath to see what tag line she had come up with. He was sweating profusely and removed the handkerchief that decorated the breast-pocket of his suit and used it to mop his brow. She could almost physically feel his sense of anticipation.

Stated simply on a slide with a black background in gold lettering – the colour of Sofa World's company logo – was the tag line: **"Quality Money *Can* Buy"**

There was silence in the room, no one even dared to breathe. She looked at Arthur whose forehead was creased downwards as he contemplated the tag line.

Oh shit, he hates it.

She looked at Maureen who was looking back at her with the same worried expression.

Everyone stayed silent, all waiting for Arthur to utter his verdict. After what seemed like an age, he eventually spoke.

"I like it!"

Arthur was smiling and looking around at his team to make sure they were too. His team of yes-men instantly perked up and began agreeing with him. Whispers of "fantastic" and "perfect" crept around the room.

"'Quality Money *Can* Buy!'" he repeated. "Yeah, I think it captures the essence of Sofa World perfectly. Quality Money *Can* Buy. Yes, indeed. I do – I like it."

The relief was palpable, not just between Maureen and Emma, but between Arthur and his team. It was obvious that the team didn't like it when Mr Pilkington was in a bad mood. If he was happy, their lives were easier.

"And what about the TV campaign?" Arthur shouted boisterously at Emma.

Emma's confidence was now buoyed up by their reactions. "Of course, Mr Pilkington. I will now show you our proposed TV campaign." She thanked Jesus and all the saints in heaven that she had done this. Normally it wasn't required in an initial pitch but she had learned from Arthur's ad manager's emails that he was a demanding individual and she had dealt with his type before. 'Expect the unexpected' was her motto when it came to these sorts.

She pressed play on the projector, which flashed to a thirty-second film showing a homely mother, maybe 5 feet 5 inches in height, with a shapely figure. She was dressed in a cashmere cardigan and beige slacks, and she cuddled a five-year-old blond-haired angel in the crook of her arm as they both leant back into a plush sofa. A beautifully decorated Christmas tree twinkled in the corner and the log fire crackled. The mother was reading a story to the child before his heavy lids closed for the Land of Nod. Then it cut to a full-screen image where a voice-over in a reassuring tone stated: 'Quality Money *Can* Buy.'

Arthur punched the air with his fist. "That's it, *that's it*!"

His team, now having the sign they needed, also started to whoop and holler in agreement.

Emma stared up at the screen for a few seconds too long after the clip had finished. She had played this video over and over when she was preparing her pitch but suddenly now she felt her throat go dry. All the men in the room plus Maureen were staring at her expectantly. She wasn't sure whether it was because she felt vulnerable in front of these people or stressed about doing the pitch, but her eyes began to fill with tears. She could see Maureen mouthing at her to continue.

"Well, gentlemen, has –" She tried her best to sound normal but her voice was too high and threatened to break. "I'm sorry – I have to . . ." She couldn't keep it together. Running out of the room, she left Maureen and the team from Sofa World stunned in her wake. She could hear Maureen apologising profusely behind her.

She ran back down the corridor towards the bathroom where she stood in front of the sink sobbing. She splashed cold water on her face as she stood there crying. Thank God the rest of the cubicles were empty.

Moments later, she heard the door swing open. It was Maureen.

"Look, I'm sorry, Maureen – I should have let you do it. I'm sorry I ruined it," she whispered.

"No, it's okay – it's only to be expected – I knew I shouldn't have left you on your own to do it – I should have stepped in and given you a hand."

Emma shook her head. "I should have been able to do it – I don't know – I had gone over it a thousand times in the last week and I was fine with it but the video clip just got me there. I'm sorry – I don't know what happened."

"Look, you were doing a fantastic job and I could see they were impressed – in fact, you had practically done the whole thing – the only thing remaining was the questions and I could handle them."

"I'm sorry for landing you in it."

"Nonsense, he had a few general ones about the cost of a TV campaign and whether I felt the price point was right for the target market. Nothing I wasn't able for. They seemed impressed, and Arthur nearly shook the hand off me on the way out so that's a good sign." Maureen put her arm around her shoulders. "C'mon, Emma, it's only to be expected."

Maureen handed her a tissue and Emma blew her nose.

"Do you want to head home early – maybe have an early night?" She smiled kindly.

Emma shook her head defiantly. "No, I'm better off in here, keeping busy. But thanks anyway." She sniffed and dabbed at her nose.

"Are you sure?"

Emma nodded.

After six Maureen turned off the lights in her office and came by Emma's cubicle, while wrapping her scarf double around her neck.

"Emma, love, I really think you should be heading home now. You've had a tough day."

"Yeah, I'm just finishing up now."

It was a lie but it was easier to pacify Maureen than start up her concern again.

She killed time surfing the web and eventually, around eight, when there was no one else left in A1 Adverts, she decided she'd better call it a night and head home.

12

Some days after, Steve rang Zoe with an update on how Dave was doing. He told her how it was like having a small baby in the house and that now he knew what new parents were talking about when they complained about sleepless nights. He had tucked Dave up in a basket with a hot-water bottle wrapped in a blanket but he could still hear him whimpering from the kitchen. He didn't have the heart to leave him like that so he had ended up taking him into his bed. The toilet training was also a bit hit-and-miss but all in all they were getting on well. Then nervously he asked her if she wanted to meet up at the weekend to see Dave.

"You can try some of my pâté and tell me what you think?" he added.

"Sure," Zoe agreed while thinking in her head again how strange the whole situation was. But after she had hung up the phone and was thinking about him, she found herself wanting to see him. His personality was infectious, being around him made you feel good about yourself. He had a natural way with people and he was charming without being smarmy. He was easy-going too, like nothing would ever faze him. He had a funny way about him – you couldn't not like him.

Over dinner the next evening she told Emma the whole story about Dave being thrown out of a car window, their trip to the vet and their dinner afterwards. Emma had been amazed by the irony of meeting someone in the street.

"He must like you," Emma said.

"Why do you say that?"

"Well, he wouldn't be asking you to meet up again at the weekend if he wasn't interested."

"I'm not sure, Emma. I'd say he's the kind of person that would be like that with everyone he meets, y'know."

"Are you going to go?"

"I think so – I know it sounds mad but he seems like a genuine sort."

"Well, who knows where it could lead."

Zoe laughed.

* * *

Zoe set off on Saturday morning with the directions that Steve had given her. She turned off the main road onto a narrow winding back road with only room for the width of one car. She could see the sea in the distance with foamy white waves topping it. The land rose up as she drove down the winding roads which weaved through the stone-walled fields. The place was so remote she hadn't passed a house for miles. Not for the first time, she began to doubt herself: what was she doing going driving out into the middle of nowhere to meet up with a man she had only met for the first time last week? She pulled over into a gateway at the side of the road and rang Steve.

"Hi there, are you on your way?" His voice was friendly and instantly she felt better.

"Well, I think I might be a bit lost – I followed the directions you gave me but it just seems a bit . . . remote?"

"Oh, people always think they've gone wrong – but keep following the road straight until the headland dips down to the sea and you'll see a turn up to the right, with my sign on it."

"Okay, well, I don't think I'm too far away then."

"Great, I'll put the kettle on so."

She pulled out in her car again and continued along the road. It really was beautiful out here, so quiet and peaceful. Living in the city she often forgot just how loud and in your face it could be. She finally saw a swinging sign for '*McCredden's Artisan Foods*' and she turned up an impossibly narrow track that had grass growing up the middle. Finally, a whitewashed cottage with small blue-painted windows came into view on the headland. When she looked down to the right she could see the sun glistening off the calm sea beneath her. It was amazing. She swung into the gravel driveway and Steve came out of the door to greet her.

"You found me okay, then?" he said, grinning at her.

"Just about," she smiled back.

"Come on in. Dave is dying to see you."

Zoe noted that he was dressed even more casually today – he was wearing jeans and a pair of green Hunter Wellington boots and the wax jacket was now replaced with a fleece, under which he wore a red check shirt. His blue eyes twinkled as he spoke and his dark hair was long but it suited him like that. His skin had a shadow of stubble. She had to admit he looked quite handsome, in a rugged kind of way.

Zoe walked into the country kitchen. Pots of herbs were scattered randomly on the windowsills, with jugs of wild flowers decorating the place. There was a big farmhouse table with mismatched chairs.

Dave was curled up in his basket in front of an Aga on which a kettle was boiling. When she stroked his ears, he opened up his brown eyes and wagged his tail. She was amazed to see how much he had grown. She had brought him some doggy treats and a red collar with his name on it. She played with him while he tried to nip her fingers with his razor-sharp teeth. As Steve recounted his antics during the week, she could tell that he had already grown very attached to him.

"Ah, the kettle is boiled." Steve made tea in a blue-and-white teapot and then left it to draw while he laid out a loaf of rustic bread and an earthenware dish of his homemade pâté.

He poured two mugs of tea – one mug was spotty and the other had a picture of a pig.

"Spots or pig?" he asked, holding up both mugs.

"Erm – oh, go on, I'll go for the pig!" she laughed. She sat at the table while Dave snuggled blissfully in her arms.

He sawed through the loaf of rustic bread and served it to her spread thickly with his pâté.

She picked up the thick crusted bread and bit a piece off.

"Well?" he asked after she had chewed the mouthful.

"You made this yourself?" Zoe said.

"Of course!"

"It tastes really good . . . mmmm . . ." She chewed some more. "It's completely different to the supermarket brands."

"That's because I only use locally sourced ingredients – everything I use comes from the farmers around here." He gestured in a circular motion.

When she had finished that, he took out a grey slate cheeseboard with a selection of smoked cheeses that he had cured himself and a small bowl of pitted olives for her to nibble on. She loved everything and made sure he knew it.

After lunch they strolled along the deserted beach, with Steve carrying Dave in his arms. She was amazed they had so much to talk about.

"How long have you lived here?" she asked.

"I bought it a few years back – I always used to come walking down here at the weekends when I was working in the bank up in Dublin."

"You used to work in a bank?" Zoe was genuinely shocked. He looked nothing like the slick banker types with their polished shoes and tailored suits.

"Uh-huh," he nodded. "But I got tired of the rat race. I was sick of losing sleep over shareholder dividends and hedge funds – I wanted to do something I enjoyed. I'm a great believer in the saying 'Do a job you love and you'll never do a day's work in your life' so that's what I did."

"What, you just handed in your notice and moved out here?"

"Well, not quite as dramatic as that – I had always loved food and cooking. My mother was a great one for the family dinners when we were growing up. And as I grew up on a farm I loved how everything grown on the land had a use. So I got the idea of starting my own small business. I started small, just making some chutneys and jams first and selling them on the weekends while I still worked in the bank during the week. But I got a great reaction so I began adding more produce, bread and scones and then the pâté and it just grew from there. So two years ago, I decided to take the plunge. I handed in my notice to the bank, put my apartment in the IFSC up for sale and started looking around for somewhere to live. One day I was walking down here and looked up at the derelict cottage and thought it was a beautiful setting, out on its own like that with nobody next or near you. But you should have seen the state of it! There were holes in the roof and grass growing out of the chimney! So I approached the farmer whose land it was on and he agreed to sell it to me but even the solicitor told me not to buy it, it was that rundown. I've spent the last few years doing it up in bits and pieces – I love that pottering around doing jobs, planning what project I'll take on next. Last year I extended the kitchen – that's where I make all my produce and I've sown a herb garden and vegetable patch."

"It really is the most amazing place I've ever seen. Dave is going to love exploring all around here when his leg is mended."

When they walked back up the dunes to the house, Steve put a snoozing Dave into his basket beside the Aga.

"C'mon till I show you the rest of the place."

He led her around the cosy rooms, all simply decorated with wooden floorboards and cream-painted walls. The bedrooms had cast-iron beds and small wooden dressing-tables.

After he had stuffed her with more of his food and chatted some more, Zoe reluctantly said her goodbyes. It was getting dark out and she didn't want to get lost on these roads with no signposts.

As soon as she had pulled out of his laneway, she knew she was seriously starting to like him but she really didn't want that to happen. As soon as she opened herself up to people, things never went her way. So she tried to tell herself to stop getting her hopes up. It was all just for Dave anyway. Plus he was so different to her usual type. Normally she went for the on-trend men, usually creative types from the fashion industry or the Dublin art scene. It wasn't that she chose these men – rather, because of her job, it meant these were normally the type she socialised with. But Steve was the antithesis of them. When she had first met him he had been wearing cords and a bottle-green wax jacket; she could no more imagine any of her exes in that get-up than she could imagine herself running a marathon. All her exes either had smooth baby's-bottom cheeks or carefully maintained designer stubble, but Steve looked as though he didn't shave from one end of the week to the next. He was what you might describe as a 'man's man', rough and ready. She knew he would also probably wrap you in his strong arms and hold you tight against his chest all night.

She dialled Emma's number.

"Well, is he a psycho killer?" Emma asked.

"No!" Zoe laughed. "Oh Emma, he's great – the more I get to know him the more I know I'm falling for him. I'm so scared though."

"Of what?"

"The unknown . . . letting go . . . seeing where life takes me . . ."

"Zoe, you have to let your guard down sometime," Emma said gently.

"I know, Em, I know."

* * *

On Sunday morning, Zoe's phone buzzed on her bedside locker. Sleepily she picked it up and saw it was Steve. She quickly answered it.

"Hello?"

"Good morning to you, Zoe."

Even the way he said good morning was full of infectious cheer.

"Morning, Steve. How's Dave?"

"He's doing great altogether – but he's getting a bit fond of my bed now."

Zoe laughed.

"I'm just ringing to check that you got home all right last night but I'm guessing you did?"

"Uh-huh, it's actually a lot closer to the city than I had thought but yet it feels like you're on the edge of the world out there."

"That's the beauty of it. Look, Zoe, I hope you don't mind but I was also calling to ask you something. Now tell me if you think I'm being a bit presumptuous but – well, I was wondering – well, y'see, there's this ball on – Irish Food Producers Association – it's an annual thing. Now I hate the bloody thing but, well, I was wondering if you would like to accompany me?"

"I would love that."

"Oh, thank God!" He breathed a sigh of relief. "I was worried the only reason you stayed in contact was because of Dave."

Zoe was taken aback by his honesty. "I actually thought you were doing the same thing!" she said, laughing. "When is it on?"

"This Friday."

"This Friday! Talk about short notice. I'll have to get a *gúna* sorted!"

"I know, I'm sorry. It's black-tie too. I wasn't even going to go this year and then, I thought, well . . . I thought it would be nice to go together."

"I'd like that."

"It's in Dublin anyway so you won't have to go too far – I have a friend who will look after Dave for me so at least he's sorted. If I pick you up about eight, is that okay?"

"I look forward to it."

Zoe lay back on the pillow and smiled. She felt like a giddy teenager. He had said he liked her. He really liked her back and not just because of Dave. She would make sure she looked fantastic on Friday so that he would be glad he brought her. She would need to call around to Emma and see if she had any great dresses – she used to be always going to weddings and fancy black-tie things so she should have something. She couldn't imagine him in a tux though. She tried to picture him but nothing was coming. She wanted to jump up and down and scream.

13

Zoe rooted through Emma's wardrobe while Emma sat on edge of the bed chatting to her.

"What do you think of this one?" Zoe took out a crimson crêpe-de-chine dress and held it up against her.

"I wore that to the Snow Ball myself and Adam went to three years ago – it's gorgeous on."

"I remember seeing photos of it on you – it was fab. Do you think it will fit me though?" Zoe was looking at the narrow bodice doubtfully.

"Of course it will – sure we're the same size."

Zoe looked at Emma's tiny frame and, knowing full well that they weren't, she decided not to say anything. "I'll try it on."

She got undressed and Emma helped her into the dress and zipped it up the back.

"There – it's stunning on you."

"I don't know – look at my tummy – it does nothing to disguise it."

"What tummy? You're ridiculous."

"I'd feel too self-conscious – sorry."

She got out of the dress and looked through some more on the rail.

"This one is beautiful – so elegant." She held out a black satin, strapless number.

"I wore that to a black-tie wedding – I just clipped on a wine corsage to decorate it. I'm sure I still have it somewhere."

As Zoe thumbed through the dresses Emma had a flash of the way her life used to be. Each dress marked a different occasion in their life. There was the dress she wore to their engagement party. She even had held onto the jersey summer dress she was wearing the night she and Adam had first kissed in San Francisco.

It's like my life in dresses. She smiled sadly.

"Oh my God – this one is beautiful!"

It was an empire-line full-length lace gown. The delicate lace was champagne in colour but it was spun with a fine gold thread and it had tiny beads sewn on all over.

"I think I got that one in a vintage shop actually – it's very *Pride and Prejudice*. It would be fabulous on your dark colouring."

Zoe slipped into the dress and stood in front of the full-length mirror.

"It's perfect on you," Emma said.

Zoe held her hair up messily with her hand and twirled in front of the mirror. The delicate shoulders of the dress and the empire line made her feel so feminine.

"It is amazing, Em! Are you sure you don't mind me wearing it?"

"Of course not – sure, when am I going to wear it again?"

Zoe said nothing.

"So you really like him?" Emma asked.

"Well, it is still early days but yeah – I don't know what it is – wait until you see him, Em, he's the complete opposite of my usual type but, I don't know, every time I think about him

I feel all – all tingly and I get flutters in my tummy. I just get so excited!"

"Well, he's going to be blown away when he sees you in that dress."

"I hope to God you're right, Em!"

She took off the dress then and folded it up neatly so as not to crease it. Emma loaned her a pair of shoes and pearl earrings.

"You're a star!"

"Not at all – I'm just glad to see you happy."

"I'm sorry, Emma – I'm being really thoughtless, amn't I?" Zoe said seriously.

"On the contrary, it's great to see you smiling and happy – you deserve it."

"Are things any better with you and Adam?" Zoe asked carefully.

Emma shook her head.

"Oh, Emma!" Zoe hugged her tight while Emma did her best to try to keep back the tears that were springing into her eyes.

14

While the rest of their friends were still living the helter-skelter single life – getting pissed most nights of the week, stumbling out of sweaty night-clubs and spending the rest of their time hung over – Adam and Emma were busy playing grown-ups. Both held down proper jobs, rented an apartment in the city centre and saved whatever money wasn't used to pay bills for a deposit on a house.

The spare room in their apartment was stuffed full of bits of furniture and antiques that Emma had bought over the years, just waiting on her dream home to put them into. When they had finally saved up enough for the deposit they thought the hard part was over, but finding the right house for them proved more difficult than they had originally anticipated. Inevitably, there were none that were right for them. Any that they liked were either too expensive or miles away from anywhere, with no public transport. Then there were those that looked fine from the outside but once you set foot inside you could see the rising damp and floorboards crawling with woodworm and there were so many with teeny tiny gardens where two people couldn't fit together at the same time, let alone a deck-chair. But they weren't prepared to settle – this wasn't to be just a starter home for them – this would be the house that they would live in for the rest of their lives, so they had to get it right.

Just as they were starting to question themselves, wondering if they were being too picky and if they would ever find their elusive dream home, Zoe had mentioned that an old lady living near her mother on Cherry Tree Road had passed away recently and that the house was now up for sale. Emma knew the house she was talking about. She had always loved it. It was an old two-storey red-brick Victorian house with white sash windows. The front door was painted submarine yellow with a white wooden surround and a semi-circular overhead stained-glass pane. The garden at the front of the house had a small wrought-iron railing and during the summer months it was always blooming with hydrangeas, hyacinths and sweet peas so the scent lifted you up as you walked past. Emma's heart had somersaulted when she had heard it was for sale and she knew in her bones this house was for them. She had phoned the estate agent straight away to arrange a viewing for that evening.

As Adam and Emma had walked through the house with the estate agent, their excitement began to build. So far it had ticked all their boxes plus more. It still retained all the original features, like the shutters on the windows and the ceiling cornicing. Each bedroom still had its tiled fireplace. They could see it was in need of some modernisation but that would be just cosmetic. They had to hold their breath as the agent led them out into the south-facing back garden. It had a long rolling lawn, with a small greenhouse on one side and a fragrant herb garden on the other, and as they walked down the winding path they saw there were two old apple trees, rhubarb plants and a blackcurrant bush. They could see themselves living in this house and had to try hard to suppress their eagerness in front of the estate agent. The agent had told them that the deceased lady's son was looking for a quick sale as he didn't live in Ireland and had no intention of trying to manage the house from overseas so they had put an offer in on the spot and they were thrilled to hear that it was accepted that very same day. Once the legals had gone through and the paperwork was signed they had picked up the keys to their new home and had moved in a few weeks after.

They instantly set about stripping down the floral wallpapers and had repainted the whole house from top to bottom, splashing out a small fortune on Farrow & Ball paint. They pulled up the carpets to expose the original oak floorboards. Adam had sanded down the wood and varnished them himself and they scattered rugs across them to create warmth in the room. They replaced the dated velvet curtains in each room with modern damask fabrics. In the kitchen they kept the original Belfast sink and black-and-white chequered tiles. As they couldn't afford to replace the kitchen, they painted the cupboard doors in duck-egg blue to brighten the place up. Emma now had a home for all the bits and bobs she had built up over the years. She was delighted when a small cross-legged writing bureau that she had found in a salvage yard fitted neatly into the alcove in their dining room and they now had room in their bedroom for the polished mahogany chest of drawers that she had come across in a car-boot sale.

They were so proud of their home; all their hard work had made it all come together and now it had their stamp firmly on it. 59 Cherry Tree Road quickly became the focal point for all their friends; its central location meant they would usually all meet there first before heading into town or else would come home for a night-cap after a heavy night out. There was always someone coming and going; calling in for tea or dropping by on their way into town.

Unbeknownst to Emma, as well as saving up to buy a house, Adam had been putting a little bit of money aside each month to buy the perfect engagement ring for Emma. He had been scouting in jewellers' windows and had fallen in love with a vintage solitaire dating from the 1940s. The diamond was held in place with four small clasps and was set onto a delicate white-gold band. It was breathtakingly stunning and when the stone caught the light, its clarity allowed it to shine straight through. On being told how much it was he nearly died on the spot, but after he had left the shop he couldn't stop thinking about it. The ring epitomised Emma, it was elegant and timeless, a perfect match for the woman he loved. So every week he checked back in the window praying it wasn't sold until eventually he had saved up enough for it. Coming out of the jewellers that day he couldn't keep the grin from his face. He had been so careful walking down the street, keeping his hand over the box inside his jacket pocket. His excitement was written all over his face and he was petrified that Emma would guess what was up.

He had also bought a fancy wicker picnic basket, with a red-and-white check cloth lining, in an overpriced lifestyle store. It had an inbuilt cooler bucket, proper cutlery and champagne glasses. He had stocked it with Emma's favourite foods – a salad with olives and goats' cheese, a smoked salmon and ricotta quiche – and he had also brought chilled champagne and strawberries.

They had set off for the Wicklow countryside early the next morning. They often went walking there so nothing seemed out of the ordinary to Emma. They had trampled through the long meadow grass, speckled red in places with wild poppies, walking for ages until there was no one around them. Eventually they came to the edge of the field, where the land sloped gently down towards the water's edge. They had sat up against a knobbly oak tree and Adam served up the picnic.

Emma was so impressed with the picnic basket that she hadn't noticed that he had been too nervous to eat anything. His heart had been pounding manically against his ribcage; he couldn't ever remember being this nervous before. He had swallowed hard and asked Emma Fitzpatrick to be his wife, listening to his shaky voice as if it was coming from someone else entirely. He had watched her stunned face, as her mind caught up with what was happening, change into an expression of pure joy. He opened back the lid on the small, black jeweller's box which contained the vintage solitaire and when he saw it again glistening in the sunlight, he knew he had made the right choice. With trembling hands, he had slid the ring onto the fourth finger of her left hand.

"Yes, of course. Yes. Yes. *Yes, of course I will marry you!*" she had screamed at him before throwing her arms around his neck.

He would never forget that moment as he had thought he might burst with happiness. They had sipped their champagne and admired the ring on Emma's slender finger. They laughed and cried and hugged and then cried some more.

They had wasted no time in setting a date. Emma had always dreamed of a Christmas wedding and although it was only six months away they managed to find an old manor house in County Kildare that was available. They had kept it small and intimate – she didn't want a large wedding, so it was just their family and close friends.

The night before the wedding, Adam found himself at home alone. Emma had followed tradition and had stayed in her parents' house, sleeping in her childhood bedroom. Adam had missed her in that short space of time; the house felt empty without her and the bed was cold on her side. He hated being away from her and, even if it was only for one night, he couldn't wait to see her again. After only a few hours apart, he already felt like he had so much to tell her.

He had stood nervously at the altar, shifting from foot to foot, zoning out on the conversation that his groomsmen were having. He barely registered the flowers decorating the pew ends or the organist warming up with Bach's 'Jesu, Joy of Man's Desiring' in the background. He shook hands with and greeted their guests as they came in and took their seats but his mind was elsewhere. Then he had heard the organist begin to play Pachelbel's 'Canon in D', which was the piece that they had chosen as their processional, as a hush fell on the congregation. When he had turned around and seen her standing at the back of the church linking her father, framed by the parted doors, looking serene and more beautiful than he had ever seen, he had lit up with happiness and pride. Her tall slender frame was enhanced by the delicate lace of the dress. He had felt so alive, so in love, so physically brimming with joy that it felt as though it was bubbling up inside of him and spilling out over their guests in the church. He watched in awe as she walked gracefully towards him with careful strides. They shared a smile and he had felt his eyes prick with tears.

When her father had handed her over to him, he had squeezed her hand tight to assure her that they would have a wonderful life together. He could almost feel her touch now. As the priest had pronounced them man and wife, the feeling of goodwill radiating from their guests standing in the pews was almost palpable.

Later in the day they had both sneaked hand in hand up to the bridal suite, just to take a few minutes out for each other from the madness going on downstairs in the reception. Sitting under the canopy of the chintz drapes on their four-poster bed, they couldn't help talking over each other in excited bursts about how fantastic their day had been so far. He could remember looking into her eyes, deep into their depths and she had gazed right back at him with that same intensity. This was to be the start of the rest of their lives. They hadn't needed to say anything; they just sat like that for a moment, taking it all in. It had probably lasted only for a few seconds but it had felt timeless, it would always stay with him. That feeling of pure joy – yes, they had once been happy.

15

Friday couldn't come fast enough for Zoe. She'd had Emma's dress hanging on the outside of her wardrobe all week and every time she looked at it she got butterflies in her tummy. When the day finally dawned, she was excited about seeing Steve again but nervous too. She just wished she could relax and enjoy it but instead she was obsessing over every detail. Hair up or down? She had finally decided on up. Should she wear a necklace or just leave her neckline bare? In the end she chose to wear a simple silver chain that trailed downward to form a knot just below her collarbone. Would he make sure to introduce her to everyone? What if he left her standing on her own all night?

She got dressed in the lace gown she had borrowed from Emma. When she put it on it made her feel fantastic once again. The bodice of her dress fitted perfectly over her breasts before it gently fell away, skimming over the areas she didn't want attention drawn to. Not trusting the hairdresser not to do something overly fussy, she had done her own hair by twisting it into two rolls on each side of her head using Kirby grips to pin it all into place at the back. When she looked at herself in front of the mirror, she felt good. She just prayed Steve would like it.

Bang on eight o'clock she heard her buzzer go. She hurried out and opened back the door to see Steve standing there dressed in a tuxedo with a tall bunch of gladioli in his arms.

"Hi, there!" He smiled and handed her the flowers. "You look stunning, really beautiful." He stood back, admiring her.

"Why, thank you! You're not looking too bad yourself!"

His tall stature suited a tux, his broad chest filling the jacket handsomely. He was cleanly shaven and his usually messy hair had been brushed back. His eyes twinkled and she had to do everything in her power not to jump on him there and then.

"Are you sure I look okay – I always feel a bit funny in these things?" He started tugging at the neck of his shirt. "I think after the years of wearing a suit in the bank I have a phobia of the things now."

"Well, I must say it suits you. You look very handsome."

* * *

As they walked into the room, Steve nodded and greeted people he knew standing at the bar. He was proud to have Zoe on his arm. He knew some of the people were looking at her as they tried to work out who she was. He led her over towards a group of men and women. Zoe saw a waiter go past with a tray of champagne – she grabbed two glasses and handed one to Steve before taking a long sip from hers. She barely knew him and here she was about to meet his friends.

"Well, you're a dark horse, Steve – are you not going to introduce us?"

"Barry – this is Zoe. Zoe, these are some of the other stand-holders at the market." He named each person as she shook hands with them one by one.

"So, Zoe, how long have you two been going out together?" a lady he had introduced to her as Yvonne enquired.

They both squirmed awkwardly and she could see Steve's cheeks go red.

"We're not . . . well . . ." he looked at Zoe, "not yet anyway."

"Oooooh!" one of the other women said.

"I mean, we haven't known each other very long."

"I see. Well, how did you meet?" She continued her line of interrogation even though she could see they were both wriggling in front of her.

Zoe jumped in to save Steve who was going redder by the second. "It's a long story."

He flashed her a grateful smile.

Finally they were saved by the gong calling everyone to take their places for dinner.

"Phew!" Steve sighed as they took their seats, which were thankfully on a different table to the group that they had just walked away from. "Sorry about that – Yvonne is forever trying to set me up with her friends. And she's so nosy – she just keeps digging until she finds out all the details."

"I can see that!"

Knowing that they would be serving the most discerning of customers, the hotel had prepared a wonderful banquet featuring the best of Irish produce including crab-cakes, duck and turbot, finishing with a dessert of pear-and-almond tartlets. Zoe was grateful that her dress was an empire line and would hide her stomach, which had grown after all the rich food that she had eaten.

After the plates had been cleared away it was time for the annual award ceremony. Zoe was surprised to see Steve had been nominated in two categories – one for 'Best Cheese Producer' and the other for the 'Best Artisan Producer'. He blushed when she asked him why he hadn't said anything about it.

"Ah, you know yourself – these things don't really mean anything. It's just hours of boring speeches and clapping hands on cue while some fella in a fancy suit presents a bit of crystal."

"Stop being so modest!" Zoe chided as she rubbed his arm affectionately.

Although he didn't win the 'Best Artisan Producer' award, he did receive a runner-up prize for his oak-smoked cheese. Zoe clapped enthusiastically as he went up on stage to receive it.

"I'm very proud of you," Zoe whispered when he returned to his seat and although she knew he was embarrassed, she could tell he was delighted at having won.

Once all the awards were given out, the tables were cleared away to make a dance floor and the band started.

"Here, let's dance," Steve said, and he led Zoe onto the dance-floor.

As he took her in his arms, Zoe was surprised to find Steve was a good dancer. He twirled her around the floor to sounds of the old Rat Pack, moving with ease and confidence.

"I wouldn't have had you down as a good dancer!" Zoe whispered in his ear.

"I'm full of surprises, me!"

After a while, breathless from all the dancing, they sat down for a bit.

He leaned in towards her. "Here – why don't we get out of here? It's stuffy anyway. I hate all this pretentiousness."

"Do you not want to stay till the end?"

"Nah – we'd only be attacked by Barry and Yvonne again anyway."

He led her by the hand as they left the room and stood outside in the evening air.

"That's better," he said, loosening his bow-tie. "Here, you look perished – put this around you." He placed his big jacket around her shoulders.

They were alone. The full moon cast silvery shadows across the lawn.

"Zoe, I just want to say thank you for coming tonight. I really enjoyed it."

"I'm glad I came too."

"I feel like I should do something romantic like you see in the films."

"Like what?"

"I don't know – point out the stars or something."

Zoe giggled and he took her in his arms. He leant in so that she could smell the champagne off his breath and began to kiss her slowly. She had been wondering how long more she would have to wait but now that the moment had arrived she savoured it. His lips felt so good against hers, like they had known each other for years. As they kissed deeply, she knew where he would be staying tonight.

16

Adam strolled down Grafton Street towards the pub where he had arranged to meet his brother Rob. After a long day in work, he wasn't in the mood for another evening in the house on his own, with only his feelings for company and too much time to think. Thinking wasn't good. So he had emailed Rob at work and they had arranged to go for a pint.

It was the time of the day where the street underwent its transformation for the night. He walked past shop fronts pulling down their shutters, flower sellers tidying up their stalls, while bars and restaurants set their tables and put out their chalk-written menu-boards, readying themselves for the evening trade. Crowds of shoppers gathered around a tinfoil-clad street artist pretending to be a statue. His audience took up the width of the street, forcing people to walk around. Adam kept on walking, weaving left and right through the hordes of people coming at him like shoals of fish.

Rounding a corner, he walked down Castle Street. Its narrow paths were crowded with gangs of smokers standing outside so he turned onto a quieter cobble-locked side-street where crowds were sitting along the outdoor terraces under café-bar awnings, friends laughing and joking.

He caught sight of a man standing under a shop front wearing heavy-set frames with a huge bouquet of blush roses in his hands. He was checking his watch and his eyes darted around the street. The woman he had obviously been waiting for came up moments later, surprising him from behind by putting her slender arms around his waist. He watched as he swung her around to face him. As they embraced and smiled fondly at one another, they were unaware of the man standing watching them only a short distance away. It was the look in their eyes that did it. It caught him off-guard like a blow in the pit of his stomach. Emma used to look at him like that. They used to do this. That couple used to be them. He stared over at them, happy in each other's arms, chatting animatedly, oblivious to the street life going on around them. They were the centre of each other's world. 'I used to have that too!' he wanted to shout over to them out of sheer petulant rage. *'That used to be me!'* He watched them walk off then, the man's arm draped lazily around his lover's shoulders.

* * *

They used to meet in town every Friday evening after work; it was something they had always done. Friday was their night. The streets were always alive with suits filtering out of offices, relieved to be escaping work for the weekend. You could almost feel the infectious excitement in the air. A stressed Emma would hurry out of A1 Adverts flustered and apologising for being late. She would complain that A1 was sucking the life out of her and how Maureen had landed her with something that was so urgent that it had to be done *'now'* just as she was about to leave the office for the weekend. But no matter how bad her humour was, she would always light up as soon as she saw him. He knew how to make her smile and lift her out of any mood.

They would have a table reserved, usually in a new restaurant that they had read about in the Sunday papers and they had been dying to try. They would start by ordering a bottle of red wine, instantly helping them both unwind from the pressures of their work. The heavy clunking sound it made as it poured out of the bottle was the sound that said the weekend was here. They would take their time poring over the menu, trying to guess what the other was going to order.

After dinner they would normally stroll hand in hand up to their local, Brown's on the canal, to meet the rest of the gang: a mixture of his and her friends. There was always someone there. In winter they would try to get the seats closest to the turf fire and in summer they would sit outside on a wooden picnic bench overlooking the lock gate until it began to get chilly and they would move back inside. More often than not, whoever was left at the end of the night would pile into a taxi and head back to theirs in Rathmines for another bottle of wine.

The next day neither would have the energy or the inclination to move very far and it would be spent hung over, snuggling on their sofa, eating crisps and chocolate, watching old films like *Breakfast at Tiffany's* or *Chitty Chitty Bang Bang* which they knew off by heart. They were always happiest when they were in each other's company. That was their routine, as comfy as old slippers, but that was them.

* * *

Adam made his way towards the back of the dimly lit pub, which was quiet enough that evening, but then again the good weather meant most people chose to sit outside. They found a quiet alcove and Rob ordered pints for them both. They sat in and sipped the creamy heads on their pints.

"So how are you? How're things in work?" Adam asked.

"Good, y'know, busy so can't complain. How about you?"

"Yeah, same old, it's grand."

"And how's Emma?" Rob knew when his younger brother rang him to go for a pint it was usually because he needed to talk.

"Good." He paused. *It's fucking shit.* "Well, as good as can be expected, I suppose." He took a slow sip of his pint and placed the glass back on the table.

"Yeah?" Rob said.

The silence sat heavy in the air between them.

"I don't know if we're going to get through it, Rob," Adam blurted out.

"Hang on – what are you saying things like that for?"

"I'm serious, Rob. I don't know if we've much of a future left together. She stays holed up in her room whenever I'm in the house. She won't speak to me. It's as if she can't bear to be around me."

Rob was taken aback by his brother's admission; he'd had no idea things were so bad. "Jesus, I had no idea!" He took a swift intake of breath before adding, "Jesus, sorry, bro'. I didn't know it was that bad."

"Sure, you weren't to know."

"Has it been like that since you came home?"

"Uh-huh." Adam nodded his head.

"Fuck. Look, I don't want to say some shit like 'give it time' or 'time is a great healer', but I, well . . . I don't know what to say. Sorry."

"I'm trying, I really am, but she doesn't seem ready to move on and I know this is awful but . . ."

"But what?"

"I'm starting to lose patience." He lowered his voice, shamed by his own admission.

"Look, I don't know what to say," said Rob. "I hate all this shit, y'know I do, but you and Emma, well, you've been through a lot . . . so give it time, yeah? You can't just expect her to forget what happened, Adam." Rob whistled softly. "Whoooah there – Jesus, listen to me, I sound like Jeremy Fucking Kyle!"

"I know, I know, you're right. It's just I don't even know if that's what she wants any more."

"Jesus, I don't know – just talk to her or something."

"Yeah, you're probably right – I think we need to have it out."

"Look, I'm sorry, I'm crap at all this."

"Yeah, I know you are!" Adam laughed at his brother who was shifting uncomfortably in his seat.

"Fuck off, you!"

The conversation changed to the steadier ground of Leinster's chances of winning the Heineken cup and eventually, after midnight, Adam called it a night and went home.

17

Adam woke abruptly and bolted upright in his bed. His mouth was dry. Panicking, he tried to take in great gasps of air against the will of his constricted throat. He started to cough and splutter as the air made its way deep into his lungs. Lying there, at last still, he kept on breathing.

He was covered in sweat and his heart was rattling wildly against his ribcage. It was always the same dream.

He put a hand down to feel the sheets underneath him. They were damp and cool to the touch against his flushed skin. In the darkness he automatically felt blindly over to the other side of the bed but then he remembered. He turned back and looked at the clock sitting on his locker: its illuminated red LED display told him it was only 5.44 a.m. He groaned; his alarm wasn't due to go off for at least another two hours. Knowing that he wouldn't be able to go back to sleep now, he threw his legs over the side of the bed and got up instead.

Switching on the side-lamp, he took his dressing gown from its home, hanging on the bedpost, and wrapped it around himself tightly, swathing his body against the early-morning coolness of the house. He looked at the damp imprint that he had left on the sheets. He pulled them off the bed to leave the bare mattress exposed and bundled the pile into the laundry basket in the en-suite. The bathroom tiles were a welcome coolness against his feet. Tugging on the cord on the shaving light above the bathroom mirror, he lit the bathroom in an eerie glow. He was almost frightened by the pallor of the man staring back at him: the lines were deeper, the circles blacker than ever before. He pulled the cord down, cloaking the bathroom in darkness once again.

Tiptoeing out onto the corridor, he glanced at the door behind which she lay sleeping. Or maybe she wasn't sleeping, he thought. He stood briefly in front of it, before continuing past.

He crept downstairs and went into the kitchen. He flicked the switch on the kettle and waited for it to boil. It seemed unnaturally loud against the stillness of the house. He made himself a cup of instant coffee with two sugars and no milk and some toast. Sitting down at the table, he flicked through the sports section of yesterday's broadsheet to pass time.

A while later, he rubbed his head and looked at the clock on the wall: it was just after seven. He supposed he might as well go into work early. At least then he would be gone before she woke. He would be doing her a favour, he thought to himself, by saving her the hassle of avoiding him for once.

As he left the house, the sun was starting to rise, filling the sky with its awesome red glow. The grass was bent double under the weight of its dewy cover. He cycled along the canal bank, its body of water still save for the odd ripple from life carrying on underneath its surface. His head was spinning with fragments of his dream. Fragments were all he was ever left with when the night was over. Fragments of frost-covered trees, a watery sunlight, his car, his hand on the grey leather of his steering wheel. It was always the same, it wouldn't leave him.

They needed to talk. He couldn't do this any more, live in this void of despair, it was smothering him whole. Things had gone on like this for too long now and there was an ocean between them. One of them had to do something. He decided he would cook her dinner that night and then he would broach it with her. His stomach was somersaulting even just thinking about it.

* * *

That evening Adam set the table with the Newbridge canteen that they had received from his Great-Auntie May as a wedding gift. If the truth were told they had never so much as taken it out of its polished wooden case before now – it was far too formal for the pair of them but he felt he wanted to make a special effort for tonight. He was following a recipe for slow-braised beef and he studied each line thoroughly in case he missed a bit. He was measuring the ingredients precisely because he wasn't confident enough to throw a cup in here and a spoon in there *ad lib* – if it said fifty grams then fifty grams it was, no more or no less. He had bought a big sticky pecan-nut tart in an artisan bakery that had set him back more than the beef and ingredients for the starter and mains combined, but it was Emma's favourite dessert and he wanted everything to be just right. He knew it was cringey but he just wanted her to remember what they had once been like and, if she could remember that feeling, well then, maybe there was a glimmer that they could save their marriage.

He set the table with the runner and place mats, the way they did it whenever they had people over for dinner. He had a bottle of Sancerre chilling in the fridge and a Montepulciano on the worktop in case she would prefer red. The starter he had prepared was a Caesar salad with no Parmesan or anchovies, because that was how Emma preferred it. Now all he had to do was get changed and wait. He had emailed her at work a few hours ago to ask her to come home early that night but she hadn't even bothered to reply, let alone ask why. But he still held out hope that she would come soon. He had been thinking about it all day, playing over and over in his head how he hoped the conversation would go.

By half past eight there was still no sign of her. The beef was well braised at that stage so he lowered the temperature of the oven and waited. Quarter of an hour later he checked on the beef again which was now way overdone. Frustrated, he turned it off and just let the dish sit there.

At a quarter past nine he opened the bottle of wine in the fridge and poured himself a large glass. Eventually just after half nine, he heard her key in the lock and started.

"Hi, Emma!" He swung his head around the door into the hall.

"Hi." She was purposely monosyllabic.

"You're working late?"

"Yeah."

That was as much as she was offering by way of an explanation.

"Come in, I've made dinner."

"Well, I'm not that hungry."

"Oh right – well, sure the beef is probably inedible at this stage anyway." He laughed nervously, alone.

She followed him into their kitchen, her cool eyes taking in the set table. There was the unmistakable smell of burnt meat. He hurriedly poured her a glass of wine in case she decided to go back upstairs. He needed to keep her here.

He cut her a slice of the tart and put it in front of her.

"I said I wasn't hungry." Her tone was terse.

"Sorry, it's just it's your favourite, that's all, I thought you might like . . ." He trailed off. She wasn't even listening.

"Emma – we need to talk," he blurted out.

Emma looked down at her fingers wrapped around her

glass and felt them tighten automatically. "I already told you, I don't want to talk about it," she said coolly.

"Emma, please just hear me out. Can you just sit down for a minute?"

Amazingly, she did as she was asked and took a seat on one of the high stools at their breakfast bar. He knew he had only a short period of time to say what he wanted to say so he came straight out with it.

"We can't keep on living like this, Emma."

"Like what?"

"Emma, please, I'm begging you, don't make it any harder for me than it already is. I'm just asking to talk to you."

"I've told you before I don't want to fucking talk about it!"

"Look, I'm worried about you. Maybe you need to see someone?"

"Like who?"

"A counsellor or a doctor – I don't know – maybe just someone to talk things through with."

"Oh and talking is really going to fix things, is it? Now why didn't I think of that?"

"Emma, please – there is no need for sarcasm. I'm trying to help you here."

"Well, don't bother!" She practically spat the words at him.

"Emma, we're going to have to talk about things sooner or later – it's sitting between us like a gulf. We can't just keep ignoring it."

"*Ignoring* it? Who's *ignoring* it?" She was shouting now. "If anyone is *ignoring* anything, it's you! Should I just be like you and forget everything that has happened and get on with my life – go back to work straight away, go out drinking every night and think everything will be the same as it was before? Is that what I should do?" She was roaring bitterly at him, her voice full of contempt.

Adam felt as though her words had pierced through his skin and into his chest.

"I haven't forgotten," he said.

"Really? Well, you're doing a pretty damn good job of pretending that everything is normal!" She practically said the words as if they were on fire in her mouth. They fell out on top of one another, landing like hot coals on Adam.

"Emma, it's been over a year now."

"Oh and after a year I'm meant to be feeling okay again, am I? Is that the magic number?"

"I didn't say that." He lowered his voice. "I just thought . . ." He trailed off. "Emma – it's hard, it's a bloody nightmare, but sooner or later you're going to have to realise that life goes on. Whether you like it or not there will come a time when you have to move on."

Emma was stunned as she tried to process the words that Adam had just uttered. They hit her with an almost physical force. She felt winded, as if Adam had just put his mouth over hers and sucked every last breath of life from her lungs or punched her in the chest so hard that she couldn't breathe. Had he really just said what she thought he did? She looked at him in disbelief and Adam knew instantly that he had said the wrong thing. He could see the anger infused with hurt washing over her face, working its way down from her forehead to her mouth, like a venetian blind being shut. *Fuck*. But it was too late, he couldn't take it back.

"Well, I don't *want* to move on, Adam!" she screamed. Her face was red, her eyes wide. Her face was consumed with hatred and anger and it was all directed at him. "How dare you!" Her voice was shrill but trembling, the pitch of her voice rising rapidly. "I cannot believe you just said that!"

Never in all their years together had he ever seen her react like this. Never. *Oh, Sweet Jesus*. Her face was contorted in such rage that he didn't dare answer.

"Time to move on? Do you think I am supposed to just forget everything?"

"No . . . I . . . Oh God, Emma, I'm sorry. That wasn't what I said . . ." Adam buried his head in his hands.

She grabbed her bag off the worktop and ran out to her car. Somewhere on the periphery she could hear Adam calling after her but she wasn't looking back. She jabbed her keys into the ignition and somehow managed to start the car.

She drove on autopilot for a few moments until she felt her mouth water and a rush of nausea forced its way up her throat. She pulled the car over to the side of the road and brought it to a sudden halt, causing another car to swerve out of the way to avoid her. She could feel the sick making its way up her throat. She swung the car door open and leant over, retching onto the road below her. No sooner had she sat back in the seat than she could feel her mouth fill with saliva again. *Oh Jesus.* Emma watched as vomit was projected from her mouth onto the road again.

She sat back into her seat and waited for her body to cool down. She wiped the beads of sweat off her forehead and searched inside her tote for a tissue to clean the spittle from her mouth. She looked at the ground beneath her which was splattered with the liquid that she had spewed up. She closed the car door again and breathed in deeply in an effort to calm her body.

* * *

Emma drove aimlessly around south County Dublin for hours. She had gone through roundabouts, traffic lights and driven down roads she didn't know until she eventually found herself in Dun Laoghaire. She got out and walked the length of the pier and wondered what would happen if she just kept walking until she fell off the end of it. It was tempting to think that with just a few short steps she could be free from all of this. It could all be over. But she knew in her heart and soul that she would never have the balls to do it. She watched a passenger ferry set off majestically on its voyage overseas before she turned around and walked back to her car and sat inside it in the darkness thinking through it all. She was reeling; she couldn't believe Adam could be so callous and have such a lack of awareness of her feelings. After all they'd been through together, she had thought that he knew her better than that. Her chest ached and she was almost certain it was physical; it felt as though her ribcage had been crushed inwards and she found it difficult to draw breath. The ever-present questions kept looping inside her head: *Why, oh why? Why them? How had this happened? It was too cruel.* The injustice goaded her. She felt the warm tears flowing uncontrollably down her face until she could taste the salt in her mouth.

18

Adam sat on his own at the kitchen table. All he could do was sit in stunned silence and let the thoughts and the fear play over and over in his head. He was utterly deflated, all his hopes of having a heart to heart had been quashed before he had even got started. *How have we ended up like this?* He was racking his head for something. Anything. He needed something to cling onto that would make everything okay. He was at the end of his tether. His wife didn't want to be around him, couldn't bear to be around him, as if she resented his very presence in her life. She had effectively shut down on him. He wasn't sure where they went from here. He wasn't religious but he even found himself asking God for an answer. He needed bloody divine inspiration because he didn't know what else to do or what more he could do. He had apologised to her over and over, he had tried to talk it through with her, tried to put himself in her shoes. But it wasn't easy for him either. He couldn't undo what had happened, there was no 'undo' button in life. They either moved on or . . . well . . . he wasn't sure what they would do.

Her words had cut deep; his way of dealing with things was to keep busy, bury his head in work, watch TV, go for a run, meet people – anything at all to take his mind off what had happened – but it didn't mean he had forgotten! He knew he had effectively shut down that part of his brain because it hurt too much but there wasn't a day that went by that he didn't think about what had happened, no matter how often he wished to forget. He was angry now and thinking of all the things he wished he had said. It wasn't easy for him either. It wasn't his fucking fault! Why did she blame him? It was all swirling around in his head. He felt as though he was competing against an egg-timer and his side of the sand was running out rapidly.

The reality of how desperate things were between them had begun to hit home and it both frightened and angered him. He felt like he was banging his head off a brick wall. Emma was his *wife*, they were best friends, he should be able to talk to her. Did she really think she was the only one hurting? He had a right to be upset too – didn't his feelings count? Well, fuck that, there was only so much grovelling he could do. He grabbed his jacket off the coat stand in the hallway. He was going out and he was going to get slaughtered.

He walked to the top of the road and flagged a passing cab. As he sat back in the taxi, he was already starting to feel more relaxed, now that he was out of their house.

When he arrived into the pub, the usual crew was there. He nodded at them all before heading straight to the bar. He needed something stronger than his usual beer so he ordered a double Jameson and Coke. He inhaled the vapour of the whiskey while still standing at the bar, before taking a long sip, allowing it to flow straight back, feeling it burn its way down his throat. He instantly felt warmer, *happier,* as he made his way back to the gang.

They were all well on, having been there since after work

and he was playing catch-up. He had finished the Jameson five minutes later and went back up and ordered the same again plus a round of Mickey Finn's for everyone. A cheer rose up when they saw him returning with the tray of shots. It was a cue to play their usual game where the last person to knock back the shot had to buy another round of shots for everyone. As this game had no discernible end-point everyone ended up in a right state but that was exactly how Adam wanted to feel. He wanted to get shit-faced and forget his own name, where he lived, what had happened, and mostly he wanted to forget that he was married.

* * *

Two hours later and Adam was in a worse state than any of them. He was feeling buoyed up and merry when he went for a wander around the pub. He saw some of the lads were huddled in together talking about something before they all threw their heads back at the same time, exploding in laughter. That was where the *craic* was at.

He made his way over and listened to his mate Tim recount how he had been chatting up an air-hostess on a flight from London recently. As they descended into Dublin, he had asked her what her plans were for later.

"So she was there writing down her number, chatting away, and she goes to open the door and the next thing there's a fucking humongous yellow slide blowing itself up right outside the door! She had forgotten to cross-check the door! So she roars '*Oh fuck!*' and you should have seen the looks on the faces of the other passengers! So as soon as they deflated the bloody slide, we all had to stay in our seats until airport security came on board and she was escorted off the flight. And that was the last I saw of her!"

They tilted their heads back and roared with laughter again.

He tried to keep up with the conversations going on around

him but he found he wasn't able to hear as well as he normally would. It was as if he was listening to everyone at the end of a long tube. He couldn't talk and found it hard to follow what people were saying so he just stood there smiling to himself at Tim's story. He needed to use the bathroom. He squinted his eyes and scanned the bar and eventually he saw a green neon sign down the back of the pub. It was like a beacon. He stumbled from side to side as he made his way down towards the back of the packed pub. "Shorry, mate!" He was aware that people were looking at him and clearing out of his way, in case he should fall on top of them. "I's okay!" He tried to tell them but the words wouldn't come out properly. "Shorry, there!" He tried to straighten up but his body wouldn't listen to his brain's commands – he was too far gone at that stage.

Once inside the single cubicle, it was a relief to have some quiet from the noise outside. He sat on the toilet bowl for an age as his head spun round and round and sloshed from side to side like he was sitting in the middle of a tippy boat. He tried to steady himself but he needed to close his eyes for a minute.

Sometime later there was a loud rapping on the toilet door. He opened his eyes to see he was still sitting on the toilet bowl, trousers gathered around his ankles. How long had he been here? He must have fallen asleep.

He held onto the toilet-roll holder to get his balance as he hauled himself off the toilet seat, then using one hand he bent down to pull up his trousers. He did up his fly and buckled his belt and, sliding the flimsy brass latch across, he went outside. He scanned the blurry queue of angry male faces. *"Shhorry. Fell shleep,"* he mumbled to the waiting crowd by way of explanation. He stumbled back into the bar, bumping and apologising his way down to the lads.

Zoe and Steve came out of Figaro restaurant hand in hand. They'd had a delicious meal and were both stuffed. She had been dying to try out Figaro's menu since she had read a review about it in a magazine a few months back, so when Steve suggested they should go there, she was delighted. The menu had certainly lived up to the review – there was an eclectic mix of dishes, including ostrich meat and shark as well as more local favourites like organic Wicklow lamb. Steve was far more adventurous in his tastes than she was and he had ordered the wild boar, while she went for the safer option of Wagyu beef.

Since the ball, things had been going well between the couple. They saw each other most evenings, when Steve would call in on his way home from whichever market he had been at earlier that day. He always brought Dave with him and Zoe had bought a little wicker basket for him to sleep in, for whenever he stayed over at her place. She had also made him a cushion for inside it from a remnant of some blue gingham fabric they had been using at work. She had stuffed the fabric with some foam before sewing it up. But Dave had chewed up the cushion within hours of Zoe giving it to him, shredding stuffing all over her apartment. So, lesson learned, Zoe now lined the basket with a towel.

"Fancy one more?" Steve asked, draping his arm lazily around her shoulders as they strolled along. They had shared a bottle of red wine with their meal and he fancied another one before they went home.

"Sure!" Zoe said. "There's a lovely pub which I go to sometimes, it's really cosy and it's only a short walk up the canal. How about there?"

"Sounds good to me."

They chatted easily as they walked along. There was a bitter wind blowing and Steve pulled Zoe in tighter against him. Their height difference meant Zoe's head fitted snugly under his arm.

As they approached the pub, they could see a man stumble as he made his way out the door. They both watched the guy, who was as drunk as a lord, but as they got closer Zoe exclaimed, "Is that Adam?"

"Who's Adam?"

"My best friend Emma's husband!"

"Oh yes, of course," Steve mumbled, abashed. She had told him all about Emma and Adam.

"Adam?" Zoe said at they reached the guy who was finding it hard to walk straight.

"Huh?" he said, looking up and taking a while to register who had been calling him.

"Are you okay, Adam – you're looking a bit the worse for wear?" Zoe asked, her voice full of concern.

"S'hure, Zoe, I'm grand." He tried to speak clearly but he was finding it difficult. "Jusht heading home now."

"Right," Zoe said doubtfully, as she and Steve watched Adam stumble away.

"Jesus, that fella will go into the canal if he's not careful. I'll flag a taxi for him," Steve said.

"Good idea," Zoe said gratefully.

Zoe tried talking to an incoherent Adam while Steve kept an eye on the passing traffic. Taxi after taxi went by them with their roof lights off until finally Steve saw a yellow light in the distance. He stuck out his arm and waved at the driver who pulled up at the path beside them.

"Can you give this friend of ours a lift?" Steve asked, smiling at the driver.

The driver looked hesitant about letting Adam into his car when he saw the state that he was in.

"Don't worry, I'll pay for it," Steve said, taking out a twenty-euro note from his pocket and handing it to the driver.

"Well, he'd better not get sick in my car," he said grumpily. "I'm fed up of cleaning the cab after drunken passengers vomit on the seats."

"Not at all, he hasn't had that much to drink," Steve lied even though they all knew Adam was plastered.

"Where am I taking him?"

Steve looked to Zoe.

"Sorry, yeah – it's 59 Cherry Tree Road, Rathmines."

They helped Steve into the back of the car and watched the taxi as it pulled away.

"He'll have some head on him tomorrow!" Steve said, trying to sound light-hearted. He knew Zoe was disturbed about her friend.

"He sure will," Zoe replied distractedly. She was deeply worried. She had never seen Adam so drunk in all the years she had known him. Sure, he enjoyed a few drinks like anybody, but he never normally went overboard like he had obviously done tonight. She knew things were hard for him too and he was going through a lot but she had already tried talking to Emma about it and she hadn't got anywhere. They went into the pub, Zoe vowing to talk to Emma about it again.

19

The next morning Adam was woken by his screeching alarm clock. He didn't dare open his eyes – instead he felt blindly over to his locker to shut the blasted thing up. He drifted off to sleep again and later woke with his heart hammering. He looked at the clock. The red display told him it was 9.03 a.m. *Shit, I'm late.*

He was dying. His head was thumping and his throat was dry. He reached over to his locker for the pint of water that thankfully he had somehow remembered to bring up with him. He gulped it back, leaving only a dribble to run back down the side of the glass. He looked down at himself: he was still in his jeans and T-shirt from last night. *Look at yourself! You're a disgrace.* He lay back and kept still, not daring to move as every part of his aching body screamed in punishment at the amount of alcohol he had consumed the night before, physically telling him he had overstepped the mark.

He forced himself to get out of bed and stand up. But his head was spinning so he sat back down again for a few minutes to steady himself before making his way into the shower. As he stood under the water, every nerve-ending in his body was on a go-slow, his skin almost numb as the droplets danced along his body. When he got out of the shower he felt feverish and thought he might get sick so he opened the window and lay back on the bed until his stomach settled.

He got up at last and dressed slowly and torturously. He walked past Emma's bedroom door and didn't bother to check if she had come home last night. He'd had enough of the anger and hatred she had for him so he kept on walking.

He cycled into work along the well-worn tow-path, forcing himself to breathe the fresh air deep into his lungs to sober up. Although he was feeling like death, it was almost a relief to be going to work; the routine of his job was a welcome escape from his home life. He was respected; people cared what he thought and valued his opinion. They didn't use every excuse to keep away from him or deliberately avoid him. Nobody treated him like he was invisible there.

He sat at his desk in Parker & Associates, just staring at his screen. Being hung over didn't help, but no matter how many times he tried to give himself a shake or reprimanded himself for not concentrating, he still couldn't get what had happened with Emma last night out of his head. He had been in denial for too long now and last night it had really hit home just how bad things were between them. There was nothing left there any more and he didn't know how to get it back. Or even if they would get it back. He felt panicked now; everything was dangerously off track, spiralling out of his control.

* * *

Emma lay still, wondering what time it was. Light was showing around the narrow gaps of the window shutters and was the only wash of light able to enter the room. She lay there with the duvet pulled right up underneath her chin. She stared up at the ceiling; she knew every inch of it, every paint splodge that shouldn't have been there, the cracks in the cornicing and the wispy cobwebs that were getting bigger in the corner. She was too upset to go in to work that day but her mind wouldn't allow her to sleep, as it ran over last night's events; it was running and racing and competing with itself in its thoughts. It chased thoughts like a dog chased its tail.

Earlier that morning she had lain there as Adam's alarm repeatedly went off but he had continued to sleep through. It had enraged her how he was able to sleep through that high-pitched beeping. She'd heard him stumbling in sometime after one as she lay in bed. He'd plodded up the stairs and then had gone quiet and she'd thought that he had finally gone to bed, only for him to resurrect moments later as he staggered along the landing.

Eventually, after the alarm had been blaring on and off for ages, she'd heard him moving around the house: getting out of bed, showering, dressing, plodding downstairs, banging around in the kitchen, before finally banging the front door closed. Even just hearing him moving about was enough to make her body go rigid with tension; everything he did, every move he made, every footstep, every cupboard door banging, made her angry. How could he have said those words last night, how could he tell her it was time to move on? How did he not feel like she did, the hurt, the anger, the injustice all rolled into a sickly ball?

Sometimes, when she looked at Adam now, it was like looking at a stranger. How could he just get on with life like nothing had ever happened? How could he do that – just pretend that everything was normal? It wasn't unusual for her to wonder if she even knew this man any more. Maybe she had never known him?

Now she lay in bed thinking, the anger building inside her. She resented how his life could still go on whereas hers had all-but-in-body ended *that* day.

She needed to see his face so she slid open the drawer on her locker and took out the book where she kept the photo, but looking at him like that wasn't enough. She desperately craved more, she *needed* more, something to touch physically, to hold onto tight and never let go. She slotted the photo back in between the pages of the book and closed it again. The tears began to spill down her face and she wondered when they would ever stop. She had cried so many tears over the last year she thought she would have no more left, that her body should be depleted of its tear reserves at this stage, but there was always more to replace the ones she had freshly cried. Her eyes were red and swollen and her cheeks were patchy and stingy from the salt.

She felt exhausted but her mind was too alert. She reached into the drawer and took out the plastic vial. She took off the cap and shook out two tablets. She swallowed them back without the need of a drink and waited for sleep to take her.

20

That night Adam tossed and turned and eventually, exhausted and worn out from his nightly battle, fell into a deep sleep but he had only brief peace before he found himself back in the dream again. He was driving down the road he knew so well. His arm was stretched out onto the grey leather of his steering wheel. The white winter sunshine glared in through his windscreen, flickers of trees and leaves passed in front of his eyes. Frost wrapped the blades of grass on the ditch in its chilly coat and in places there was the sheen of ice on the road. He passed the farmhouse with the red door and its chickens roaming around amongst bits of old farm machinery and scrap lying idle, having been discarded in another era. He rounded the bend and was gently pulled to the left as the car hugged the curve of the road. Ahead of him a car zipped through a crossroads at speed though it didn't have right of way. Christ! If he had reached the junction a few seconds earlier the idiot would have hit him! Crossing the junction he heard the roar of acceleration. He looked to his left. Oh shit, it was coming straight for him! *Why wasn't he waking up? He normally woke up at this stage.* He waited for what felt like an eternity for the bang. And then it came louder than he had expected: the awful sound of metal crashing upon metal. Simultaneously, he fell forward onto a hard cushion of air and then backwards as instantly. His car was spinning now, his tyres locked, sliding along the icy surface, and he had no control. He was tossed high up in the air, turning over and over like a leaf blowing in an autumn gale and then he was tumbling down, falling, falling. *Bang.* Twisted metal crumpled in around him as shards of silvery glass rained down over his body. Then there was just silence. Deafening, thunderous silence.

When he came around, he didn't know how long he had been there or indeed if he was dead. Every part of his body was roaring in pain. *Is this what death feels like?* He was cold, so, so cold and his clothes felt damp and sticky against his skin. There were voices somewhere and he thought they were calling to him but he couldn't answer. He opened his eyes and looked squarely at the man who kept shouting at him, but it was easier just to close them back down again. He could still hear him, roaring at him now, demanding his attention and he wanted to tell him to fuck off. He just wanted to rest for a while but the stranger wasn't getting the message. He tried to turn his head to check on Fionn but a steel prop was pressed against the side of his face so he couldn't move. The wreckage of steel had anchored him to his seat. He tried to talk to Fionn – *It's going to be okay, son, you're okay* – but no words left his mouth. *Am I dead? Maybe this is what it feels like.*

He could hear a brigade of piercing sirens that were getting louder and higher until they were on top of him, deafening him. He wished they'd go, it was tiring him out. He needed to rest. Then there was a sawing noise cutting so close to him that he could actually see the sunlight gleaming off the blade. He felt tugging as the reverberations from the cutting vibrated through his body until eventually the rays rushed in and blinded him. And then he was being lifted up and laid down. *Maybe now I'm dead?* They were trying to talk to him but he didn't want to talk. They strapped him in and then he was travelling with the siren chasing him. *Fionn. Did they remember to bring Fionn?* He had to close his eyes again, he was so tired.

Part II

21

November, 2009

Jean McParland stumbled sideways, free-falling. She scrabbled to try to grab onto the locker to break her fall but missed it and kept careering forwards, waiting for her head to smash off the wall at any second. Finally it came. She heard the smash of bone against concrete as she tumbled forward, her forehead hitting off the wall. She rebounded again as she fell so that her skull bore the brunt of it this time. She lay slumped on the floor, momentarily stunned, her head looking down on her own body from an awkward angle as she tried to figure out what had just happened.

Almost instantly the pain began to radiate from her skull down through her body and she thought she might be sick – she wasn't sure if it was from the shock or the bang. The 'Hello Kitty' posters looked blurry above her on the wall from where she was lying between the radiator and the plastic-pink doll's house. She could hear Chloe's small voice whimpering in fear.

"Shut the fuck up, y'little bitch, or you'll be fucking next for a slap!" he roared at her terrorised daughter.

Chloe stopped crying immediately, afraid that she would be

next for the brutal treatment. Jean went to shift herself upright in a half-sliding manoeuvre against the wall but her head was spinning so she lay where she was for a few minutes longer. He was standing over her now, looking down at where she was lying on the floor. She swore she could see hatred in his eyes.

"Please, Paul," she begged with her hands covering her face.

He turned and walked calmly out of the room and slammed the door behind him. It wasn't until they heard the car engine that either of them dared moved. Chloe rushed to help pull her up onto her feet.

"Are you okay, Mam?" Chloe was sobbing. "I'm so sorry, Mam, I'm sorry for fighting with him. I should have just given it to him."

"It's not your fault, love. I'm okay, I promise. It's just a bump on my head." She put her hand to her head and already she could feel the swelling grow. Everything was swaying before her eyes but she forced herself to act normally for her ten-year-old daughter's sake. She sat on the edge of the single bed to steady herself.

"I'm scared of him, Mam – I wish he'd just go away and leave us alone."

"I know, pet. I know. Come here." She hugged her daughter in her arms so that Chloe wouldn't see the tears that were streaming down her own face. She was scared too. That was the first time he had actually hit her. God knows he had come so close to it several times before but never before had he actually done it. *Her son had hit her.* She was left reeling with the shock of it all.

"How about you sleep in with me tonight? We can cuddle up together and watch a film in bed. How about that?" She knew it was safer to have Chloe sleep beside her as she couldn't predict what kind of a mood he would arrive home in. She had seen his Jekyll and Hyde behaviour before – he could either be a total monster or else he act like nothing had happened just hours earlier.

Chloe nodded her head emphatically, relieved that she wouldn't have to go to sleep on her own. At ten years of age, she was at that stage where she didn't usually like her mother fawning her with affection but tonight she was vulnerable and upset and was happy to let her mother take care of her. Thank God Kyle was at a sleep-over in his cousin's house, Jean thought to herself. It was one less thing to worry about.

Jean was still trembling as she set up the DVD player while Chloe chose what DVD she wanted to watch. She picked *Shrek*, one of her favourites. Jean sat up against the wooden headboard with her daughter's head resting on her chest as the colours danced from the screen to the wall. Chloe was sucking her thumb, which she did only when she was really tired, and had the duvet pulled right up under her chin while her mother stroked her hair softly. Jean watched her daughter's eyes repeatedly grow heavy and the lids begin to close before she would open them wide again as she tried to fight the tiredness. Eventually she gave in and dozed off in her mam's arms.

Jean lowered the volume so that she was watching the rest of film in silence, as her daughter slept peacefully in her arms. Her head was pounding. She listened to every sound, to see if it was Paul coming home, and she had her phone in her hand just in case. Every sound she could hear outside caused her to tense up with fear in case it was him. She couldn't fall asleep, she was too scared of what might happen if she did, so instead she stayed there staring at the ceiling all night watching Chloe's chest rise and fall in shallow beats.

When morning dawned, Jean was relieved to find that he hadn't come home. It wasn't unusual for him to stay out all night, but there was always the lingering worry of what he was up to. Chloe was still asleep beside her; the poor mite was exhausted by the events of the night before. She managed to wriggle her way out from underneath her and went into the bathroom. She took two more Paracetamol but they didn't seem to be shifting her headache. When she looked in the mirror, the damage was plain to see. It was far worse than she had thought. Her whole left eye was inflamed in an ugly mass of blue-black tissue. How was she supposed to hide that? She splashed cold water on her face before dabbing it dry with a towel. Her sister Louise would be calling to drop Kyle back later on that morning; she would be wondering what had happened. She tried to dab some foundation over the skin to conceal it but it was painful under her fingertips. She persisted, trying to layer concealer, foundation and powder, but no matter what she did the bruising still came through. She knew she was wasting her time; no amount of make-up was going to hide it. She racked her brain to come up with a decent excuse, one that wasn't the usual one women used about walking into doors. She decided to say that she slipped on the floor in the kitchen after she had mopped it and fell against the kitchen table. She would blame her flip-flops. Yes, that was it. They were lethal on wet surfaces, everyone knew that, and in fact she *had* nearly slipped on several occasions in the past when she had been mopping the floor so it was a very easy thing to do. The more she thought about her story, the more she began to believe it herself.

When Chloe woke up, she padded into the kitchen where Jean was seated at the table with a cup of tea. She was startled by her mother's face.

"Your face looks really sore, Mam!"

"Oh, it looks worse than it is," she brushed her off.

"Are you sure?"

"Of course I am!" Her tone was upbeat. "Now, do you know what I'm in the mood for?"

"What?"

"How about pancakes?"

"Pancakes?" Chloe's eyes were wide with excitement.

"And maple syrup!"

"Oh yes, please, Mam!" Chloe squealed at the rare treat.

Jean moved around the kitchen mixing eggs, milk and flour before pouring some of the batter into a heated frying pan. She turned the pancake over and as soon as it had browned, she flipped it out of the pan and onto a plate. She squirted maple syrup in lines across it and served it up to Chloe, then set about cooking more and piling them up on a heated plate.

"He's not here, sure he isn't, Mam?" Chloe asked through a mouthful of pancake.

"No, love, he didn't come home last night."

"Good – I hope he never comes home."

"Chloe!" Jean was taken aback with her daughter's forthrightness. "You don't mean that!"

"I do, Mam!" She defiantly shook her head, her brown eyes wide and serious. "Every time he goes out, I hope he never comes back."

Dear God, thought Jean. She had no idea her daughter was that scared of him. *In her own home.*

"It'll be okay, love."

"Will it, Mam? Because he just keeps getting madder and madder."

She was only ten years old but already she had seen so much and was speaking more sense than Jean ever could.

"I'll talk to him, love, okay? Don't be worrying about things." She took a deep breath. "Now, y'know your Auntie Louise will be dropping Kyle home later?"

"Yes?"

Chloe was smart; Jean knew she would have to tread carefully. "Well, she'll probably be wondering what happened to my face, so I was thinking it might be a better idea to say nothing to her about last night?"

"Why not, Mam?"

"Well, we don't want to worry her. I'll just say I slipped after mopping the floor."

"Mmmh," her daughter said, giving a half-hearted reply, and Jean could see she wasn't really buying into it.

"Please, Chloe, we'll just keep it between ourselves, yeah?" Her voice was desperate.

Chloe looked up at her and Jean begged her with her eyes.

"Okay, Mam, if that's what you want."

"Thanks, love. Did you have enough pancakes? Will I put on another batch?" She was disgusted with herself – trying to butter up her own daughter.

She was dreading facing her older sister. She considered getting Chloe to tell her that she was sick in bed but she knew she would insist on coming up to the room to see how she was, so she would see her either way.

Chloe sat chewing away on her pancakes in small bites while Jean played around with the one on the plate in front of her.

Soon after she could hear the heavy engine of her sister's black Range Rover SUV pulling up beside the footpath outside the house. A gang of teenagers began to circle around it before Louise had even had time to step out of it. They eyed up Louise as she climbed down from the jeep. It looked completely out of place in the forlorn council estate with its graffitied walls, boarded-up houses and foot-high weeds shooting up through the cracked pavements. Louise looked nervously at the teenagers and held her Louis Vuitton tote tight to her chest. Kyle hopped out of the back seat and came running up the path ahead of her.

Although the sisters were separated by just two years in age, Jean and Louise's lives couldn't have turned out more differently. Louise was the wife of an adoring husband who was always whisking her off for romantic breaks or giving her thoughtful little gifts such as flowers or jewellery. He was a senior partner in one of Dublin's leading accountancy firms, which allowed her to be a stay-at-home mum to their two boys, Ronan and

Seán. They had built a huge seven-bedroomed house in the country on acres of land, with its own stables and paddocks and Louise had kitted it out with luxuries that Jean could only dream of, like a mahogany walk-in wardrobe, a kitchen island that was as big as Jean's entire kitchen and a bright and airy living room with floor-to-ceiling-height glass. Louise had employed a designer to choose the wallpapers for the feature walls and complementary fabrics for the curtains and cushions. The house wouldn't look out of place in an interiors magazine. Louise and her family were living the country dream. It was in stark contrast to Jean's three-bedroomed house down the back of a tough local-authority housing estate.

Kyle came in the door. He dropped his bag on the floor and stared at his mother. "What happened to you?"

"Well, hello to you too! Did you have a good time? I hope you were good for Auntie Louise?"

He nodded his head.

"Jesus, Jean, what happened to your face?" Louise's eyes were riveted to the bruise on her younger sister's face. It looked tender and, judging by how she winced every time she made a facial expression, it was painful.

"Oh that? It's nothing!" she replied, trying her best to sound nonchalant. "I was stupidly mopping the floor yesterday in my flip-flops and I slipped and fell against the table. No matter how many times I tell myself never to mop the floor in flip-flops, I never learn, and I ended up with this shiner!" She forced a smile on her face to sell her story.

"My God – that is some bruise!" Louise leant forward to take a closer look.

"It looks worse than it is," Jean lied, because it was bloody sore, as was the egg-shaped lump on the back of her head.

"You gave yourself some bang."

"Bloody flip-flops, you know how slippy the things are."

Something in Jean's eyes wasn't quite right and Louise looked over at Chloe for confirmation.

C'mon, Chloe don't let me down, Jean begged silently.

Chloe sat at the table, saying nothing. Her expression gave nothing away. Jean thanked her inwardly.

"You should get that seen to," Louise continued.

"Sure they can't do anything about a bruise, I'll just have to hide under a pair of dark sunglasses for a couple of days." She laughed, trying to make light of the situation.

"I suppose you're right," Louise said somewhat hesitantly. She looked at the lines on the face of her younger sister, her grey pallor, her brown velour tracksuit, her lank hair pulled back. She was stick-thin from years of worry. You would never think she was the younger one of the two of them.

"Are you sure you're all right?"

"I'm grand, it's just a bruise. I'd hate to see the fuss if I really injured myself."

"Mmmh . . . well, are you sure you're okay?"

"I'm fine, Louise, stop worrying. Will you stay for a coffee?"

"Sorry, love, I have to pick Seán up from karate in five, but if you need anything just give me a ring, yeah?"

Jean let out a huge sigh of relief as soon as she closed the door behind her sister and from the window watched her pull off from the kerb. Chloe and Kyle had moved to the sitting room to play on the X-Box. They were twins and were as close as they came. She could hear Chloe's animated voice talking to Kyle so she moved towards the door so she could hear them better. Their backs were to her and their faces were concentrating on the graphics on the screen.

"He just started screaming because I wouldn't give him my money and then when Mam came up he pushed her and she banged her head and now she has the bruise."

"You should have just given it to him, Chloe."

"I wish I did because it's all my fault that Mam hurted herself."

"Where is he now?"

"Dunno." She shrugged her small shoulders. "He didn't come home. I hope he's gone away forever."

"Me too."

They continued playing their game, as if it was the most normal thing in the world and Jean felt her heart twisting with sadness. She was supposed to be the adult here, she was meant to be in control, but this whole situation was her fault and it was now starting to affect Chloe and Kyle. *How could he try and take her pocket money from her?* She was only ten years old for God's sake! She was saving it for a trip to the toy store that Jean had promised her.

She went into the kitchen and sat at the table drinking a cup of tea. She knew she needed to do something but she hadn't told anyone about the nightmare that was her daily life. No one knew of the constant terror that followed her around, the anxious waiting and wondering what kind of a mood he would come home in. And now that the line had been crossed into violence, what would come next? She constantly lived in fear in case the smallest thing set him off into a rage. He could have killed her last night – her head had missed the edge of the radiator by millimetres, but what was worse was that Chloe had seen the whole thing. What kind of an environment was that for the twins to be brought up in?

After dinner there was still no sign of Paul and she didn't know if that was a good or a bad sign. On the one hand it would give him more time to calm down but on the other he could be building up into a rage again and could fly through the door in a mood worse than when he had left. That was the thing with Paul – he was completely unpredictable.

Later on, after she had put Chloe and Kyle to bed and gone

back down to watch TV, she heard his engine revving outside the house. Automatically her breathing quickened and she prayed he would be in good form. She heard him come through the door and walk straight into the kitchen. He was opening the fridge and then she heard plates banging. He walked out of the kitchen and straight past the sitting-room door and continued upstairs. *Please leave them alone.* She was relieved when she heard him go into his bedroom but minutes later the sound of dance music was pumping throughout the house. She really didn't want to have to confront him.

The sitting-room door opened inwards and Chloe's small face appeared around it.

"Mammy!" Chloe started to cry.

"Come in, pet, what's wrong with you? Is it the music?"

She wouldn't say and just buried her face in her mother's lap, sobbing.

"What is it, Chloe – has he been in to you?"

She shook her head.

"What is it, Chloe – come on, love, you can tell me."

"My bed is all wet." She looked at her mother with shame in her eyes as her face convulsed in tears.

"Oh love, it's all right, these things happen."

She hadn't wet her bed since she was being toilet-trained at the age of two.

"I'm sorry, Mam."

"Don't be silly. C'mon and we'll get you changed."

Afterwards, Chloe didn't want to go back to her bedroom so Jean let her snuggle up onto her knee on the couch. Soon after it was Kyle's turn to come down to the sitting room.

"I can't sleep, Mam, the music is too loud." He rubbed his sleepy eyes as they adjusted to the brightness of the room.

"I know, love, I'm sorry." *Sorry for being too scared to do anything about it.* "Sit down here with myself and Chloe."

Later she sat upright on the sofa with her two children lying on either side of her in sleeping bags as they eventually nodded off to sleep. She watched the hours change with the small hand on the carriage clock, the music still blaring down from upstairs until she drifted off in a hazy sleep at some point herself.

22

On Monday morning Jean busied herself with the morning routine of buttering bread and packing lunchboxes for Chloe and Kyle. They ate their cereal with painstakingly small mouthfuls while she looked on in exasperation.

"Hurry up, you two – we're going to be late."

They looked up at her but continued to chew at a frustratingly slow pace. When they finally finished, they all bundled into her car. They were just reversing out the drive when Chloe realised she had forgotten her PE kit. Jean sighed wearily before getting out of the car again and letting herself back into the house, running around frantically trying to locate her daughter's tracksuit and runners. She ran back out to the car and they set off on the school run. She dropped them outside the school gates, giving them each a kiss as they hopped out.

Although it was only nine o'clock she was already exhausted. She hadn't slept a wink after Paul's antics over the weekend. She looked at herself in the rear-view mirror. The swelling in her face had now turned to a dirty yellowy-green colour but at least it was starting to fade. She had masked it as best she could, using layers of carefully applied concealer and different shades of foundation but if anyone in work asked what had happened, she would tell them the same story as she had told Louise. She locked her car and, taking a deep breath, made her way into the small solicitors' office where she worked as a legal secretary.

As expected her colleagues looked at her face with concern but her recounting of the story to Louise at the weekend had served her well and she told the story like it was real and even managed to throw in a laugh at her own stupidity. She knew they bought it.

She sat down in front of her computer and got stuck into the cases she was working on. Her desk was a mass of paper – she had several letters to type, she also had to serve the proceedings for a family dispute. Plus she needed to do the preparation for a High Court case for her boss Sheila by this evening. Normally secretaries didn't get involved in that sort of work but the partners had grown to trust her over the years and had been giving her bigger and bigger projects until now she was often doing the work of the solicitors herself. She liked the fact that they knew she was capable of the extra responsibility so she gladly took it on, plus it was break from the tedious administration side of her job.

When the rest of the girls were going out for lunch she declined because she wanted to get through all the paperwork on her desk. At half three, just as she was putting her signature on yet another notice letter, her mobile on the desk beside her started to ring. The number of her neighbour Rita Maguire flashed up. She knew immediately something was up at home so she excused herself from the office and stepped outside to answer it.

"Rita – is everything all right?"

"Jean, I'm sorry for ringing you in work again but it's Paul."

Jean felt her heart sink. She knew where this was going. "What's he done now?"

"He's gone and locked the other two out again, I saw them out my window – standing shivering outside in the garden, the poor things."

"Oh God, are they okay?" *I'm going to kill him.*

"They're grand, don't worry, they're fine. They're over here now, having a cup of tea and some bread and jam with me."

"Right, I'm on my way."

"You take your time, love. Sure amn't I glad of the company?"

"Thanks, Rita, I'll be there as quick as I can."

When Jean hung up she was trembling with rage. Enough was enough. This was the third time in the last month that he had locked them out after they had come home from school because he wanted the house to himself. Effectively he was barring them from their own home and it wasn't on. She went back into the office and a sea of heads turned to look at her but she kept walking past her desk and knocked on the glass pane of Sheila O'Malley's office.

"Come in!"

"Hi, Sheila."

"Jean, is everything okay?"

"Look, Sheila, I'm really sorry, but there's a family emergency. I have to leave early."

"But what about the Gallagher case – you were meant to be preparing a summary for the court case tomorrow?"

"I'm really sorry, Sheila, it's halfway there. I know that isn't good enough," she lowered her gaze, "but I really have to go."

"Jean, this is the third time this month you've had to run home for a *'family emergency'*." She said the words with emphasis to imply that she didn't really believe her.

"Sheila, I'm awfully sorry, I really am – I know this isn't acceptable – but I have to go." She couldn't meet the other woman's eyes.

"You're right, Jean, it *isn't* good enough – do you think I can stand up before the judge, in front of the senior counsel and whoever the hell else in the High Court tomorrow and tell them my summary is half-ready? You can be bloody sure I can't!"

Jean squirmed awkwardly in front of her boss. She knew everyone outside would be able to hear the exchange.

"Well, you'd better go then if you have to go," said Sheila curtly. "But we'll talk about this tomorrow."

"Thanks, Sheila," she mumbled before leaving the office. She could feel her cheeks burning and she knew her colleagues would all have been earwigging and trying to figure out what had just gone on.

* * *

When she rounded the corner to the road where she lived, she saw Paul's car in the driveway. She parked on the road outside and got out quickly. She knew the twins would be okay with Rita for a few minutes longer. She was livid; she needed to speak to him now. She let herself in and stormed into her living room, where Paul was sprawled out on the couch watching some daytime TV show about police chases. She walked straight over and turned it off.

"What the fuck d'you think you're doing?" he roared at her, rising up from the sofa.

"I could ask you the same question – what do *you* think you're doing? This is *my* house, Paul – *my* house. As it is also Chloe and Kyle's! How dare you! How dare you stop them going into their own home!"

"Ah, would you ever fuck off!"

"No, Paul, no, I won't. This is the third time this month you've done this, left your brother and sister sitting on the doorstep on a bitterly cold day and left me explaining to my boss yet again why I have to run home. Well, that is it. I won't tolerate it any more. Are you listening to me, Paul – that is the end of it!"

"Whatever." He got off the couch.

"Come back here, Paul! *Paul!*"

She was screaming now she was so infuriated but he ignored her and walked out the front door and got into his Honda Civic. He had modified the white Honda Civic Type R so that the modifications were worth more than the car itself. You could hear the sound of the chrome exhaust pipe as it roared before he got near the house and the gears hissed into action when you changed them. He had got the windows tinted, bucket seats fitted, and had recently had enough cash to have a spoiler moulded onto the back. Jean didn't know how he paid for it all and she wasn't sure she wanted to.

His indifference enraged her. She just didn't seem to be able to get through to him. No matter how much she shouted and screamed and ranted and raved, he didn't pay any heed to her. He didn't respect her authority any more; he hadn't done for a while now. The last time he had done this, she had tried getting through to him by taking away the one thing he loved: she had hidden his car keys as punishment but he just went and took her car instead even though he wasn't insured to drive it.

Of course she knew it was her own fault that Paul was like this. Coming from a broken home and not having his father in his life were bound to have an effect. She knew what the child psychologists and parenting books would say. She had let him down over the years and it was payback time now. Her son had so much anger built up inside and she was his target practice. But over the last year Paul's behaviour had gone from bad to worse. He was out of control. He lay around the house all day; she had given up on asking him to get himself a job. Then he would go off at night in his car to God only knew where. She had asked her own father, who Paul had always been close to, to have a word with him but to no avail. He wouldn't listen to anyone; there was no getting through to him. She was at her wits' end and, what was worse, the effect it was having on his younger brother and sister broke her heart. They were afraid of his mood swings and what they would face each day. Chloe would be watching a cartoon in the sitting room and Paul would just walk in and switch channels and the sad thing was she didn't even dare challenge him on it any more. He terrorised the whole house. One wrong word and he would rise up, like a lion awakened – it could be something simple like asking how he was that day or serving him his dinner slightly burnt.

Jean went across the street to Rita's house. The woman was in her mid-seventies and lived alone. She had been widowed young and all her children had grown up and moved on. She loved making a fuss of Chloe and Kyle and often gave Jean a hand to keep an eye on them if she had to go out somewhere. Jean didn't know what she would do without her. She let herself in through Rita's back door.

"Hi there, Rita."

"Come in, love, they're in here."

The twins were seated around Rita's kitchen table eating freshly baked Madeira cake and washing it down with cups of tea.

"Hi, Mam!" said Kyle.

They both smiled up at her and Jean felt her heart twisting with guilt for them again.

"Will you have a cup yourself, love? God knows you could probably do with it – you look exhausted!" She eyed Jean's bruised face but made no reference to it.

"I'm okay, thanks, Rita – are you two ready? We need to get cracking on your homework."

The disappointment on their faces at having to leave Rita's homely kitchen and the feast in front of them was obvious.

"C'mon," she said firmly so they knew there was no point protesting.

As Chloe and Kyle walked ahead of her over to their house, she stood on the step with Rita.

"Thanks again, Rita."

"Will you stop – sure isn't it nice for me to have their company for a while?"

"No, I mean it, Rita, thanks for keeping an eye out for them."

"Well, y'know how fond I am of the pair of them and they don't stay small for long – don't I know it from all of mine?"

Jean smiled at the older woman whose lined face was the very essence of human kindness.

"Look, Jean, is everything okay? I'm not prying and you can tell me to mind my own business if you think I am but . . . well . . . just with Paul?"

"I'm doing my best, Rita."

"Heavens above, I know you are, love, I know you are. That's not what I meant! It's not easy on your own – but just give me a shout, any time, if you need anything, you know where I am."

"Thanks, Rita. For everything."

* * *

When Paul came home that evening he was his usual gruff self. He ate the dinner put in front of him without so much as a thank-you. Of course Jean knew better than to expect an apology for what had happened at the weekend or even today. And she was too worried about Sheila's parting words to push things further with Paul. Sheila's 'We'll talk in the morning' had seemed ominous.

* * *

The next morning, as Jean walked into the office, she braced herself to face her boss. Knowing Sheila, and knowing she'd had even more time to stew, she knew she would be in for a severe telling-off. Oh well, she would just have to grin and bear it, she thought to herself. She sat down at her desk and, while the rest of them chatted about last night's *Coronation Street*, she kept her head down and tried to finish off the summary for Sheila's case in the High Court in the afternoon; she hoped it might appease her a bit. As she typed out a list of precedents she could feel a presence and she looked up to see Sheila standing at the side of her desk.

"I'm just finishing off that summary for you, Sheila. Sorry, I know I'm cutting it fine but I should have it for you within the next hour."

"There will be no need, Jean –"

"No, honestly, I'm almost done now."

"No, Jean, I don't think you understand. We need to speak with you in my office."

Jean wondered who the 'we' were? She began to feel flustered and her heart was beating wildly. She walked behind Sheila and made her way into the office to see the managing partner, Billy Walker, already sitting there waiting for her. Sheila shut the door behind them before taking a seat alongside Billy so that the desk divided them from Jean. Jean knew things were serious if Billy was here.

"Jean, firstly I would like to thank you for coming in to see myself and Billy." Sheila was being overly formal. "Now . . ." She cleared her throat before proceeding "The last few weeks, Jean, have seen you need to leave work early on three separate occasions."

"Sheila – and Billy – again I apologise, I admit I haven't been very professional over the last month or so but . . ." she lowered her voice – it killed her to bring her personal life into things, "well, I'm having some family difficulties at the moment."

Silence descended upon the room.

"Jean, we don't wish to delve into your private life but we need someone who is reliable, not someone likely to have to run home after only starting work five minutes beforehand. We have clients' deadlines to meet, legal deadlines that have to be fulfilled. You of all people will understand that."

She found herself nodding in agreement.

"Now, we both know you are a very valuable employee, in fact you are our most capable secretary, but your behaviour over the last few weeks has left us with no option and it is with great regret that we have to inform you that unfortunately we will no longer be able to keep your position open for you. Jean, I'm sorry but we have no choice but to let you go."

Jean felt as though this was all being said to her from afar. She was being fired? She hadn't been expecting that – she thought she was in line for a warning at the most. A warning – she would have understood that – but surely they were overreacting by firing her? In fact, they couldn't. Legally, they wouldn't be able to do this. There had been no written or even verbal warnings and a solicitor especially would need to be seen to be going through due process.

These thoughts flew through her mind. Then, "I understand," she found herself replying although she wasn't sure why. She only knew she had no energy left for a fight of this kind. And she knew in her heart that, inevitably, there would be more crises with Paul in the very near future.

They nodded at her, obviously relieved that she seemed to be taking it without protest.

"Now we will of course pay you one month's notice and we'll give you a good reference."

"Thank you," was all she could think of to say. She stood up to go, and let herself out.

As she walked back to her desk, she was stunned. Why had she been so complicit in all of this? As usual she had done what she was told. When was she ever going to learn how to stand up for herself? But instead she found herself standing at her desk packing up her things.

She went home a broken woman. She tried her best to hold back the tears but she was devastated. Her work was important to her; it was the one thing that gave her a sense of self and made her feel like she wasn't just scrounging off the state. It afforded her a small bit of independence, things like having her car or being able to buy little things for the kids. It was only small money but it meant so much for her to have it. Plus the routine of going into an office every day and not just meeting the same depressing faces from the estate did her good. She knew if she sat at home all day long, looking out the windows, the hopelessness would eventually get to her. But it went beyond her own personal reasons – she had desperately wanted to save up enough to get Paul out of the estate; she was trying to save up to rent a house in the town and to take him away from all his friends and the trouble. That was her goal, to get out of the bloody hell-hole where they were living. Without her job, she knew her future was bleak. All her dreams of giving her children a better life had just been wiped out. She didn't know how she would ever get out of the poverty trap now.

23

Ballydubh Village, 1991

Jean had met Gavin Grimley when she was just fifteen years old. She vaguely knew who he was; he was one of *them*, the gang of lads that hung out on the wall outside the school. She and Louise had to walk past them every day on their way home. She knew their faces – they had been a couple of years ahead of her in school, but one by one they had all dropped out. They had never bothered to look for work, it was easier just to draw the dole. They now filled their days hanging around the town and would always be waiting on the school wall at the end of the day. They would shout down at the sisters from where they sat on top of the railings. Sometimes they would even throw things at them, but never anything that would hurt, just random objects like sweet wrappers or pieces of paper. They always singled Jean out because they knew they got the best reaction from her. They would make a comment about how she looked or what she was wearing, anything at all that they knew would embarrass her. She was painfully shy and her cheeks would go bright red until her whole face felt as though it was burning up to match her wine-coloured gabardine. Her reaction egged them on even more. She wished they would leave her alone, she didn't want their attention. Louise would tell her to ignore them, that they were just looking for a reaction, but she couldn't help it. She felt as though Louise thought it was her fault, that she was drawing it on herself. She began to dread their journey to and from school and, if for some reason Louise wasn't able to walk with her, she would lower her head and quicken her pace almost into a run until she was past them.

When Louise went to university, Jean knew she would have to walk home alone every day so she began to heed Louise's advice and tried to act cool as she walked past them, pretending not to hear them when they shouted at her. On the first day she tried it, they kept on shouting but on the second day, the shouts were fewer and by the end of the week they never shouted again. She was amazed when this had the desired effect. She slowly began to get used to them and, although they would watch her and take a drag on their cigarettes as she passed, for the most part they left her alone.

One day just after she had walked by them, she heard heavy footsteps running behind her. She felt her blood run cold; there had been no one else on the path but the boys. She swung around in panic and immediately saw it was one of them. He was dressed in baggy jeans with a hoody pulled up over his head. She tried to break into a run but found herself rooted to the pavement, her legs were frozen in fear.

"Hi, there." He came up beside her and slowed down to walk on the path next to her. "Sorry, didn't mean to scare you." He pulled down his hood.

He was smiling and he didn't seem like he was going to hurt her.

"You didn't," she lied. She felt a bit silly now.

"Where are you going?"

"Home."

"Can I walk with you?"

"Why?"

"Because I like you."

Jean was startled by his forthrightness. This was the same boy who had tormented her since the age of fifteen and now he was telling her he liked her!

"But you always tease me and shout!"

"Yeah, sorry about that. It was only a bit of fun. What's your name?"

"Jean."

"I'm Gavin."

They walked the rest of the road in silence. Jean didn't know what to make of him. She wondered if it was a dare from the lads and tomorrow she'd be the subject of more ridicule. When they reached the top of her road, she told him he had better go. She didn't want her mother to see her with him. She knew she'd be in trouble.

The next day, the lads had stayed quiet as she approached and Jean inwardly said a prayer of thanks that she wasn't going to be mocked for having fallen for one of their stupid pranks. When she walked through the convent gate, Gavin hopped off the wall and walked up beside her again. He continued doing the same thing each day, until it became a daily routine that he walked her home.

When it became clear he wasn't trying to cause trouble for her, she began to lower her guard with him. She was surprised to find herself thinking that he was a nice guy; he was completely different to what she had thought. Plus, because she was so shy, she didn't have too many friends in school, so she enjoyed their chats. As she talked to him and got to know him she learnt that he was from the town. He was very open with her and he told her that his mother was dead and he lived with his father who had hit the drink very hard after his mother had passed away. He wasn't violent or anything but he was just buried under his grief. Jean was shocked by his story and felt so sorry for the childhood he'd had but he just shrugged his shoulders at her and said "That's life!"

As he told her more about himself on their walks she couldn't help but compare his upbringing to her own. While she had two loving parents, breakfast served before school every morning, a clean pressed uniform laid out, warm soup waiting on the cooker in the evenings, piano lessons, speech and drama and ballet and hopefully, if she did well enough in her Leaving Cert, university next. Gavin didn't have any of that. He was only two years older than her but he had grown up years ago. However, he didn't want pity. He accepted that this was his lot and just got on with it.

Soon she found she loved being around him. When she walked out of the school every evening she was so excited. Her heart would leap when she caught a glimpse of him waiting for her outside the gate.

She dared not tell her mother or Louise; she knew what they thought of the Grimleys. She had heard her father talking about how he had seen Gavin's father falling out of O'Looney's pub and her mother would tut and say that that he had "never got it together after his wife had died" so she knew they would never approve of their friendship.

Soon after, the daily walk from the school to her house became too short and she longed for more time with him so they began to take a detour and go down to the weir on their way home. They would sit and watch the rushing water until Jean would look at her watch and know her mother would be starting to wonder where she was.

One day out of the blue as they sat on the meadow grass, their voices drowned out by the rushing water, he had leaned over and kissed her. It was the first time she had ever kissed a boy and she could have sworn she had been lifted off the ground. She wanted more and they had kissed deeply for hours.

Pretty soon they started to climb over the old stone wall to the weir every day. When the summer came, she would fling off her gabardine and roll down her long wool socks. She would loosen the knot in her tie, undo the top button of her blouse and run through the grass until they reached their spot near a big ash tree. He would sit back against it and she would lean back into his arms. He would stroke her hair or plant delicate kisses along the skin of her neck, so light that they caused the hairs on her skin to stand up. They would pick blades of grass and split them down the centre. She felt so comfortable with him. He understood her and he was the only other person who she had ever opened up to outside of her family.

As the exams drew closer, she began telling her mother she was staying back after school to do supervised study just so she could have an extra two hours with Gavin. She knew she was way behind on the amount of revision that she needed to have done at this stage but she still couldn't bring herself not to meet him every day. She cringed inwardly whenever she heard her proud parents telling friends and family how she "had the head down" and was "working very hard" and that they were "expecting great things from her" – it just made her want to run out and escape and to spend even more time with Gavin. It was a vicious circle. She had such a mountain of revision that she needed to do, she didn't even know where to begin. She felt the pressure building inside her and the more she avoided it, the harder it became. She began to block it from her head and pretend it wasn't happening.

The weeks went on and soon it was the night before the Leaving Certificate. The first exam was English Paper I and, as she opened her copy of *Othello*, she began to panic when she realised that she didn't have the first idea what the play was even about. She had been in class but had been too busy daydreaming, as evidenced by the pencil scrawls that littered every page. She tried to remember what her teacher had said about the characters of Iago and Desdemona. She knew one of them was meant to be evil but for the life of her couldn't remember which one. She knew there was no way she would even be able to blag her way through this. She slammed the text book shut. It was too late; the volume of work to be done at this stage was insurmountable.

* * *

Jean climbed out of her bedroom window and ran down the road into town. She knew which house belonged to Gavin because he had pointed it out to her before. She knocked on the door with the paint long since cracked and faded and prayed he was home. She was relieved when it was opened to see him standing there.

"Hey, what are you doing here? Are you okay?" He was surprised to see her. She had never been to his house before.

"No!" She began to cry. "I've left it too late to study, I can't take anything in. My mam and dad are going to kill me."

"Hey, it's okay!" He wrapped his arms around her and brought her inside.

Jean stepped inside into the hallway and took in the gloominess of the room. She tried not to look shocked by the state of the house. The wallpaper was coming unstuck from the wall in parts and the ceiling was stained with black mildew spots. The brown swirly carpet on the floor was filthy and as Gavin led her upstairs to his room Jean noticed the stair rail was covered in a layer of dust. She quickly removed her hand. As she followed Gavin into his room, she was hit by the stale air. Even his room was grimy. She sat on the edge of his bed, amongst piles of CDs and clothes strewn about the floor.

"C'mon, you're going to be fine." He rubbed her shoulders "You're really clever."

"No, I'm not."

"Yes, you are. Some of things you tell me – like that time we were sitting out in the rain and remember there was thunder and lightning and you told me that you could calculate how far away it was from us?"

"But that's not going to pass my Leaving Cert for me, is it?" she wailed. "Oh I'm in such deep shit. I'm not going in tomorrow."

"You have to go!"

"I don't!"

"At least give it a go – it might all start coming back to you again once you get in there."

She looked at him doubtfully.

"Please, Jean, you have to – your parents will freak if you don't go in. Then they'll find out about us and they'll stop us being together."

The thought of not being able to see Gavin frightened her. She knew he was right; if she didn't do her Leaving Cert, her parents would leave no stone unturned until they found out what was wrong. She could see it now; she would be wheeled into counsellors or brought to the best education advisers money could buy. It would just make everything a million times worse.

"C'mon, do it for me. Please?" he begged.

"Okay, only for you – I'll give it a try."

"That's the girl!"

He walked her back down the stairs. As she passed the sitting-room door, she could hear loud snores, presumably coming from his father. At the top of her road he gave her a kiss on the forehead and told her he would be waiting for her after the exam finished.

* * *

While all her classmates had chattered nervously outside the exam hall saying that this year it had to be "Yeats because

142

Clarke had come up for the last four years in a row" and that "the character sketch better be based on Iago", Jean hadn't joined in. She had kept to herself because she didn't have a clue what they were even talking about. They had looked at her and assumed she was just quietly confident.

With trepidation she turned over English Paper I. All the words in black print looked jumbled together. Phrases like *'Compare and Contrast'* and *'Give an Account of'* jumped off the page in front of her. She told herself to calm down and to breathe deeply. She read the questions and read them again but she couldn't think of anything to write. Whatever bit of knowledge she had retained from class, that she was hoping would get her through, was still locked inside her head. She looked around the exam hall at the heads buried in concentration. Hands were writing furiously trying to get hurried thoughts onto the paper in case they were forgotten again. She wrote her name and exam number on the top, hoping that that might quick-start her memory, but nothing was coming.

Someone coughed she could hear the heavy footsteps of the invigilator as he wore a path up and down the hall. He stood beside her breathing heavily and she could tell he was looking at her empty answer book. She kept her head down and pretended she was just reading the paper again. She looked up at the black and white clock on the wall and watched the hands moving around. *Tick, tick, tick.* She knew she was obliged to stay for the first half an hour and after that she could go. She watched the hands turning around until they read ten o'clock. She shoved back her chair, causing a screech along the floor tiles. A sea of heads turned to stare at her. She got up from her desk and walked up towards the invigilator and handed him her paper. She could see the looks of confusion on her classmates' faces as they wondered where she was going: *She's only been here half an hour – she couldn't be finished yet!* She could see them looking at each other, amazed.

Jean was one of the top pupils, she was one of the ones that should be there right until the last second frantically trying to scribble down every last bit of knowledge onto the paper before she was forced to stop.

As she walked towards the door Jean could feel ninety pairs of eyes boring holes in her back. When she got outside she cried. *Her life was over, she had just ruined her life.* She was forever being told that the Leaving Cert was the most important exam of her life and it would determine her whole future. She went outside into the yard and through tear-filled eyes could make out Gavin's outline as he waited for her on top of the railings like he did every day. As he climbed his way down, she ran up to him and flung her arms around his neck. She was relieved to feel his strong arms around her, tight and reassuring.

They walked hand in hand and climbed over the stone style and walked down to the weir. She sobbed as he held her tight in his arms. She started to kiss him, hard and passionately. She wanted to feel his skin, she needed to be close to him, closer to him than she had ever felt before. She took off his T-shirt and lay on his bare chest in the heat of the June sun. They fumbled with each other's clothes until they were both half-naked and he was lying on top of her. Then he entered her and she felt a sharp stabbing pain momentarily.

"Are you sure you're ready?" he asked, feeling her body tense.

"Uh-huh," she nodded.

He moved inside her, their bodies united. She had never felt closeness like this.

"I love you, you know?" he said.

"I love you too."

* * *

They lay there together in the heat of the sun for hours until Jean checked her watch and knew her mother would be waiting for her at home to hear how the exam had gone.

Gavin helped her back over the wall and she jumped onto the path below. He walked her to the top of the road and they kissed goodbye. She loved Gavin Grimley and he loved her, that was all that mattered. She couldn't believe she had just had *sex*. She tidied herself up and smoothed her hair so her mother wouldn't become suspicious and walked on cloud nine back to her house.

As her mother fussed and fawned over her, serving up her favourite dinner of lasagne, followed by home-made chocolate brownies, Jean knew she couldn't do it to her. She couldn't shatter the high hopes that she held for her so she lied and told her that it had gone well, a bit tricky in parts but otherwise okay. She didn't have the guts to tell her that actually she had handed the paper back to the invigilator as blank as it had been given to her in the first place. She was amazed at how easy the lies came. She knew the truth would come out eventually but she would get a plan together by then.

* * *

By the end of June, Jean's period was overdue by a week or so. She tried not to think about it. She pushed it out of her head. She was irregular anyway. Now that school was finished, she had loads more time to spend with Gavin. They spent long endless days by the river in each other's arms talking about what they would do in their future together, making up scenarios about where they would live and what they would work at.

By the middle of July, before Jean could even get out of bed in the mornings, she had to rush to be sick. She felt wretched; she was pale and drawn and was constantly exhausted. She couldn't stomach the dinners her mother prepared for her; even the smell of her favourites were enough to send her running to the bathroom to throw up again. Her mother, worried that she had a vicious stomach bug, insisted on bringing her to Dr

Thornton. Jean tried to tell her she was fine but she insisted they were going and that was the end of it.

Jean couldn't make eye contact with Dr Thornton as her mother outlined her symptoms. When he asked Mrs McParland to step outside because he wanted to have a word alone with Jean, her mother began to protest but the doctor stayed firm and an annoyed Mrs McParland found herself sitting outside in the waiting room.

"Now, Jean, nothing to be frightened about, I just want to ask you a few questions alone if that's okay?"

Jean nodded.

"So when did you have your last period?"

"May or June."

He looked up from where he was scribbling his notes. "Can you remember which?"

"End of May maybe."

He began to write again. "Now please don't be offended but I have to ask the question – is there any possibility that you might be pregnant?"

Jean said nothing. She felt her eyes getting heavy as they filled with the weight of tears which overflowed and spilled down her face. She tried to wipe them away but they still kept coming.

"It's okay, Jean, it's going to be okay. I'm going to get you to do a pregnancy test just to confirm, okay?"

She nodded, incapable of speech.

"There's a toilet in there and I want you to get a urine sample for me." He handed her a brown plastic vial.

Jean sat on the toilet knowing what was going to happen. She knew she was pregnant; she had known it since she noticed her period hadn't arrived in June. She knew she would come out and hand this jar of piss to the doctor and he was going to tell her that she was pregnant and her life would be changed forever. She knew her mother was going to hit the roof, that was a given. She didn't know how Gavin would react, she hadn't told him her period was late. Would he stick by her and tell her they would raise the baby together? Or would he do a runner like the nuns in school and her mother had always warned about when young girls got pregnant? She considered staying in the small toilet cubicle forever where she could be protected from all their reactions. There was a soft knocking on the door.

"Jean – are you okay in there?"

"Yes, I'm coming now, Dr Thornton." She did up her jeans and went back out to the surgery and handed the vial to him.

She didn't watch as he went about the test. Instead she prayed that maybe it was just a bad bug she had picked up after all, like her mother thought.

The minutes ticked by, then she became aware that he was checking the test.

"Jean . . ."

She looked up and met his eyes.

"It's positive."

She was pregnant. Her life was over.

Her mother had been called back into the room then and Jean felt as though she was watching all of this from above. As Jean was incapable of speaking, Dr Thornton had broken it to her mother that her seventeen-year-old daughter was actually not sick at all, just pregnant. Jean watched her mother's face crumple as the shock took hold and she looked at her daughter for confirmation that it was true. But instead of shouting and screaming like Jean had thought she would, she remained silent which unnerved her. She almost wished she was angry.

"You couldn't be – are you sure?" was all she could muster up.

They left the surgery and a stunned Mrs McParland drove home with her daughter in the passenger seat, clutching a bundle of leaflets all offering advice on how best to deal with a crisis pregnancy. Every so often her mother would ask a question. "But how? Who? Where?" but Jean stayed quiet.

Later that evening, when both had had time to digest the turn of events, Jean told her mother everything, from how she met Gavin, to her appalling Leaving Certificate. She watched as each confession broke another piece of her mother's heart as she realised that her daughter's future had been dramatically altered from the path she had hoped and dreamed for her. Even though she had been bright in school, Úna McParland had never gone to university herself; her parents could never have afforded it in a million years. She had a tough childhood, helping out on the farm early in the morning before school and afterwards every evening too. She had left school at the age of twelve to work in the local sewing factory. Most of the girls in her class had done the same thing; it was only the privileged few, the daughters of doctors or solicitors in the town that had gone on to secondary school. That was why she had wanted so much more for her daughters, she had made it her life's work to make sure they had everything that she didn't have and now her youngest daughter was about to go down a radically different path despite everything she had done for her. Úna had not seen it coming.

As expected, her father had hit the roof when he was told that evening, but Úna had begged him to stay calm and pointed out that his reacting like that wasn't helping anybody.

Louise came in from college a while later, in her long skirt and granddad-style cardigan – she had recently become a convert to the grunge look. When her mother had told her about Jean, she had looked at her little sister with a mixture of disgust and pity. Later, when they were alone, she had cornered her. "How could you be so naïve – have you never heard of a condom? All teenagers have sex nowadays but they use protection for God's sake!" she said angrily. It was Louise's reaction that had hurt the most. She had always looked up to her older sister.

Over the next couple of days her family discussed what Jean

was going to do, but she wasn't included in the plans. She tried telling them that Gavin was a really good guy and that he loved her and it wasn't his fault that his dad was an alcoholic. She told them that she and Gavin would raise the baby together and that she knew Gavin would stick by her even though she hadn't even told him yet that she was pregnant, but her parents forbade her to go anywhere near him ever again. She listened as they planned her whole life out for her. She was going to take this year off and have her baby, then she would go back and repeat the Leaving Cert the following year and go on to university. Úna would take care of the baby. They never asked her if this was what she wanted.

24

As the weeks went past, Jean missed Gavin desperately. Her mother stuck to her like glue and Jean found it impossible to sneak off and meet him. She had no way of communicating with him and she was worried about what he must be thinking of her, when all of a sudden she didn't show up to meet him. She had just vanished on him and he didn't even know she was pregnant. It didn't help matters that his dad didn't have a phone in the house so she couldn't even ring him when she was at home alone. She begged to be allowed go for a walk on her own, but her mother refused saying she couldn't be trusted and that if she really wanted to go for a walk, she would happily go too.

One day her mother accompanied her to Dr Thornton for one of her antenatal check-ups. After an hour Úna looked up from the magazine that she had been licking and thumbing for the umpteenth time and sighed. The waiting room was still packed – there were still nine people ahead of them. She knew it would be hours before Jean would been seen and, sighing heavily again, she put the magazine down and said she was going off to get a few messages and would be back shortly.

150

Jean knew this was her one and only chance. Gavin's house was located two streets behind the surgery. She knew if she hurried that she could be there and back in a matter of minutes and her mother need never know. She had butterflies in her tummy just thinking about seeing him again. She waited for a few minutes after her mother had gone, before getting up and telling the receptionist that she needed some air. Taking in her growing bump, the receptionist smiled at Jean sympathetically and told her to take her time and she was sorry they were running behind schedule.

Once outside the door, Jean looked left and right to make sure there was no sign of her mother before she tore down the street and around the corner to Gavin's house. She knew people were looking at her but she needed to get there fast, she didn't have much time. She prayed he was at home. She pressed the bell and stood on the step and waited anxiously. She strained to listen for anyone coming to the door but she was met with silence. *Please be here, Gavin. Please.* She pressed the bell again and pounded on the door with force and waited a bit more but there was still no reply. She felt cheated that he wasn't in; this was the first chance she'd had in months to see him and likely the only chance she would get for months again. She turned around defeated and walked slowly back towards the surgery. She had just rounded the corner back onto Market Street when she heard her name being called.

"Jean!"

She swung around to the familiar voice, the voice that instantly comforted her and told her things would be okay.

"Gavin!"

They ran towards each other on the street and embraced, momentarily forgetting they were in Ballydubh village where people weren't used to this kind of carry-on. People were stopping in the street to look at the pair of them. Gavin took a step back as he noticed Jean's bump.

151

"You're not . . ." he lowered his voice, "pregnant, are you?"

Jean nodded. She watched his excitement at seeing her wane before her eyes as the shock took over. They were starting to attract the attention of the town busybodies so Jean pulled him down a side street.

"Jesus! Why didn't you let me know?"

"My parents won't let me out of their sight. I've been trying to think of ways of getting to see you but they're all over me."

"But I posted a letter to your house! Did you not get it?"

"No! I never got it!" she cried angrily. "I bet my mam opened it before it got to me. I can't believe she's reading my post too!"

"I thought you just didn't want to be with me any more. God, I've missed you so much." He hugged her tight.

"I haven't much time, I'm supposed to be in Dr Thornton's waiting room for my check-up – if Mam finds me here she'll kill me."

"Come away with me."

"What?"

"Yeah, you and me . . . and now our baby. Jesus, I can't believe you're having a baby!"

"Really?" Jean's eyes had lit up. All she wanted was to be with Gavin and get out of this godforsaken town.

"Yeah, I'll find us somewhere to live, I'll get a job. We can be a family!" His idea was starting to gain momentum and he was being carried away by his excitement.

"Meet me at midnight tomorrow night, down by the weir. We'll go away together, miles from here. I'll have everything organised. I have some money saved –"

"I have some put away at home – I'll bring that."

"Great!"

She kissed him on the lips and ran back to the surgery with a huge smile all over her face.

"Where were you?" Her mother, who was already back, asked with a face that would turn milk sour.

"Sorry, Mam, I just needed some air. I felt faint."

"Well, you look perfectly fine to me."

"That's because I just had some air."

"Don't use that tone with me, young lady!"

Jean was going to reply but she bit her tongue. Tomorrow she would be free from all of this. In little over twenty-four hours, she and Gavin would be together again.

* * *

The next night, Jean sneaked out of her bedroom window and tiptoed down the garden path. She held her breath, praying the neighbour's dog wouldn't start barking and blow her cover. As soon as she was away from her house, she started to run. There was a full moon out, lighting the path for her. All she had managed to bring was a backpack with a few of her clothes, some toiletries and a photo of her family. She was beyond excited at the thought of her and Gavin running away together, setting up a new life for themselves and becoming a proper family.

They hugged as they were reunited. Gavin told her that he had managed to find an abandoned shed that they would stay in until morning but he assured her it was only for tonight and that tomorrow would be different. Jean was so buoyed up that she didn't care that they would be sleeping in a shed. Luckily it was a mild October night and the winter frost had yet to bite. As they lay there in each other's arms, under the moonlight, she couldn't help but think how romantic the whole thing was; they would be telling their baby this story in years to come.

At first light they got on a bus to Cork. They both slept the whole journey long as neither had slept properly in the shed. They didn't wake until the driver turned off the engine. Looking out the windows, they realised they were in the terminus. They got off the bus and took their bags out from the hold. Gavin had the name of an auctioneer who let houses and they asked a man for directions before setting off.

The city was coming alive for the day ahead. Traffic filled the quays, the pavements were filling up and shops were opening up. Jean looked around in excitement; she couldn't believe they would be living in a city. She had been living in the small village of Ballydubh her whole life, but this place was so alive and vibrant that it seemed like another world altogether.

25

John Grace had looked at the young couple sitting across the desk from him with raised eyebrows. They were a very young couple, he thought, hardly out of their teenage years with all their worldly possessions on their backs. And her pregnant! He knew something wasn't right but it wasn't his place to say so. After all, he was just an auctioneer – he was in the business of renting houses, he wasn't bloody Social Welfare. It wasn't his business to be sticking his oar in and wondering what folks were up to. He gave them brochures of all the houses and apartments that he had on his books but when they turned them over and saw the rents, he thought that the young fella was going to pass out. Then, when he had happened to mention the fact that you had to pay a month's rent in advance plus another month as a deposit, you'd think he had told them the sky had fallen in! And then of course the girl had gone and started to get upset. He was beginning to feel like the inn-keeper that turned Mary and Joseph away. It was pretty easy to guess that their finances were pretty dire. So much for a handy commission, he thought grimly. Then he remembered the bedsit that was adjoining his own house. His mother had lived in it until she died last year and he had never done anything with it after that. He knew it was hardly in a fit state. By now the place was damp and teaming with mildew but, sure, as his mother always said, beggars couldn't be choosers, now could they?

As he showed them the dark one-roomed bedsit, he couldn't help thinking that it was worse than he had remembered – if that was even possible. It had been nearly a year since he had set foot in the place and he was greeted with a pungent odour as soon as he opened the door. There was a flowery settee against one wall, a double bed against the back wall and a small circular table and chairs stood in the centre of the room. There was a battered TV set with a faux wooden surround. John tried to remember how long he'd had it – it must be at least twenty years old but sure it worked grand. The floor was covered in grey stripy linoleum throughout and the walls were papered in ruby-red velvet-effect wallpaper. His mother had taken a fancy to it a few years back and had gone wild with it. She'd had the entire place covered in it. All her old ornaments and china figurines stood on every space; he had never got around to tidying the hideous things up. He thought up a figure in his head for the rent, enough not to scare them off completely but sufficient for it to still be a nice little earner for him; he wouldn't get *too* stuck into helping them out.

* * *

Jean blinked back tears as she watched Gavin shake hands with John Grace as he handed over three quarters of all their money for the deposit and first month's rent alone. She didn't think she had ever seen anywhere quite so awful – granted she'd had a pretty sheltered upbringing but this place was dire. She knew John Grace wasn't doing them any favours on the rent either but, as Gavin kept on telling her, they didn't have any other option. For some reason she had thought they would be able to afford somewhere a bit nicer, a proper home, small but cosy, but she had underestimated rental costs. She tried not to let her disappointment show.

While Gavin signed the lease, Jean stayed standing. She was afraid to touch anything in the place and there was no way she was going to sit on the furniture. As soon as John Grace had gone, she set about cleaning straight away. She put on rubber gloves and wiped away layers of greasy dust that had built up over years. She swept away wispy cobwebs from the ceiling but, no matter how much she sprayed her deodorant, she couldn't mask the musty smell. She was sure she could still smell the old woman who had died here. She shivered at the thought.

She thought about home as she cleaned. Her family were probably in a panic now that they had realised she was gone. She didn't want them worrying about her; she just couldn't live there any more. She would ring them in a few days to tell them she was okay when hopefully they would have calmed down.

After they had bleached and dusted the place as best they could, they sat back wearily onto the settee, which they had now covered with throws which Gavin had gone out and picked up cheaply in a discount homewares store on North Main Street. This was their first night together in their own place and already the excitement of living together was starting to pall. They had only ever spent short amounts of time with each other but here they were playing house. It was odd deciding what to watch on the TV, when to go to bed or asking what the other wanted to eat. They had bought a small few bits to eat in a supermarket and Jean was shocked at how much everything cost. She began to fret that their money was being swallowed up rapidly but Gavin told her not to worry and that first thing in the morning he was going out to look for a job.

That night as she listened to him snoring gently beside her in the bed, a tear rolled down her face.

* * *

Days went by with Gavin trawling through the job notices in the windows of the employment office. He soon realised that jobs were not as easy to come by as he had hoped. The building sites didn't want to know him as he was too young and anyway, even if they were to overlook his age, his scrawny body didn't look like it would be capable of the heavy work. He spent an entire day walking to all of the factories but none of them were hiring at the moment. He tried shops and offices but they all wanted people with experience.

He knew he needed to get something fast. They were down to their last twenty pounds and the rent was due again at the end of the week. He couldn't draw the dole because Jean wouldn't let him sign on in Cork for fear that it would flag their whereabouts with the authorities. She was paranoid about going to the Social Welfare office even just to enquire about their entitlements in case they would trace her back to her parents. She wouldn't even go to a doctor down here for her check-up in case the doctors had been alerted to her being missing. Gavin himself thought she was over-reacting but she was insistent so he had no choice but to try and get a job somehow. He could see she was getting more upset by the day and he knew she was having second thoughts about running away together. And even though she denied it, he could hear her crying at night. She was nearly now in her third trimester; she was getting bigger and wasn't as mobile as before. Gavin could see she longed for the comforts of her old life and the novelty of them running away together had quickly worn off. He was trying his best to be positive but it wasn't enough. He knew that John Grace would soon be looking for next month's rent and Gavin knew that his type would have no qualms about throwing them both out onto the street whether or not Jean was pregnant. Gavin didn't want to admit to Jean that he was actually really worried, so he kept on saying that everything was fine and he hoped she believed him.

26

November, 2009

The music boomed down from the stacked speakers and echoed around the vast concrete warehouse. Beams climbed up the high walls, climbing higher still so that they illuminated the cracked windows running along the top before running back down to the floor again, scattering coloured shadows around the space. All the bodies faced forward, dancing together, covered in sweat, and their heads tilted upwards in a kind of intimacy. The blinding halogen light made the DJ appear like God above them. Someone had managed to climb their way to the top of the speakers and was now frenetically moving to the music from way up over the crowd.

Paul could feel the music reverberating from the speakers, rebounding off the floor and up through his feet, until it was like electricity, coursing through his body from the tips of his toes, travelling up his legs, pulsing around his veins and vibrating through his bones. His two hands were raised above his head as he thumped the air to the beat of the music. The music slowed; then briefly speeded up, before slowing down again as the DJ played cat and mouse with them. Then finally after he had teased them for long enough, he roared *"One! Two! Three! Are you ready?"* He spun his two hands on the decks sending the tempo faster, the music getting louder. *"Here! We! Go!"* Paul could feel the rushes building and radiating across his body to the beat of the music. When finally it reached the climax, a cacophony of foghorns blared. Paul felt as though every nerve-ending in his body was exploding in small pops of blissful euphoria like a flower bursting through its bud. He felt weightless as he floated on the sound waves being carried along by the volume of the base drum pounding.

He loved everyone. *Loved* them. Every single person in the warehouse was the best person in the world. Everyone in this room was fucking deadly. They were all rolled into this ball of love together, united on a higher plane.

A girl wearing red sequined hot pants and a white bikini top displaying a toned, tanned midriff was walking towards him. She had a pink cowboy hat on her head and a purple feather boa around her neck. She went behind him and wrapped the boa around him before putting her two hands around his neck. She began to massage his shoulders and tickled his back by running her fingertips in light feathery movements up and down his spine. He felt the rush building inside again. He swung her around so that she was in front of him and cupped her head in his hands. He leant down and kissed her dry lips. Her mouth tasted like chewing-gum.

"You're fucking ace!" he shouted at her.

"What?"

"I said you are fucking ace!" He roared back again. He wanted her, he needed to touch her. His hands reached out and started feeling her body, moving up over her breasts. She threw her head back laughing, her mouth wide open to reveal small gappy teeth. She jerked back upwards again before pulling away from him. He watched her as she walked off on her path through the crowd, kissing strangers as she went. He was left

standing, swaying gently as the music softened into a trance. His hands fumbled with the small plastic bag full of pills. He used to eat ten-penny mixes from bags like this. He swallowed two instantly and waited for the warm feeling until he could feel it rise up inside him, building from his core, radiating out to the tips of his fingers, skin, toes, until every part of him tingled in pleasure, alert and alive. His white T-shirt was stuck to his skin, transparent with sweat. He took off his top and threw it aside. He was thirsty and grabbed a plastic pint glass of water from where they were lined up on a table, gulping it straight back; he took another one and poured it over his body to cool himself down. His heart was thumping and his breathing rapid. All the while his foot kept tapping out the beat. He continued dancing bare-chested, pounding out each beat as if it were physically in the air in front of him. He danced for hours, never wanting this to end. He wanted to stay like this forever; feel like this forever.

After a while the music stopped. The lights were coming on. He could see forlorn faces. They all felt it. He searched out their God up high and begged him with wide eyes not to stop but already he was packing up. The lights illuminated bay upon bay of empty racking and for the first time he saw how vast the place was.

Despondent bodies began to filter out of the warehouse, subdued and exhausted from hours of hardcore dancing. It was raining and the droplets felt cool as they danced along his bare skin. The chemical high from before was rapidly evaporating as bare-chested men and semi-naked women stood huddled around outside with vacant faces and dilated pupils as the fear began to ascend, disenchanted that it was all over and now they were faced with reality again. The amphetamines were still racing around his body but the warm feeling had worn off; he needed something to replace this awful sinking feeling. He saw the girl that had kissed him earlier on; she was shivering in the moonlight. She looked older than she had inside. She was more wrinkled and instead of looking toned, now she just looked bony. He watched her angular body, with its bones jutting out all over as she stood taking long drags from her cigarette, exhaling grey plumes onto the night air. He could now see her teeth had yellow pockets in between. He had to get away from her. She was bringing him down. He needed to escape from everyone here with their empty faces. He whistled to the lads and they all headed over to his car. Aido asked three girls who were standing nearby in the rain if they wanted to go to a party. They shrugged their shoulders and, with no better offers, squashed in on top of the four lads sitting in the backseat of the small Honda Civic. He had to get out of there.

He drove fast, speeding along the main road. The roads were empty, with only the silvery glow of the moon keeping them company. They turned off that road after a few miles, branching onto back roads, pot-holed country lanes.

"*Da, da, da, da-da!*" Aido was humming a tune from the rave in the passenger seat beside him. He tapped his foot to the beat. "*Da, da, da, da-da!*" He kept going, repeating the same five notes on loop until Paul felt as though *Da-da-da* was boring holes in his skull and drilling into his brain. "*Da, da, da, da-da!*"

"Would you ever shut the fuck up!"

"Jesus!" Aido let out a low whistle. "Relax the fuck, Paul!"

The car descended into silence again as Paul drove faster. He swung around a corner onto the other side of the road. His passengers all swung with the gravity to the right and then back again. One of the girls started to laugh, high-pitched and squealy. It drilled through Paul's skull. Eventually he pulled up outside his home.

He let them in the door. The house was in darkness so he turned on all the lights. He walked over to the CD player and took out the CD in it that belonged to Jean, flung it onto the floor and put in his own CD of trance music. He left them all there in the sitting room while he went up to his room to get some gear. He needed to get rid of this feeling. He snorted line after line of the white powder until the membranes of his nose were tingling and his gums numb from where he rubbed it on directly. The cocaine gave him a different buzz altogether, the feeling of euphoria was gone – instead he felt alert and his heart was thumping in his chest.

He could hear the others laughing and shouting in the sitting room. What the fuck were they laughing at? The girl with the laugh let out another squeal before her and Mick descended into fits of laughter again. He wondered what was so bloody funny. Were they laughing at him? It better not be about him because it was his bloody house and no one would laugh at him in his own house.

He went back down to the sitting room and threw himself into the centre of the couch between two of the girls. He felt a hand move along his leg and when he looked to find out whose hand it was, the girl smiled at him. Her eyes were half closed and Paul knew she was in her own world. Her hand moved further along the top of his thighs towards his crotch and he felt himself instantly harden. He needed to release it. He looked at the faces in his own sitting room and pulled the girl up and led her into the kitchen.

He sat on one the wooden kitchen chairs and undid his fly. He kicked off his trainers, unbuttoned his jeans and pulled them off together with his boxers, throwing them onto the floor. Wearing only his socks, he guided her down on top of him. She swayed backwards unsteadily for a few moments so he had to hold her. He lifted her dress so it was above her waist and moved her tight lacy thong to the side and seconds later he was in. He gripped her hips and moved her up and down on top of him, until she was grinding against him. He looked up at her; her eyes were closed now. He started to go harder, pounding away on the verge for an age until finally he felt himself explode inside her. He sat back into the chair and she slumped forward so that her head was hanging over his shoulder. He held her back out from him by her two shoulders and shook her.

"Fucking hell – wake up!"

She opened her eyes, smiled at him before closing them down again and slid back into her trance. He got out from underneath her and stood up while she slumped back down on the chair. *How could she sleep through that?*

He lit himself a cigarette on the gas cooker and stood looking at her where she slumped on the chair, her skirt still above her waist so that everything was on show. *Served her right, the stupid bitch.*

27

Jean had woken up to the sound of shouting coming from her living room. She'd quickly sat up in her bed and listened, to try and figure out what was going on. It was followed by someone roaring in laughter, then more shouting and screeching. The light from the hall was flooding under her door and illuminating her bedroom. It was Paul. Her clock said it was 3.05 a.m. *This isn't fair,* she thought. Whatever about her not being able to sleep, Chloe and Kyle had school in the morning.

She'd sat there contemplating what she should do, hoping the noise might die down by itself but when it became clear that that wasn't going to happen, she got out of bed and wrapped her terrycloth dressing-gown over her pyjamas, before making her way down towards the noise.

Bracing herself, she pushed open her sitting-room door. Her eyes had to adjust to the light as she took in a crowd of teenagers sprawled across every conceivable space in her small sitting room. The air was heavy with thick white smoke and cans were littered around the floor and coffee table. As she took in the torn pieces of white paper, ripped cigarette boxes and tinfoil strips that were strewn everywhere, she could feel the rage starting to build inside. How dare he! She scanned the unfamiliar faces that didn't even look up at her. No one seemed to register her standing there and if they did, they weren't too perturbed by her presence.

"Where's Paul?" she asked a girl who was closest to her but she just shrugged her shoulders at her. *She probably doesn't even know who Paul is*, thought Jean. She looked at the vacant faces to see if there was anyone she knew but she had never seen these people before.

She stepped over legs and strung-out bodies, walked over and switched off the CD player, instantly bringing the room to silence before going into the kitchen. She stopped in the doorway and took in the sight of her son standing over beside the cooker. His back was towards her and he was bent forward onto the worktop in the process of snorting a line of cocaine. A girl sat slumped on one of the wooden kitchen chairs. Her skirt was pulled up over her hips so she could see her little thong and much of her pubic area.

"What do you think you're doing?"

He swung around at the sound of her voice, his eyes blazing and his teeth bared.

"This isn't on, Paul. This is my house – Chloe and Kyle have school in the morning!"

"Fuck off!"

"Paul, I'm serious, I want all your friends out of the house immediately."

The girl on the chair suddenly began to sway and Jean rushed over to steady her. She opened her eyes momentarily, before smiling at Jean and shutting them down again. She was out of it.

"No one's going anywhere!" he roared at her.

"Paul, please, I'm asking you – just tell everyone to go home. The party's over."

"No, it's fucking not, you stupid bitch! Who the fuck do you think you are, trying to tell me what to do?"

"I'm your mother, Paul –"

"No, you're bleedin' not! You're nothing to me!" He lunged forward so that before she knew it, she was lying on the ground and he was on top of her, thumping her in the head. She could hear herself screaming at him to stop from afar, *"Stop it, Paul . . . please . . . stop!"* She screamed for help, *anyone*, but the swaying girl merely opened her glazed eyes again and stayed slumped on the chair.

Through swollen eyes she saw Chloe and Kyle come into the room, the fear written all over their small faces. Mercifully Paul stopped punching her when he saw them and Jean thanked a God she didn't believe in. She tried to speak to them to tell them it was okay but the words wouldn't come out and instead she had to spit out a mouthful of blood. She watched the blood, mixed with spit, pool on her beige kitchen tiles. Chloe and Kyle both turned and ran out of the room and Jean prayed they would just stay in their room, out of his way until he had calmed down. She reached upwards to grab onto the edge of the table and managed to pull herself up onto her feet. Her head was spinning and she had to hold onto the table to keep steady. Through slitted eyes she saw ruby-red trails of blood were staining her pyjamas. Paul was standing holding onto the sink with his back to her. Using the wall as an aid, she managed to feel her way quietly over to the door; she had to get away from him. She had just put her foot onto the wooden floor in the hallway when she heard heavy footsteps behind her.

"Where the fuck do you think you're going?" he roared.

"Paul – stop – I –"

He grabbed hold of her wrist and swung it back until she heard it crack. The pain seared through her arm. The thumps rained down on her again, heavy and fast, as she slid onto the floor, putting her hands over her head to protect herself until she thought she was going to pass out. She didn't know how long the beating went on for.

Finally she heard a noise coming from behind the door.

"Stop what you're doing! Gardaí Síochána. Stop!"

Someone finally pulled him off her. A woman's voice could be heard talking softly to her but Jean couldn't make out her face through eyes that were almost closed now.

"You're okay now, it's okay. It's all going to be okay."

The woman helped her up and sat her at the table and Jean realised she was a Garda. She began to cough and had to spit out another mouthful of blood. She could hear the Gardaí ordering everyone out of the house. She watched as Paul was put into handcuffs and led away. The girl who had been strung out through Jean's ordeal came to, looked at the scene around her and just walked out, oblivious to what had just happened in the same room as her.

"Don't worry, the ambulance is on its way," the female Garda reassured her. "I think your wrist is probably broken and we need to get those cuts looked at – you might need some stitches."

She went to the fridge and Jean could hear her rooting around in the freezer.

"Here, put this on it." She held a bag of frozen peas wrapped in a tea towel up to Jean's head.

And then the tears started as the shock began to subside. Jean hadn't cried in years but they were flowing freely now; the worry, the fear for the last few months, the relief that the Gardaí had come when they did, the kindness of the woman looking after her – it was all released.

"It's okay, you get it all out," the Garda said, holding onto her shoulders. "It's not the first time, is it?"

She shook her head, her whole body heaving with sobs. She registered the small outlines of Chloe and Kyle as they appeared around the door before they ran over and put their arms around her. She tried to hug them as best she could.

"How did you know to come?" Jean asked the Garda.

"This brave little man here gave us a call." The Garda smiled at Kyle.

Jean looked at the shy face of her ten-year-old son and felt a horrible mixture of deep gratitude and guilt; he shouldn't have had to do that.

"I'm so sorry!" She began sobbing louder until Kyle and Chloe joined in and the three of them huddled together crying.

"Now, have you anyone who can come and look after these two while you're gone to the hospital?" asked the Garda.

Jean didn't want to call Louise, she really didn't want to do that, but she didn't exactly have many options. She nodded meekly.

"I can call my sister."

The game was up; she knew she could no longer hide the truth from Louise.

* * *

The hospital put seven stitches in the wound above her eyebrow before bandaging it with a large gauze pad that stretched halfway across her forehead. They gave her drops to take down the swelling in her eyes so she could see out through them again and her left wrist was put into a cast all the way from her forearm down over her hand.

When she finally got back home after seven in the morning she was exhausted by the night's events. Her bruised and battered body was weary. She rang the bell and Louise ran out into the hallway to let her in. She threw her arms around her younger sister. They walked in silence into the sitting room where Louise had been waiting up for her with only the lamp lighting up the room. Jean noticed the room had been tidied up from its earlier state but it still reeked of stale smoke and beer.

"Why didn't you tell me?" Louise started to cry.

"I'm so sorry, Louise, I couldn't – I just couldn't bring myself to say it."

"I'm so sorry! I knew something was up the other day. I knew something wasn't right, I just knew it, but I went off and left you. He did that too, didn't he? That bruise over your eye last week, that was him, wasn't it?"

Jean nodded.

"God, Jean, I'm so, *so* sorry. I let you down. You must have been so scared!"

"Sure, what are you sorry for? I should have told you but it's hard, you know, to admit your own son has done that to you. I just don't know what has come over him . . . the last few months, it has been like living with – a – a time-bomb."

"I wish you had told me, I could have helped you out, got Brian to talk to him or something?"

"I think he's beyond talking to at this stage."

"Jesus Christ, he could have killed you – that wound over your eye and your wrist – how could he lay a finger on his own mother? How could he do that to you?" The anger in Louise's voice was unmistakable.

Jean stayed silent; she was wondering the same thing herself. They stayed like that, looking at each other.

"How are the other two?"

"They're fine – they were a bit upset when you left but they're fast asleep now."

"Thanks."

"What are you going to do?"

"I don't know, I really don't know," she sighed.

"Hopefully getting the Gardaí involved now will have given him the wake-up call he needs."

"I hope you're right." *I really hope you're right.*

After they had talked it out, Jean tiptoed into the bedroom that Chloe and Kyle shared. Although it was nearly time to be

171

getting up for school, no one would be going to school today. Their room was divided in two by an invisible line down the middle so that only they knew where it was. Their peaceful faces were lost in the land of slumber and showed no signs of their fears from earlier on. She hoped they were dreaming sweet dreams. She felt a pang of guilt for what they had seen that night. They must have been scared out of their minds, especially if Kyle had rung the Gardaí. How brave he had been! She gave them both a kiss on their foreheads before creeping out again and shutting the door quietly behind her.

Jean hadn't realised how difficult things would be with only one functioning hand so she was glad Louise was there to help her to get ready for bed. Louise tucked her younger sister up, making sure she was comfortable, before heading home herself to get her own two ready for school but promising she would be over again later on.

When she was finally alone, an exhausted Jean fell into a deep sleep; nights of broken sleep full of raging fears and worry had finally caught up with her. She didn't wake until she heard her doorbell ringing. Her head was thumping. She looked at her cast momentarily before it all came flooding back to her. As she got out of bed, her whole body felt stiff and achy. She made her way towards the door. She caught sight of her reflection in the hall mirror. *Jesus.* She was startled by her bruised and swollen face and the white bandage across her forehead. Through the glazed panes at the end of the hall, she could make out the shape of the two Gardaí from last night standing on her doorstep again. She pulled back the door to them.

"How are you this morning, Jean?" They both smiled kindly at her.

"I've been better."

They both nodded at her. "Of course."

"We didn't really get a chance to introduce ourselves properly last night. I'm Garda Lisa Jones and this is Garda Terence Fingleton. We just want to have a talk about the events last night, the lead up to it etcetera."

"Sure. Will we go into the sitting room?"

They sat beside each other on the sofa while Jean sat gingerly into the armchair.

"Now, there's no need to worry," said Terence Fingleton. "Paul is sleeping it off in a cell but we need to ascertain what exactly happened last night."

She relayed the story as best she could remember but it had all happened so fast she wasn't sure if she was recalling everything exactly as it had unfolded. They nodded sympathetically and took notes as she spoke but for every word they wrote down against her son, Jean felt a stabbing in her heart.

"What we need to determine is where you want to go from here?" said Lisa Jones.

"How do you mean?"

"This can't continue, Jean," Terence Fingleton said. "He savagely beat you last night, you're lucky the damage wasn't more serious. He has done it to you before and, in my experience of situations like this, I would say there is a pretty high risk he will do it again. For the sake of your two younger children . . ."

"It isn't a good environment for them to be living in, Jean," Lisa Jones interjected. "And they could be in actual danger."

"I know."

"So what we need to ask you is –" Terence Fingleton looked at his colleague before continuing, "whether or not you intend to press charges?"

She was horrified at what they were suggesting. "Against my own son?"

"Jean, I realise this is hard for you but domestic violence is a crime like any other. The sad part about it is that it is usually someone we love that is the perpetrator, which leaves the victim in a very difficult and emotionally conflicting position – but that doesn't mean it should go unpunished."

Jean zoned out on what they were saying. All she could think of was they wanted her to Judas her own son.

"Of course we are very sensitive to these matters and we have dealt with similar cases in the past. Now, granted, the usual cases are husband and wife rather than mother and son, but we have very experienced staff who are available should you require their services."

"I can't."

"Can't what?"

"I can't do that to my own son. I just can't do it."

"Jean, I would strongly urge you to consider it. You are not to blame here. He has committed the act, not you."

He wasn't like that, she wanted to tell them. Paul was her son, *her baby*. It wasn't black and white like they were suggesting. What had happened to her baby boy who had been the light of her life, her firstborn that had filled her with such pride? When he was a boy, he had been sweet and gentle, constantly giving her kisses and cuddles. She still had his artwork from primary school, scrawly drawings with childish handwriting "*I love you, Mammy*" with hearts falling in an arc from a small stick-boy towards his mother. He used to be great helping her around the house, cutting the grass for her or watching the other two. In fact she had relied on him, he was the man of the house, he took pride in helping her out and they had a special bond, a different bond than that she had with Chloe and Kyle. He was older than them by a good few years so had an understanding of the situation. Maybe it was her own fault because she had been unconsciously treating him as an adult for years. They had a special trust but recently he seemed to have replaced their closeness with resentment and anger. She still could only see Paul as her son and it was her job, as ever, to protect him.

She stood up and they took this as their cue to go.

"Okay. Well . . . ultimately, Jean, it is your decision. If you decide not to pursue things any further, he will be cautioned and released today and hopefully that will be enough for him."

"It's okay. I just want to leave it for now." She could see it in their eyes: they were judging her.

"Well, it's up to you how you handle things from here but please be aware that we are obliged to inform social services about Paul's behaviour due to the fact that there are children living here who may be in danger."

"I see," Jean said.

"In the meantime please don't be afraid to ring the station if you run into any more problems with him."

"Okay, thanks." She just wanted these people gone from her house.

She showed them out and stood at the door watching the squad car as it drove off and made its way towards the top of the estate. Litter swirled along the green, dancing in the wind before it got caught in the wire fence at the edge of the estate. She shivered and went back inside and closed her door to shut out the cold air.

28

November, 1991

Jean bundled herself into the phone box and slotted in the coins and dialled the number of her home. It was her mother who picked up.

"Hello?" Jean could hear the tiredness in her voice and her heart ached with regret.

"Mam, it's me."

"Jean, oh Jean, love! Where are you? Are you okay?" She started sobbing hysterically down the phone.

"Mam, I'm fine, please, don't worry. I needed to be with Gavin. We're a family now." The guilt began to rise inside her.

"Jean, please come home!" her mother wailed.

Jean had never heard her cry like that before.

"Pleeeease, Jean. I-I'm so worried, I haven't slept since the night you left. Y-y-you're pregnant, you're not in any condition to be running off around the country. Come home, love, we'll talk it out, we can sort it out. We were probably a bit too hard on you, I can see that now, but if you just come home, we'll work it out."

Jean would have liked nothing more than to tell her mother

176

where she was and have them come and collect her and take her home. She wished desperately she could say she was coming home, get on a bus back to Ballydubh, run through the kitchen door and put her arms around her mother and sleep in her own bed, but she had to be an adult now, she was going to be a mother in a matter of weeks, she needed to grow up sometime.

"I can't, Mam." She started to cry too.

"Please. Jean, I'm begging you – for your sake and the sake of your unborn child – you're only *seventeen*, you need your family around you, love."

"I'm sorry, Mam, I'm so, so sorry. I love you all. I really do." And then she hung up on her mother.

Her body heaved with sobs as she stood in the Perspex phone booth, tears streaming down her face until an angry-looking woman rapped on the door and told her "Get the fuck out of the box if you're not using it!' Jean wasn't used to people speaking to her like that and the woman just made her feel even more wretched.

She ran down the street with tears blinding her vision. She didn't feel ready for this; she had made a mistake, she wanted to go home. She needed her mother, someone who knew what it was like, someone who would take care of her. She was frightened, alone and scared. She came up to a bench overlooking the river; she sat down on it and cried. She loved Gavin but, in the harsh light of reality, their dreams of running away together now seemed ill thought-out and immature. How were they going to afford a baby when they couldn't even feed themselves? She had never even held a baby before, she was the youngest in her family, she had never had younger brothers and sisters or even small cousins to practise on. Then there was the birth. She was scared and she didn't know what to expect and the more she watched her bump grow, the more the fear inside took over. *How was she actually meant to get it out?* But she was too embarrassed to talk to Gavin about it. She knew he was trying hard to sort them out and provide for them but as the weeks went on she was becoming disillusioned by his attempts and now he was starting to grate on her.

She sat there alone for a few hours, just watching life around her. She knew she had to stop feeling sorry for herself – this had been her choice as well but she hadn't known it was going to be this hard. She had to keep telling herself that she wasn't a baby any more; she was going to *have* a baby. She had made her bed, now she would have to lie on it.

Almost as if he could read her thoughts, when Gavin came home that evening he had a bouquet of bright, unnaturally coloured carnations in his hands for her. She groaned inwardly because they couldn't afford flowers. Flowers meant they went without a meal because their finances were so bleak but when he announced that he had managed to get a job in a pub, she jumped up and hugged him. He told her how he had been calling into every bar and pub in Cork City but no one had any work. He'd almost walked past a tiny pub, dismissing it as too small, but he said he'd try anyway. There had been an old man, about eighty Gavin reckoned, sitting on a stool behind the bar with a few old men with caps on sitting up on stools at the bar. They all turned to look at him and he was about to walk back out when the old man asked if he was all right. He mumbled that he was just looking for work but that he could see they probably didn't need anyone. He turned again to leave but then the old man said he was getting too long in the tooth for running the pub himself and was looking for someone to come and do the evenings for him. He told him he could start tomorrow night.

Jean jumped up and down and hugged him. She didn't care that this meant he would be gone every evening; she was just so relieved that he had a job.

From then on, Gavin headed off to work every day from

four to close which was usually the early hours of the morning. The work itself wasn't too hard – basically, he was serving the same few elderly men that had been coming into the pub, some every day, for the last forty years. For them it was more a social outlet than for the drink. Gavin soon learnt that the majority of them were widowers or bachelors who had never married. He grew to know them and their stories and they warmed to him too and would slip him the odd fiver here and there which he promptly gave to Jean to save up for the baby. He would come home and climb into bed beside her and sleep until lunchtime before getting up again to get something to eat before heading off on his bike to the pub.

He worked all the hours he could get and so Jean spent most of her days alone. She would usually walk into town, picking up tiny fleecy baby outfits in expensive boutiques to look at them before putting them back down again because they couldn't afford them. Sometimes she would ring her mother or Louise just to talk to them and hear their voices, but no matter how many times they asked, she would never tell them where she was. They would cry and beg her to come home, telling her over and over that they were worried about her and that the way she was living was no way to bring a baby into this world, but she wouldn't change her mind, not now, not after all Gavin had done for them. He was working so hard to make a life for them together, to take care of her and their unborn child. She didn't admit to them that she had the same fears as they had; how *were* they going to manage? Was she going to be on her own all day with the baby while Gavin worked? Would he be around to help? But even though she was scared about what lay ahead for them, she couldn't throw that all back in his face, not now after all he had done for her.

29

The stress and strain of the final months of pregnancy began to take its toll on Jean; money worries, doubts over how they would cope when the baby was born and even fears about what to do with a baby were continuously on her mind. She wasn't sleeping well at night and she was constantly tired and pale. She desperately wanted her mother near her; she needed her reassurance about what lay ahead. She would pluck up the courage and dial the house phone. She longed to say the words "Mam, I'm sorry – I want to come home" but the words would never come out. Sometimes she didn't say anything at all. She would hear her mother's soothing voice at the other end of the line saying "Hello. *Hello?* Hello, is there anyone there?" and she would hang up the phone again with tears streaming down her face.

One chilly February day, she sat shivering in their bedsit. The rain was coming down in icy sheets outside the house. It was a grey and bleak day. They had only storage heaters and as they couldn't afford the cost of them they didn't use them so the place was permanently freezing. The paper-thin walls had no insulation and you could feel the draughts coming through the sides of the windows. She walked around tidying up the bedsit, wearing a hoodie and a large woolly jumper belonging to Gavin over it, but no matter how much she moved or how many layers she put on, she just couldn't get warm. Gavin had already gone into work for the evening. She tried to read her book but she just couldn't get comfortable – her bump was heavy and awkward and was starting to weigh down on her now. She got up to make herself yet another cup of tea to keep her hands warm when she felt a pain across her whole bump. She had to lean forward and hold onto the side of the cooker until it passed. The same thing happened again some minutes later. The baby wasn't due for another few weeks yet, she told herself, it was too early for labour pains, but soon she was caught up in waves of agony and she knew that the baby was on the way.

She threw on a raincoat that was hanging on the back of the door and made her way to John Grace's front door, picking a path through the puddles. She knocked hard but he wasn't home. The lights were all off and his car wasn't in the drive. The rain was pouring down on her now. She had to lean forward and place her palms flat on to the panels of the front door to steady herself as another contraction gripped her. She knocked harder still, willing someone to answer but there was no one there. She knew she would have to walk to the telephone box down the road.

Her steps were slow and clumsy as the pressure became unbearable. She kept having to stop as another contraction took hold. Passing motorists splashed the pools of water from the side of the road up onto the footpath so that muddy trails of grit were running down her face as she bent to endure the contractions. Finally a car, seeing the hunched-over figure out on such a night, knew something must be up and pulled up on the path beside her. The driver asked if she was okay and then, when he saw her bump and the agony on her face, he told her to get in and said that he was taking her to the hospital straight away. Jean couldn't even answer this stranger. He told her it was okay, he was a father of three himself. Jean knew from his kindly eyes that she could trust him. He brought her into the hospital and handed her over to the nursing staff. She didn't even get to thank him.

She was led straight to the delivery room. The midwives looked at her, full of pity, a young girl drenched with rain and her eyes full of fear and terror. The contractions were coming thick and fast now, one on top of the other, there was no let up. They would start off down low before gripping her abdomen like a vice and then wrapping around into her back. She tried to tell the midwives to ring Gavin but they told her there wasn't time and that it was time to start pushing the baby out. She felt the pressure bearing down on her and the urge to push became overwhelming. She summoned up all her strength and pushed her baby out into this world.

"It's a boy!" she could hear them telling her from afar and then she heard the primal infant cry as they placed her newborn son in her arms. She looked down at him with his tufts of dark hair, looking so much like his father. He was small but perfectly formed, with the most beautiful little fingers and toes. She couldn't believe that this tiny little being, this small bundle, was hers.

* * *

A while later, when she was back in the ward, Gavin's head appeared around the curtain of her cubicle.

"I'm so sorry, I'm so sorry!" he panted. "I only just got the call and I came as fast as I could."

He stopped in front of her in awe of their tiny baby in her arms.

"Do you want to hold your son?"

"A boy?"

Jean nodded and placed the towel-wrapped baby delicately into his arms.

Gavin stared at him in wonderment, taking in every detail on his small scrunched-up face and his pouty lips.

"He's perfect, isn't he?" Jean asked.

"He is that all right." He couldn't take his eyes off him. "What are we going to call him?"

Jean went silent.

"What?"

"Well, I was hoping – if you wouldn't mind – I'd like to call him Paul, after my dad." She lowered her gaze and felt the familiar pang of longing for her family. There was an unmistakable sadness in her eyes.

"Sure, of course, pet. Baby Paul it is."

* * *

In the weeks that followed, Jean was snowed under by the routine that her new baby demanded. It was a never-ending conveyor belt of nappy changes, four-hourly feeds and winding. Sometimes it felt like she had just put Paul to sleep after the last feed by the time he was awake and grizzling again. She would look at the clock in disbelief but it would indeed be four hours later. She would sigh before lifting him from his crib and the cycle would start all over again. In the evenings he would cry so hard his whole body would tense up and his face would turn purple because he was screaming so hard. He just wouldn't settle no matter what she did – she tried burping him, walking with him around the room, rocking him in his crib or singing to him – but nothing she did would ease his distress. Jean herself would begin to get upset because she felt like such a failure watching her son in pain and not knowing what to do to help him. Then John Grace would bang on the wall and roar at her to "Shut that bloody child up!" She was starting to feel trapped, as if the four walls with the velvet wallpaper were coming in around her. Sometimes the crying felt as though it was drilling into her brain and she didn't think she could stand it any more. And because Paul was still so small and the weather so bitter, she didn't want to risk taking him outside until he was hardier so she was confined indoors most of the time.

The days dragged with no one to talk to but her baby son and she longed for other company, but then he would look up at her with his innocent blue eyes and she would feel guilty for her thoughts.

Now that Paul was here, neither could believe how much having a baby ate into their already limited finances. Gavin was working more than ever to pay for the nappies, formula and clothes for him, plus it was one of the harshest winters on record and they needed to have the heat on constantly. He would reassure Jean with a kiss every day that it was just for a few months and, when summer came, he would be at home more to help her – but the weeks seemed endless to her.

Gavin would come home in the early hours of the morning and, no matter how quiet he tried to be, inevitably in the one-roomed bedsit he would wake Paul, always after Jean had just settled him. Gavin would collapse into bed exhausted, leaving Jean to get up again to see to the baby. Then in the mornings she would be busy looking after Paul while Gavin slept late.

She had phoned her parents from the hospital the day after Paul was born to tell them that she'd had a baby boy and that they had named him Paul after her father. They had begged her to let them come and visit, promising that they wouldn't put any pressure on her to come home, that they just wanted to see their grandson and her, just to make sure they were both okay. She had asked Gavin what he thought but he told her it wasn't a good idea, that once her parents knew where they were living that would be it. So even though it broke her heart, she stood firm and refused to allow them to come to see her. She missed her mother desperately – she needed her help, she had so many questions about Paul that she wanted to ask. Was it normal for him to cry this much? Was there something wrong with him? She felt so alone.

One evening when Paul was a month old, he started his usual evening screaming but this time his hair was damp with sweat and his body felt hot to the touch. Jean began to worry. She stripped him but nothing was calming him.

John Grace was knocking on the paper-thin wall next door, shouting *"For the last time, would you ever shut that bloody child up!"*

She began to panic because she didn't know what to do. She didn't know if he had a pain or if he was sick, she didn't even have a thermometer to check his temperature. His crying had a shrill, high-pitched tone to it and, as his screams began to get higher and more agitated, Jean panicked. The sensation that her baby was distressed and nothing she was doing was helping him was overwhelming, until eventually she was crying with him.

And that was it; she snapped. She'd had enough; she couldn't take any more of this. She wrapped her baby in two blankets and put a woollen hat on his head before putting him into the buggy. She grabbed her bag and coat and ran down the road to the phone box, pushing the buggy in front of her. She dialled her parents' number.

"Hello?" she heard her mother's voice answer sleepily and her father asking who it was in the background.

"Mam, it's me."

"Jean, love, are you okay?"

"Paul has been crying all evening – I don't know what to do!" she sobbed.

"It's okay, love, it's okay. Where are you? We need to help you."

"I'm in Cork."

There was a short silence. Jean guessed her mother had

expected her usual refusal to say where she was and was taken aback when she told her.

"Tell me exactly where you are, love. We're coming to get you right now."

Instantly Jean felt as though a weight had been lifted from her shoulders. She gave her mother the address and said goodbye. Then she replaced the receiver with a shaking hand and stepped out of the phone box. She took a deep breath in the cool air and exhaled, watching the plume of white air form in front of her. It was going to be okay. She pushed the buggy back to the bedsit. As she sat waiting for them, for the first time all evening, she noticed there was silence. Paul had stopped crying.

* * *

It was a tearful reunion for the McParlands. Jean fell apart as the tension of months of trying to hold it all together was released. Úna and Paul peered into the cradle at their little grandson, looking so contented as he slept, showing no signs of his marathon crying session from earlier on. They were appalled by the conditions that Jean and Gavin has been living in. They had known things were bad but they had no idea just how bad.

When Gavin finally came in the door from work after three in the morning, he was shocked to see Jean's parents there sitting on the flowery settee. He knew them to see but he had never even spoken to them before. The look of contempt and anger in their eyes was unmistakable. Gavin felt as though they all wanted to attack him.

"What's happened? Is Paul okay?" He looked at Jean for answers.

She nodded and dried her eyes with a tissue.

"I can't take it any more, Gavin."

"*What?*"

"This!" She gestured around the bedsit. "You being gone the whole time, me left on my own looking after Paul with him screaming the place down every single evening. I just can't take it any more."

She could see the hurt register on Gavin's face. She felt as though she had betrayed him.

"I thought this was what you wanted?"

"I do, Gavin, I did – I love you but I can't live like this."

"Christ almighty, I have been working my ass off just to pay the rent, the bills. Do you think I enjoy being away from you and Paul the whole time? We're parents, we're grown-ups now, that's life!"

Mr and Mrs McParland sat with their eyes looking at the floor. They said nothing; this was up to their daughter.

"Well, I can't do it any more," Jean said quietly.

"So what are you saying?"

"I want to go home."

"You're leaving me?"

"No – I want you to come too."

"I'm not going back to that shithole!"

"Please, Gavin!"

"No fucking way am I going back there!" He looked at her and shook his head before walking out and slamming the door behind him so hard that it rattled against its thin frame.

"Would ye ever keep it down in there!"

John Grace banged on the wall again and Mr and Mrs McParland looked at each other in horror, wondering for the hundredth time since they had arrived here how their daughter ended up in a place like this.

They all sat in silence for a while until eventually Úna plucked up the courage and asked Jean softly what she wanted to do, saying that either way it was her decision and they would support her.

Jean was torn, she hated having to choose between the people she loved like this but she was at her wits' end. Her mind was made up.

187

"I'm coming home, Mam."

They helped her pack up her small amount of belongings. They wrapped Paul up in warm clothing and put him into the car while she finished off inside. She wrote a letter for Gavin, telling him that she was sorry but that she needed to be close to her family. She told him that she still loved him very much and begged him to reconsider and come home with her, that they would work something out together. She placed the note on his pillow and then closed the door behind her for the last time.

30

When Jean arrived home into the familiar house of her childhood, instead of feeling sad all she felt was an overwhelming sense of relief. It was bliss when her mother tucked her up that first night under a mound of blankets and duvets, with her bed already warmed with a hot-water bottle.

Her parents' house was warm and comfortable and didn't smell of dampness. The little things that she had taken for granted before now seemed like great luxuries. The feeling of soft carpet underneath her feet made a welcome change from the sticky lino in the bedsit with holes that were worn through to the concrete floor below. As did not having to wear layers of clothing just to keep warm. She knew it was a much better place for Paul too who seemed calmer from the moment they had arrived.

She rang Gavin in work the next day but the man who answered told her gruffly that he hadn't shown up for work.

"I had a funeral on today," he complained to her. "That fella will hear it from me now when he shows his face and you can tell him that too if you see him!"

She left her number and told him to call her or get Gavin to call her if he showed up. She was worried about him now on his own. They didn't know anyone else down in Cork. She plucked up the courage and decided to ring John Grace to check if he had seen him but he said there was no one there and that after the racket they had made the other night he was glad of the peace and quiet over the last few days. She hung up on him.

She went back into the kitchen, sat at the kitchen table and put her head in her hands. Her mother was holding Paul in her arms singing a lullaby to him. She looked up at Jean.

"Any luck?"

"No, he hasn't shown up for work and John Grace our landlord hasn't seen him. I'm really worried about him, Mam."

"Give him time, love, I'm sure he's okay – he probably just needs a bit of space, a bit of time to think."

"I feel so guilty, Mam, just leaving him like that – walking out the door with our son after all he has done for us!"

"There, there, love, I know it's difficult for you but you need to put yourself and baby Paul first. You couldn't stay in that place with a baby, Jean, c'mon! Sure the damp alone would have had you running in and out of hospital with him. And him weeks early and everything! It's no way to raise a child."

She looked over at Paul snoozing in her mother's arms and, granted, he seemed like a different baby since she had come back home. She didn't know if it was because of the comforts and warmth of where they were or if he could sense that his mother was more relaxed, but all Jean knew was that he didn't scream any more. She lifted him out of her mother's arms and smiled down at his gorgeous plump face. He smiled back at her.

"Did you see that, Mam? Paul just smiled at me!"

"Well, would you look at that! There's nothing like those

first smiles – I remember when you and Louise first smiled at me, I thought I might just burst with happiness."

Her mother busied herself making Jean a cup of tea and serving up a plate laden with cream cakes. Having full presses was another thing Jean used to take for granted but now she could really appreciate it.

* * *

The days went on and she didn't hear from Gavin. She had tried the pub on several more occasions and also John Grace, who was now losing patience with her, but they hadn't seen him or heard from him.

One day when she was up changing Paul's nappy she heard the doorbell go downstairs. Her parents were out at the time. She cursed inwardly as she tried to change Paul's nappy as fast as she could while he kicked his legs in the air and gurgled up at her. She picked him up and went down the stairs. When she pulled back the door she was shocked to see Gavin standing there. She threw her free arm around him in relief as her eyes pricked with tears.

"I'm sorry, Gavin – I didn't run out on you, I just couldn't take it any more." She sobbed into his shoulder. "But I've been trying to ring you. Honest I have. I phoned the bar – I even phoned John Grace every day!"

He reached out, took Paul in his arms and smiled down at his baby son who had got so much bigger even in the short while that he hadn't seen him. His pudgy fists thrashing about, Paul beamed back up at him.

"It's okay, I'm not angry with you." He looked at her. "I was angry – I was raging for a few days but I've calmed down now and I've had time to think and see it from your side. I know I was always working – I didn't have much choice but it can't have been easy being on your own all day with a new baby."

191

"Here, let's go inside, it's freezing out here and I don't want Paul to get a cold."

"What about your parents?"

"They're not here but don't worry. They've been great, really they have. They're not shouting and screaming at me like I thought they would, they've just been really supportive. And they *love* Paul – you should see my dad with him – he ooohs and aaahs over him – Mam says he was never like that with me and Louise." She paused and put her hand on his arm before leaning in towards him. "I'm so glad you're here, Gavin."

When her parents came home they were shocked to see Gavin in their living room. For their daughter's sake they tried to act calmly and not let their disappointment show. After all, he was Paul's father but, deep down, they had both been secretly hoping that they had seen the last of Gavin Grimley. They left the two of them alone to talk things out, praying that he wouldn't talk Jean into leaving home again. They were relieved when a couple of hours later they heard Jean letting Gavin out the front door. She came back into the kitchen and told them that he was going to stay with his father. They both breathed out a sigh of relief.

31

Gavin let himself back into his father's house, pushing back the heavy door. He was met by the stale air. He had never noticed it before. He made his way in to his father who was sleeping off the excesses of a bottle of whiskey in his armchair. Gavin couldn't believe the state he had got himself into. He seemed to be wearing the same filthy clothes since the day Gavin had left and he smelt dirty.

When he woke and saw Gavin there, he didn't seem surprised to see him. It was as if he hadn't even noticed that his son had been gone for the last few months. Gavin tried talking to him but he didn't seem to register him sitting there, he was so caught up in his own drunken haze.

The house was filthy, the kitchen had used plates and cups piled high, the curtains were closed and Gavin wondered if they had ever been opened since the day that he left. He walked back out and went up to his room. He couldn't believe he was back in this shithole.

* * *

Gavin knew he would need to get another job. He tried the village pubs first as that was what he had experience in and was offered a job in O'Casey's Pub. It was a lively place where all the young people in the town went. The place was literally heaving with people every Thursday, Friday and Saturday night and they had a DJ playing. It was worlds away from the place where he'd worked in Cork. Here there were four barmen on a shift, all young fellas like himself. The queue for the bar was always ten deep, with people ordering pints and shorts. The barmen were allowed to drink a few pints on the job as well – as long as they weren't falling around the place no one minded. At the end of the shift they would all sit down and drink a few nightcaps before heading off for home. Sometimes a few girls would stay back too and they would have a right laugh playing drinking games as the girls flirted to get more free drink. He loved going to work; there was always banter and *craic*.

He would call over to see Jean and Paul each evening on his way to work but he never felt as though he could fully relax in the McParland household. They watched his every move, waiting for him to make a cock-up before they would pounce on him. Of course Jean assured him that they weren't but it was clear as day in the looks he would get from Úna and Paul. They would look over his shoulder as he played with baby Paul; if he swung him in his arms they would tell him "Be careful with him!" or if he heated a bottle for him, they would double-check it again to make sure it wasn't too hot. They didn't trust his judgement or didn't seem to see that he was trying his best for his son. Some days if Paul was overtired, he wouldn't come to Gavin and he would scream crying if he tried to pick him up. Jean's parents would hurry over and take him out of his arms and of course he would instantly quieten then. He felt like roaring at them *'He's my son for fuck sake – I've a right to hold him too!'* but instead he internalised it and it went with all the other put-downs and the 'not feeling good enoughs'.

Jean never spoke up for him and Paul wondered whether she just didn't notice or if she was afraid to speak up against her parents, but either way it infuriated him how she could be so oblivious to it all.

He knew something had changed between them since they had come back to Ballydubh. Although he would never admit it, he resented the fact that she had chosen her family over him. He had been willing to give it all up for her but when push came to shove, she hadn't been willing to do the same for him.

He had asked Jean several times to come out with him to O'Casey's when he had a night off. He had told her it was a great spot but she rarely came; she wasn't one for drinking and found the crowd that frequented O'Casey's raucous. It was only then that Gavin realised that they were essentially different people. Sometimes she seemed so innocent to the ways of the world. How had he ever thought that she would be able to survive on her own in Cork without the back-up of her family? He'd had to do it for years since his mother had died but Jean wasn't tough like him.

He saw her as 'one of them' now. Her mannerisms were the same as her parents' and the way she would ask her mother first if there was a decision to be made about Paul drove him demented. *'Should I put a cardigan on him, do you think, Mam?'* she would ask her mother instead of asking him, as Paul's father, what he thought. He couldn't even remember the last time they had been intimate. The only time they would get alone together was if they brought Paul out for a walk. Gavin knew she was a great mother to Paul – she would cuddle and kiss him and they had a bond like no other – but he found himself looking at her and wondering how they had even been together.

32

As the years went on, things stayed the same. Gavin would call in for an hour on his way to work in the evenings. Jean's parents would mumble a greeting to him and he would grunt one back, even though they despised each other. He knew the McParlands looked down their noses at him; their feelings hadn't thawed with time. But he didn't really care what they thought. Paul was old enough now to play with him and he would come running up to him as soon as he came through the door. He loved the rough-and-tumble play with his daddy.

When Paul started in primary school, Jean had got a job in the mornings in a solicitor's office in town, doing a bit of admin work. She seemed to like it and they were impressed with her aptitude so they had begun to give her more work on higher-profile cases and trust her with more complex issues. They suggested she should study a legal course part-time and said that they would even pay for the course but when she reluctantly told them she didn't have a Leaving Cert they had been shocked and never brought it up again.

* * *

One night Gavin came home from O'Casey's feeling warmed up by the couple of whiskeys they'd had after work. "Hey, Dad!" he shouted in to his father. He didn't respond so Gavin went into the dark sitting-room to check on him. He saw he was fast asleep in his armchair. Gavin stumbled over an empty bottle of whiskey that he had left on the floor and sent it clattering across the bare floorboards until it careered loudly against the radiator. He picked up the bottle and went up to bed.

When he got up around lunchtime the next day he went back into the sitting room to see if his father had even moved since the night before. When he saw him in the exact same position, his arms resting at the same angle, his mouth half-open the same way as when he saw him in the dark the night before, he knew something was up with him. His heart somersaulted and he ran forward and put his hand on his father's arm which was cold and stiff. He tried to pull him forward and listen to see if he was breathing but there was nothing. He realised then that he was dead. *No, Dad, please don't be dead!*

On autopilot he phoned Dr Thornton who hurried over and, using his stethoscope to listen, shook his head. "I'm sorry, Gavin, he's gone," Dr Thornton lowered his head.

Even though they hardly had anything remotely resembling a father and son relationship, Gavin was acutely aware that, apart from Jean and Paul, his father was all he had left in the world. They had long since lost touch with his relatives on his mother's side and his father had been an only child like himself. The loss brought back all the old feelings of when his mother had died when he was only seven years old, old enough to understand what had happened but young enough still to need her desperately. The anger and grief he felt overwhelmed him.

He got through the next few days and the funeral in a blur. Jean was by his side throughout and she even stayed over in the house with him so that he wouldn't be alone. She held him as he cried at night and they had a togetherness again that had gone missing years ago.

He went back to work the week after the funeral; he needed the distraction. For every pint he drank behind the bar, he would sneak a quick short as well. Pint, short, pint, short. Alcohol was the only thing that allowed him to forget. If anyone noticed, no one said anything to him because they knew he was grieving. But, before long, he couldn't get out of bed in the mornings without taking a quick swig of whiskey to knock the edge off the pain and get him through the day. He told himself that it was only temporary to help numb the pain of his father's death. An image of his dead father sitting in rigor mortis in his armchair with an empty whiskey bottle beside him would flash into his head and he would push it out again. He wasn't like him, he told himself, and he could control it. He would stop soon.

Jean began to worry about how he was coping. Some days he seemed to be dealing with it quite well and other days he would go to pieces. So that he wouldn't be alone, she decided to move in with him with Paul. He was delighted at first but once Jean was in the house it became harder to hide his drinking from her. At least in work he could drink all he wanted – it was a pub for God's sake, he was supposed to drink – it wasn't his fault that his job involved so much drinking. Of course he did try to stop, especially for Paul's sake – he didn't want Paul growing up the same way as he had – but he couldn't help it, he needed it to get him through the day.

* * *

One day after he had collected Paul from school, he went up to the bedroom and gulped back an entire naggin of vodka in one go. Instantly feeling warmer, he came back down to his son who wanted to go outside to play. Outside, the fresh air hit him and as he swung Paul around he started to feel dizzy.

"Faster, Daddy, faster, Daddy!" his son roared.

"You want to go faster? Okay then, you asked for it, matey!"

He spun and spun in rapid circles, the trees whizzing past his eyes and the sound of his son's infectious giggles filling the air until he found himself careering headlong into a spin that he couldn't stop, until eventually himself and Paul both came crashing down against the garden fence. He managed to protect Paul from the fall, taking the brunt of it himself, but Paul had got a fright and began to cry. When Jean had come in from work, Paul relayed the story to her as she cuddled him in her arms. Gavin told her they had just tripped up over a rock in the grass but it was a wake-up call for him. He swore he was never going to touch a drop again. For Paul's sake.

He took the bottles from his hiding-place in the wardrobe and poured them down the sink. He resisted temptations all around him in O'Casey's and was the only person sober in the place.

* * *

Paul was six years old when Jean sat Gavin down and announced that she was pregnant again. He was dumbfounded. For a start he could count on one hand the number of times that they had slept together in the last year. He normally came in so late that he automatically slept in the spare room so as not to wake her. He had asked her how she had let that happen and she had got really upset with him and stormed back to her parents with Paul in tow. He had reached for a bottle of whiskey again and, as he gulped it back, with every sip he wondered what the hell he was going to do now? It was hard enough providing for Paul but now, if there was a second baby on the way, how were they meant to afford it?

He knew his reaction was out of line so the next day he had swallowed humble pie and called over to the McParlands to apologise to Jean. He told her that of course he wanted this baby and that they would figure it out. They made up and Jean came back home. He made a promise there and then to himself to stop drinking. With a second baby on the way, they couldn't afford it for a start. But within three days he had succumbed to the pressure of the lads as they stayed back after hours in O'Casey's.

* * *

As the weeks of her pregnancy progressed, Jean was beginning to put pressure on him to get a more agreeable job with regular hours so that he would be at home more in the evenings to help out with Paul and the new baby that was on the way. She would give him the newspaper every day with jobs already circled and then she would ask him what ones he had applied for. He could feel the pressure mounting on him. He tried fobbing her off, saying that what he had was the best for everyone because he would mind the children when she was in work and be with them all day and that if anyone should change their job it should be her. She got upset with him, asking him why he was being so difficult, but he just couldn't contemplate leaving O'Casey's. It was the only thing that kept him going. It was the one place he could drink freely, no one noticed if he took an extra shot of whiskey or had a double vodka on the go. It was acceptable to drink there. If O'Casey's was gone, then he would be too.

* * *

At Jean's first scan the ultra-sonographer had probed around her belly for longer than normal.

"Is everything okay?" Jean had asked worriedly.

"Mmmmh . . ." The ultra-sonographer stared intently at the screen.

"What is it?" Gavin asked, scared.

"Don't worry, everything is fine, guys, but . . . well . . ."

"*What?*" Gavin demanded.

"Well, you're actually having twins!"

Gavin felt the blood drain from his head.

"Oh my God! Did you hear that, Gav – twins! That is unbelievable!"

He looked up at Jean and the ultrasound technician who were smiling wildly at one another as if this was the best news in the world.

"Is there a history on either side?" she asked.

"Not that I know of!" Jean replied, laughing.

He began to sweat; a mixture of water and vodka came out through his pores until he could smell the salt on his skin. *What the fuck? Twins! Jesus, things were bad enough as it was – he was barely getting used to the idea of another baby being on the way but twins! They didn't even fucking run in the family!*

He felt as though the walls were closing in around him. The pressure was unbearable. He looked at the two of them grinning at him like a pair of Cheshire cats. He looked at the door, which had a porthole window and, although he didn't know why, he suddenly found himself bolting out of the room. As he ran through the hospital corridors, trying to avoid bumps large and small, he could hear Jean's voice calling behind him but he had to get away.

33

A letter arrived on the doormat a few weeks later, with a postmark from Spain. It was from Gavin, explaining why he had left and that he was sorry but that they would all be better off without him. There was no return address. Jean ripped the paper into shreds and threw it onto the fire and watched it until the paper had singed and eventually dissolved in the heat of the flame.

Initially she was shocked at how Gavin had just walked out on her like that. How can you think you know someone only to discover that you never really knew them at all? But as the shock began to subside, she became angry. She never in a million years would have thought he would do that to her. Never. Her parents had been right about Gavin all along. She knew that if he ever so much as showed his face back in Ballydubh again, she would run him out of the village herself.

She moved back home with her parents once again. They stepped in as best they could but Jean knew they were bitterly disappointed in her. They had got over the fact that she had fallen pregnant with Paul, these things happened, people made mistakes, but to do it again, a second time – well, they had no understanding of how she could let it happen again and to be carrying twins was a whole other ball game. They knew the town gossips were having a field day but at the end of the day she was their daughter and they would do the best they could to support her.

It broke her heart how Paul, who was old enough to understand that his father wasn't around, asked where he was constantly. He was only six years old and he couldn't understand why his dad wasn't waiting for him outside the school gate like he used to. She tried to keep it together for his sake and for the sake of the two little babies growing inside her who were now starting to make their presence felt with small kicks and wriggles inside her rapidly growing tummy.

A few months later, Jean gave birth to a boy and girl. She named them Chloe and Kyle.

The first few years were tough. Jean had her hands full with a seven-year-old boy and newborn twins. Her parents tried their best to help out but the house wasn't big enough for all of them. Jean returned to her job in the solicitor's office in an effort to pay their way while her parents minded her three children. They brought Paul to school in the mornings and she collected him on her way home from work in the evenings. But Úna and Paul found themselves resenting the fact that although this was the period of their life when, having reared their own kids, they should be winding down and starting to live their lives again, instead they were back in the baby stage. Jean could sense that they were growing tired of having the house overrun by three small children so it was a relief for all concerned when Jean managed to get a council house in a village nearby. They would still be close enough to help out but they would have their house back to themselves again.

The house that Jean was given was basic and in many ways the leaking windows and lack of proper central heating reminded her of the bedsit in Cork, but it was a roof over their heads and it was a relief to be out of her parents' hair. At least now if the twins cried during the night, she didn't feel under pressure to keep them quiet, or when Paul was tearing about the place pretending to play cops and robbers she didn't have to keep on telling him to be quiet.

She set about putting her own touches to her new home. Paul chose a cornflower blue for his room and she put a sunny yellow in the twins' room. Her dad helped her to paint the walls. He pulled up the ancient carpet and put down some semi-solid wood flooring, he sealed the leaking windows and hung pictures and photo-frames around the place. They gave her their old sofa and she decorated it with throws and cushions. For the first time in her life she felt as though she was finally taking control of her own life. For years she had been doing what her parents told her to do, then she had let Gavin take charge. Now it felt good to have her own independence, to do the things she wanted, to be a mother in the way she wanted without her own mother looking over her shoulder. In fact, she found it was quite liberating.

34

As the months after Gavin had left went by, Paul began to mention his daddy less and less. Jean was relieved that he didn't seem to be as upset as he first was. He loved his new school and was doing well. His teachers were happy with his progress. He still asked for his dad occasionally, usually after he heard other boys in his class talking about the things that they did with their dads. Her heart would break for him. It was different for Chloe and Kyle. They had no memory of Gavin so in some ways that was just the way things were for them, they didn't know any different. But Paul had memories of his father, he knew what it was like to have a dad and to have him taken away. She didn't know if it was because they had been together for seven years on their own or for what reason but she had a special bond with Paul, different to the bond she had with the twins. They had been through a lot together and she knew she treated him differently to the other two because of that. She relied on him. He would keep an eye on the twins if they were outside playing and he helped her do little jobs around the house. She called him her 'big strong boy' and when she said that to him, his face would burst with pride. She would let him stay up after the twins had gone to bed at the weekends and they would snuggle up together and watch a film with bowls of popcorn and goodies. It was their special time of the week together and they both looked forward to it.

Every year on Paul's birthday, Gavin would send him a card with money in it. But there was never anything for the twins. She assumed it was because he didn't know their birthday. She had heard through people in the town that he was running an Irish bar somewhere in the Costa Del Sol and she had remarked that it was very apt with more than a hint of bitterness.

But as the years went on Jean couldn't help but notice that the absence his father was having a huge impact on Paul. When the boys in his class realised that he came from a broken home, they had started bullying him. Jean had tried talking to his teachers but they didn't take it seriously and told her that that was just "what boys did" – they were just "playing". But she knew it wasn't right for a ten-year-old to come home from school with a black eye or ripped uniform; that wasn't "playing". She had tried to teach him how to stand up for himself but he was embarrassed and would tell her to leave him alone. She asked her father to have a chat with him but Paul had pretended that everything was fine. She had wished his father was still around to help him. Chloe and Kyle had each other but she couldn't help thinking that poor Paul was on his own.

The bullying had marked a change in Paul. No longer was he her sweet innocent son. He had grown up, almost too soon, and was tougher now and less inclined to let his feelings show. Whereas, before, he would walk up to her openly and put his arms around her, now he put on a brave front and he wouldn't show her any affection. Then he made new friends in the estate, friends that were a little older and from similar backgrounds as himself so he wasn't laughed at by them for not having his father around. His new friends were in the classes above him and as soon as the bullies saw who their victim was now hanging around with, they left him alone. The new friends became a shield around him.

Jean didn't like these boys. She knew their faces from where they hung around the estate every day, messing and smoking, but there was no doubt that Paul had seemed happier since he had made friends with them. For the first time in two years, he was sure of himself – a new-found confidence that Jean didn't want to take away from him, so she knew she had to tread carefully. She tried her best to distract him from his new friends but he wasn't having any of it.

Things began to go downhill. At eleven years of age she had smelt cigarettes on him, at twelve he had stumbled in drunk. It became a daily battle to get him to go to school and keep him in there. Whereas once he had excelled, now in secondary school Paul was one of the troublemakers. She was forever being called in to discuss his behaviour and Jean had to beg for second chances from disgruntled teachers. She knew he was doing drugs at fourteen; he would come home with his eyes rolling in his head and his tongue bulging in his mouth. He brought girls up to his room and no matter how Jean tried to stop him, he wouldn't listen to her. He would lash out in temper, kicking holes in the door or the wall or throwing her belongings on the floor. One time he had flushed her phone down the toilet because she wouldn't give him money. He was finally expelled at the age of fifteen. Jean didn't blame the school, she knew there was nothing they could do for him any more, but it now meant that he was at home all day with time on his hands and his temper seemed to grow. She began to fear his outbursts. She was afraid to be in her own house and it was her own fault for giving in to him over the years. It was as if he blamed her first for his dad leaving and second for being bullied at school, and her guilt meant that she made excuses for him. But he was out of control. She knew she had no one to blame but herself because when his behaviour had first started getting out of hand, she hadn't stood up to him. She hadn't challenged him on it and now she was paying the price.

35

November, 2009

When Paul came home from his night in the Garda cell, Jean was shocked at how calm he was. She had expected him to storm straight into the house and go ballistic but yet again her son surprised her by acting completely the opposite to what she had feared. While he didn't talk to her, he did stay out of her way up in his room. There was no music blaring and no shouting at Chloe and Kyle. Jean was dumbfounded by his behaviour but maybe the stint in Garda custody was the wake-up call that he had finally needed. When he was hungry that evening he didn't come in like he usually would and demand that she cook something for him, he just went and made it himself. Even the twins were gobsmacked and they all looked at one another with surprised faces.

When Louise called over to check how she was doing, she told her sister about the complete change in his personality. They both hoped it was a lesson learnt for Paul. He went out quietly that evening and Jean prayed he wouldn't come home in a state. She knew he could be fine when he was sober but under the influence of drugs and alcohol there was no telling what he would do.

She didn't even hear him come home that night. Usually he would come in slamming doors and turn up the stereo but she hadn't heard a sound last night. As she was getting breakfast ready for the twins the next morning, Paul stuck his head around the kitchen door and asked if she wanted anything in the shop. She was stunned by the gesture; it had been years since he had done anything remotely like helping her. She longed to walk up to him and draw him close into a hug and tell him that she loved him, but she knew that would be pushing it so instead she replied that she was okay for everything but thanks for the offer. When he left she let out a long sigh of relief. *My son is back.*

The atmosphere in the small house perked up instantly. Chloe and Kyle didn't seem so weighed down with worry and fear, and Jean could relax a bit more now that she knew Paul wasn't going to descend upon them all in a vicious rage. The Gardaí had rung to check how things were since he had been released and she was glad to report that things were great, in fact better than they had been in a long time. Imagine if she had listened to them and pressed charges like they had wanted her to do! Of course she was very grateful that they had stepped in when they did but all that was required was a caution and he was back to his old self again. Her son had learnt his lesson; he wasn't a violent man like they had made him out to be.

For the first time in weeks, she began to sleep at night without fear. Chloe and Kyle began to do better in school; the combination of being able to get their homework done in peace and getting a good night's sleep had worked wonders and made Jean feel awful because it was only now that she was realising just how badly they had been affected by Paul's violence.

Paul seemed to have a new-found respect for her and her house and no longer saw it as his own stomping ground to invite his friends over and do whatever he wanted. Whatever they had said to him in the Garda station, it had worked.

She stopped making excuses when her mother or Louise suggested calling over to her – she was no longer afraid of what state Paul would be in. He began to talk to her again – granted, there was no in-depth conversation, only greetings like 'Hi' or 'See you later' but it was a start. She hoped that maybe he was finally beginning to grow up. He still went out with the lads to God knew where and she was pretty sure he was still doing his assortment of drugs but, if he was leaving her and the twins alone, she was going to leave him alone.

36

December, 2009

Saturday morning was the one morning of the week that the Kinsella family all sat down and ate breakfast together. Morning time on the weekdays was a blur of trying to coax the girls to sit down to eat a few bites of breakfast cereal while Nora flustered around making lunches, finding missing school-ties and packing schoolbags that she had been promised were already packed. Her husband Pat was usually on the road early every day to beat the commuter traffic from their County Wicklow home into Dublin City Centre. But on Saturday mornings they normally all sat down together and had big blow-out late breakfast. Of course it was Nora who was left cooking the fry, flipping pancakes or pouring maple syrup over the waffles, but it was as much a treat for her as it was for the rest of the family. The three girls were seated around the breakfast table whilst Nora tossed the eggs over in the frying pan.

"I no want guggy-egg," Emily, the three-year-old, roared at her mother.

"No guggy-egg, love – I'll make it hard, so."

"But *I* want guggy-egg!" Katie, her four-year-old daughter, protested.

"All right, here you go then," Nora said in exasperation as she walked over to the table with the frying pan and placed the egg onto Katie's plate before bring the pan back over to continue cooking Emily's egg. Nora knew Katie was just doing it to be difficult – whatever her sisters did or wanted Katie had to do the opposite.

"What way do you want your egg, Orla?"

Orla was six and was a mini-adult in comparison to her two younger sisters.

"Guggy-egg is for babies, I want it hard."

"No, it's not!" Katie whined. "Mammy, tell her it's not!"

"Orla, guggy-egg isn't for babies – stop winding Katie up!"

"Ha!" Katie said goadingly to her sister.

"Now that is enough, the pair of you!" *Jesus, Sweet Mother of Divinity, why do I bother at all with family breakfasts? They aren't worth the stress!*

"But I need soldiers, Mam!" Katie was looking at the lonely egg on her plate.

"Right, sit back down. I'll put toast on for you now."

"I want soldiers too!" Emily was roaring again.

"Emily, I can hear you perfectly well – there is no need to shout."

Nora popped bread into the toaster and wondered how she would get through the day. It was only eight o'clock and already she was worn out from the demands of her daughters. And Pat was enjoying a lie-in as usual. It irked her that, even though she was up early with the kids all week, just because he went out to work he automatically felt entitled to his weekend lie-ins. It didn't matter to him that her job as a stay-at-home mother didn't operate from Monday to Friday with the weekends off and an hour-long lunch-break. In a few minutes she would shout down the hall to wake him up and he would wander into the kitchen with a big sleepy head on him and have his 'family breakfast' served up to him on a plate. She sighed and opened the fridge door and a carton of milk that had been hastily stuffed onto the edge of one of the glass shelves fell out and spilled all over the floor.

"For Christ –" she shouted but, when she saw her daughters looking at her wide-eyed, fearful of the tone of her voice, she stopped herself in her tracks. "Who left that there?" She took a deep breath. *Patience*, she reminded herself, *patience*. She knew already that today was going to be trying.

She had bent down on her hunkers and was looking into the cupboard under the sink for kitchen-roll when suddenly there was a huge screech from outside. Its pitch sent a chill down her spine. *What was that?* It was followed instantly by the sound of metal crashing upon metal. She felt goose-pimples rise on her skin. *Sweet Jesus.* She looked over at the three girls who now, instead of being frightened by her, were frightened instead by the noise coming from outside.

She hopped up and looked out the kitchen window. Her eyes scanned the garden as she saw clumps of leafy green foliage scattered all around the grass. *The hedge, there was a hole in the hedge. What had happened to the hedge?* Then she noticed the trampoline had been upended and was turned upside down, lying on the opposite side of the garden instead of in its usual spot. Deep ugly brown track-marks now divided the green lawn in two. Her eyes followed the tracks until they rested upon a car lying on its side. *A car!* It all seemed so out of place. *Why was there a car in their garden?* She could hear a commotion coming from the road.

"Pat! *Pat!*" She shouted down the hallway of their bungalow towards their bedroom. But he was already running towards her; he had heard it too. He ran past her and the girls and out the back door. The four of them followed in haste behind him. They all stood momentarily on the doorstep, just surveying the sight before them, trying to process what they were looking at.

Pat sprang into action. "Get the girls inside, Nora! Quick, call an ambulance!" he roared at her.

And at last she realised what was happening and ushered the girls back into the house. Her daughters looked at her for explanation, their small confused faces trying to make sense of why their dad was shouting and why there was a car lying sideways in their garden. She hurried them into the playroom and told Orla to put on the *Peppa Pig* DVD for the girls. Emily was thrilled by the impromptu viewing of her favourite cartoon without even having to ask for it. She started jumping up and down, repeating giddily, *"Peppa Pig! Peppa Pig!"* Orla was about to protest, probably something along the lines of her not wanting to watch *Peppa Pig* and how it was only for babies but something about her mother's voice and demeanour told her to do as she was told. She led her younger sisters into the playroom and turned on the TV for them.

Nora fumbled with the phone, trying to dial 999 while simultaneously peering out through the frosted glass in the side panels of their door.

"Hello, yes . . . There's been a bad accident. At the crossroads on Newtown Road – a car has gone off the road and tumbled into our garden. I'm not sure how many are in the car." Her voice was trembling. They took her address and said they would dispatch an ambulance and the fire-brigade.

She ran back out to Pat who was trying to peer into the car through the shattered front windscreen but the millions of small cracks made it impossible.

"They're on their way," she said.

He ran around to the back of the car, where the back window had fallen through and peered in.

"There's a baby in there, Nora. Holy Jesus!"

Feeling utterly useless, Nora willed the emergency services to hurry the hell on.

She watched, fearful that the car might explode or something, as Pat tried to climb up the undercarriage of the car so that he could look in through the side window.

"It's a man. There's a man in the driver's seat!" He started shouting into the car. "Hey, can you hear me? The ambulance is on its way. Can you hear me? What's your name?" Pat watched the man's eyelids flash open for a second before closing again. "You're going to be okay, just hang in there."

Eventually sirens could be heard in the distance, getting closer. The fire-brigade arrived first and mobilised themselves into action immediately. They cut through the roof of the car as if they were opening a tin of bins. The ambulance pulled up swiftly after. One crew immediately began trying to free the baby and another began to remove the man. Both were removed gingerly and placed on stretchers. And then the ambulance sped off in the direction of Dublin County Hospital.

Nora and Pat were guided back into their house by a Garda who had arrived on the scene also. He told them to sit down and made them sweet tea as if they were guests in their own kitchen. They all sat in silence for a while before he asked them for their version of events. They tried to tell him what they knew but the shock made it seem surreal and they weren't sure if they were making any sense. Eventually the Garda left and told them they would let them know as soon as they had any news on the victims.

Later on some of the neighbours had called around and they all sat huddled together around the rectangular table, adding in their pieces of the story. Nora and Pat soon learnt that there was another car involved too but it was a hit-and-run. It had gone into the ditch in front of the McDermotts' house but had reversed out and driven off before anyone had time to stop it or get its number plates. They shook their heads in despair as to how anyone could be so callous. The neighbours would fall silent as they all prayed inwardly for the man and the baby before someone would speak up again as they tried to process their disbelief at what had happened on their quiet country road that morning.

When the Gardaí phoned later that afternoon, they learnt the worst. The baby had died at the scene. It had been a baby boy, only six months old.

"Oh, dear God! In our garden!" Nora found it hard to take. She felt the blood drain from her head and her legs felt weak beneath her. She had to sit down on a chair and catch her breath. Although it was a baby she had never known, she was a mother herself so she could only begin to imagine what the parents were going through. The man was in a coma in intensive care but his condition hadn't deteriorated any further which they were hoping was a good sign. Pat had asked the Gardaí what had happened, what had caused the accident, but they weren't inclined to comment until their investigations had been completed.

That night as Nora tucked her three white-haired angels up in bed, she hugged them all so close that they tried to wriggle away from her arms in laughter. She was grateful that they didn't seem to pay much heed to that morning's events. Orla had asked what had happened and they had explained to her that there was a car-crash but never mentioned that there were people involved and she didn't ask. She seemed more concerned by the fact that their trampoline had been uprooted. How blessed Nora felt to be able to hold her daughters. To think that only that morning she had been groaning inwardly, losing patience at their ever-increasing demands! What that baby's parents wouldn't give for that! They would never get to experience it now. And what would have happened if the children had been playing in the garden at the time? Her blood ran cold at the thought. You really had to cherish each and every day, she thought.

Once the girls were asleep she went back out to her husband. He wasn't normally one for affection but he wrapped his arms around her so that her head was buried into his chest. She didn't need to be able to see his face to tell he was crying. The reminder of the fragility of life that day had shaken them and they both knew that they would never be the same again. She said a prayer for the family of the baby boy, people she didn't know but that were now living through every parent's worst nightmare; she prayed they would have the strength to get through it.

37

The first thing Jean noticed when her son walked into the kitchen was a large gash right above his left eye. He was also limping badly and grimacing at each step he took. She got a fright and instantly rushed over to attend to him but he pushed her away and sat down.

"What happened to you?" she asked worriedly.

"Leave it, Ma, will you!"

"That is some gash, Paul – you need to get that seen to." She looked down at his leg where it was swollen to twice its size. "Jesus, Paul, it looks broken. I'm taking you to the hospital."

She flustered around the place, moving papers and pushing jars to find her keys.

"Not now!" he said, raising his voice.

He looked out of it and Jean wasn't sure if it was because of the pain he was in or for other reasons so she backed off. She placed her keys back down on the counter. On the one hand he looked to be in tremendous pain but still he was insisting he didn't want to get it looked at.

She went out to the hallway and through the glass panels of her front door she saw that Paul's car was completely crumpled on one side. The metal was raised and folded and the white paintwork scraped off to reveal the tin underneath. She realised what had happened. She went back to the kitchen.

"I saw your car!"

He said nothing.

"What the hell did you crash into?"

"Ah Ma, stop, would you just give over, you're wrecking me head!" He hopped up from the chair, taking a sharp intake of breath, then hobbled in obviously excruciating pain upstairs to his bedroom.

She wondered what had happened and what trouble he had got himself into now. And worse – what kind of a state had he been in at the time? Suppose he had been driving faster? He was lucky he wasn't killed. She shuddered at the thought. Her heart lurched as she realised it could have been very different; at least bones would heal. She would allow him sleep off the effects of last night and then she would insist that they go to the hospital and get the wound and his leg treated.

She turned on the radio and went about the kitchen doing her chores. She cleaned out the fridge, throwing away a load of out-of-date yoghurts that Kyle had begged her for the week before but hadn't eaten. She shook her head despairingly; she couldn't afford to be throwing out food like this. She made a note to herself to tell Kyle later that the next time he begged her to buy him something in the supermarket he had better eat it. She cleaned down the counter-tops and swept and mopped the floor. She had to stop for a minute to flex out her wrist – she had only just got the cast off and, although the break had healed well, it tended to get sore if she did too much with it. She listened to the songs on the radio – it was one of those eighties hours. She sang along to A-Ha's 'Take on Me'. She remembered how she had thought that song was the best song ever when she was younger. She had bought the record and everything and had the band's posters all over her bedroom wall.

Then the serious tones of the newsreader could be heard as he broadcast the lunchtime news and the events that had taken place overnight.

An earthquake measuring Force 7 on the Richter scale had hit Chile; the workers of Aer Lingus were going on strike on Monday; a baby had died after a serious road-traffic accident in Newtown Village and the male occupant in the car was in a serious condition in Dublin County Hospital. The Gardaí were appealing for witnesses.

She knew that road well. It was a peaceful country road but all it took was for someone to hit those bends at speed and they could easily be gone – and there was one blind junction where there had been more than one accident in the past. Her heart went out to the family – to lose a child like that was every parent's worst nightmare.

Jean then set about dropping the twins to their Saturday activities: Chloe was going to her horse-riding lesson and Kyle was going to soccer practice. She was grateful to her parents who paid for their activities since she had lost her job – it would have broken the kids' hearts if she'd had to tell them that she could no longer afford it. Plus, she hoped it would give them an interest and a broader outlook on all the possibilities that life had to offer, and maybe stop them going down the same road as Paul. She wanted them to make something of themselves, be comfortable financially and not to make the same mistakes that she had.

When she got back to the house, she went up to check on Paul. She pushed back the door to his bedroom, cursing silently as it creaked, but he didn't wake. He was still sleeping off the effects of whatever was in his system.

It had been months since she was last in his bedroom and

she nearly gagged on the stale smell of smoke and overflowing ashtrays that littered the place. Posters of half-dressed pin-ups hung on the wall now – they hadn't been there the last time. She looked at the rise and fall of his chest. The gash on his head wasn't bleeding but it was gaping and could probably do with a stitch before it got infected. She couldn't see his leg and she didn't dare pull the blanket back to take a look. She tiptoed back out of the room and closed the door gently behind her. She would wait until he woke up.

Jean had half an hour to spare before she had to pick up the twins. She sat down with a cup of coffee and a digestive and switched on the TV. The news was on and they showed the mangled car involved in that crash on Newtown Road being lifted up by a tow-truck. She dunked her biscuit in her tea and tutted at the wreckage. *The poor baby didn't stand a chance*, she thought. She watched the Garda appeal for witnesses to the horrific hit-and-run.

Her blood ran cold. She hadn't known it was a hit and run. Jesus Christ. She thought about Paul: his crashed car, his wounded forehead and most likely broken leg and his reluctance to get them seen to. *No*, she told herself. *Don't be silly. Stop over-reacting, putting two and two together and getting twenty-two.* Paul wouldn't do that. He might be capable of a lot of things but he would never crash into another car and leave the scene of the accident. *Would he?* No matter how many times she tried to suppress the thoughts, they kept popping up again like one of those pop-up games that the kids had when they were babies that no matter how many times you hammered down the shapes, another blasted one would always pop up again. The doubts kept niggling at her and for some reason she just had a bad feeling about all of this. She really hoped she was wrong.

Almost on autopilot she got up and went to collect Chloe and Kyle. She walked past the wreck of Paul's car. She stood momentarily and surveyed it. It was damaged but not nearly to the same extent as the wreckage of the other car that had been on the news. There was no way it had been Paul's car. Sure he had driven it home. If it had been Paul's car, it wouldn't have come out of the crash with just a crumpled front bumper. She felt better as she drove away. She would talk to Paul about exactly what had happened. She was sure it was nothing major but she would have to broach it with him. She needed to make the point that, if he was driving under the influence of drink or worse still drugs, even if he had a lucky escape this time, he mightn't be so fortunate next time. He was going to have to cop himself on.

* * *

Chloe and Kyle hopped into the car and immediately started chatting to her, Chloe regaling her about how high the jumps were and Kyle about how he had scored the winning goal. They were both buoyed up and excited and she wanted to hug them close. She knew they were at that age where their childhood innocence would soon disappear. She wanted to keep the fragments and savour their excitement at small things for as long as she could because, as she had seen with Paul, in the blink of an eye they would grow up.

When she pulled up in the driveway and they saw Paul's car they both looked to her for an explanation.

"Oh, I think he just hit off something last night."

They both looked confused by her brief explanation but knew by her tone that they shouldn't push it any further.

When Paul finally got up the twins had gone to bed. Jean was glad because at least it would allow her to ask him without them overhearing. He hobbled into the kitchen, barely able to walk, his face etched visibly with pain at every movement.

"Have you any painkillers, Ma?"

"Sorry, love, only Paracetamol and I think you need something stronger than that – look, I really think we need to get that leg looked at."

"Not now. Just leave it, yeah?"

"But, Paul, you could really do serious damage. What happens if it doesn't set properly or if that wound gets infected? Jesus, you could get septicaemia in that!"

He was about to argue back but he let out a groan of agony instead. "In the morning," he said with a grimace.

* * *

The next morning, on their journey to the hospital, Paul became increasingly agitated and wound up. She put it down to the pain but when he kept telling her what to say and what not to say, the niggling worries about that hit-and-run on Newtown Road began to bother her again. He told her that she wasn't to mention anything about a crash; he had just fallen over at home. And she was to say it happened only last night, she wasn't to mention anything about Friday and if anyone did ask her where he had been on Friday night, she was to say that he was at home with her.

She looked at her son, deep into his blue eyes, and she knew.

38

Jean was thankful that she didn't have to lie to anyone at the hospital because she wasn't sure if she would be able to do it. No one had batted an eyelid at their circumstances and whatever story Paul had spun them, they believed it and assumed it was just your run-of-the-mill domestic accident. Although the sweat was pumping out through her pores, Jean sat shivering in the waiting room. She rubbed her arms to get warm and tapped her feet. How could he do that? *A baby had died.* And a man was seriously injured. That poor family torn apart because of *her* son. *Jesus Christ. Jesus fucking Christ. What the fuck was she meant to do now? Paul was her son, her firstborn baby, but he had gone too far this time.*

When he came back out to her with his leg in a plaster-of-Paris cast, balanced on crutches with his bandaged forehead, he smiled at her. It was the first time he had smiled at her in years. Just days ago she would have begged the gods up high to let her son smile at her but now, under these circumstances, it made her feel ill. She could have sworn there was a tinge of relief in it – she wanted to go up to him and wipe it off his face.

Slap his face hard and scream at him. *How could he have done that?*

They walked in silence back to the car. The news came on the radio and said they were still looking for witnesses to the crash. They were appealing again to anyone who knew anything or anyone who might have seen a white car in the vicinity. Paul leaned forward and turned it off. They both sat listening to the squeak of the wipers going back and forth.

"It was you – wasn't it?" Jean turned to him.

He didn't answer her but he wouldn't make eye contact with her. That was all the answer she needed.

When they got home, Paul went up to bed. She busied herself in the routine of making a snack for Chloe and Kyle but she couldn't stomach anything herself as the worries kept on circling around and around in her head. What should she do? On the one hand, she knew she should report him to the Gardaí. Somebody had died. But he was her son. She couldn't be a traitor to her own son, could she? She was the reason he was like this. It was her fault; he had a difficult upbringing and she needed to take her share of the blame on board.

She watched the other two innocently eating their tea, oblivious to the dilemma she was faced with. She opened a bottle of wine and they looked at her – she rarely drank but she needed something now. The heavy noise it made as it filled the glass calmed her. The stress was taking its toll; she was only in her thirties but she felt in her eighties. She wished she was that age – at least she would be close to death's door.

Why did this have to happen? Why her son? He had a tough enough life as it was and just as she finally felt she was getting through to him! If she let him down again, that was it, his life would be over. He would probably get a long jail sentence: driving under the influence, dangerous driving, failing to stop – the list of possible charges was endless. He would probably get life imprisonment. No judge would have sympathy for him.

They would look only at the black-and-white hard facts of the case. They wouldn't care if he was bullied in school or had a tough childhood or that his dad had walked out on him when he was small – none of that would matter in a court. This was the one time in her life that she could do something to protect him. But on the other hand a baby had died. *A baby!* She thought back over all the times where she had failed him: letting his dad walk out like that, the bullying in school, maybe she had been over-reliant on him, he'd had to grow up too quickly, he didn't have the childhood that the other two had. Every mother was hardwired to protect their child. The protective instinct was present as soon as he had been placed in her arms. No matter what, he was still her son, he always would be. Her mind was made up; she wasn't going to let him down again. She couldn't do that to him.

39

It had been Aido's birthday. He had a free house for the weekend, so they were heading over there for a session. They all sat around the living room drinking from tins of beer.

"All right, boys!" Paul came through the door, grinning at the lads.

"Jesus, where the fuck were you?"

"Patience, J, *patience* – all good things come to those who wait. Did your ma never tell you that?" He piled his tray of cans on top of the rest.

"Here, dish it up the fuck, would you? We've been waiting long enough!" J was irritated.

Paul took a small bag full of white powder from inside his jacket and threw it onto the table. J sat forward and immediately started untying it.

"Hold on a sec, what do you say?"

"Cheers, Paul."

"Louder."

"For fuck's sake – *Cheers, Paul!*"

"That's better – after all I do for you! I thought the pigs were onto me."

"What d'you mean?"

"There was a copper car behind me most of the way back here, so I pulled in to a garage but he kept on going."

"Ha, ha!" laughed Aido.

J proceeded to tip some of the cocaine onto the glass coffee table. He measured it out with a card before chopping the powder into individual lines, using the card to even them up. He took a fifty out of his pocket, rolled it up and began snorting up his nose before passing it on to the rest of the lads.

They knocked back tins and snorted line after line of cocaine until eventually they could no longer feel the insides of their noses. Paul was starting to feel good about himself. The stereo was pumping out the lyrics of Dizzee Rascal. He paraded around the living-room floor like it was him on stage. He stepped over the legs of the lads who were sprawled around the floors as he waved his arms and synched his lips to the music. He knocked over a half-drunk can that had been sitting on the floor and watched as it spilled out, forming a foamy pool across the carpet. He stepped over it and kept on dancing.

"Here, give us some more of that Charlie, J!" Paul said as he plonked down on the sofa again.

"Fuck off, you, get yis'er own!"

"What the fuck are you saying, and me after buying it for you?" Paul's eyes grew wide and angry.

"I'm only buzzin' off, ya' muppet ya! Here!" He slid the bag of white powder over to where Paul was sitting.

They sat around all night, drinking tins and hoovering up the last of the cocaine until the sun started to come up outside. Some of the lads had started to doze in their chairs. Someone was snoring in the corner. But Paul wasn't feeling sleepy; on the contrary he had never felt more alive. He was feeling thirsty but there was no drink left. The stereo was still blaring away and the room reeked of stale beer.

"Here, who wants a race to the shops? C'mon, me and Aido against J and Noel!"

"You're on!"

They went outside into the cool morning air in their T-shirts but they didn't feel the chill. J and Noel got into one car, while Aido got into Paul's passenger seat. When he turned the key in his ignition, the rest of the song from where the CD had stopped last night started up again but the beat was too fast and too loud now so he lowered it rapidly. He lit a cigarette and put it between his lips, then reversed at speed out of the driveway so the tyres screeched. He could see some of the neighbours coming to their windows to see where the racket was coming from. He gave them the finger out the car window and made the engine rev even louder.

He drove along with the window down, letting the chilly morning air into the car. The lads were following behind and as soon as they got out of the estate they tried to take him on the outside. He swerved across the road to block them. Aido turned the mirror around to see them and started laughing. When the road widened, he moved to the left but when J went to overtake again, he moved out right across the road to block him. But J bounded back to the left, managed to undertake him and moved ahead. Paul pressed his foot to the floor to catch him. They came up to a bend and Paul went up the inside. It was tight. He didn't know if he was going to get through. Aido looked over at him but there was nowhere else to go. His car was inches from J's wing. At the last minute, he got through. J swerved to the right, into the path of an oncoming driver who swerved to avoid them both.

"Fuck, that was close!" shouted Aido.

Paul's heart was thumping; the adrenaline was rushing through his veins. J was chasing close behind him now, sitting on his bumper. He zigzagged to the left and right, J trying to overtake. They bounded left then right and left again. They came up to a wider part of the road and J moved out to the other side so that they were neck and neck, taking up both sides of the road.

"Here we go! *Woo-hoo*! Floor it, Paul, c'mon!"

He pressed his foot down on the accelerator. The wind coming in through the window filled his ears from the speed. Their car moved marginally ahead before J's caught up again.

"C'mon, Paul! *C'mon!*" Aido was roaring in his ear. "*C'monnn!*"

His foot was to the floor but J's car shot ahead, Noel raising his fingers in a mocking L-shape to them as they passed.

The trees whizzed past as he tried to catch up. He tapped his jittery fingers on the steering wheel. They came up to a crossroads with a stop sign. J drove straight through, he wasn't stopping. There was no visibility right or left and Paul hesitated instinctively, his foot coming up off the floor. Then he accelerated out onto the junction at precisely the same moment that a silver Volkswagen came through from the right. He spun his wheel and swerved but it wasn't enough and he braced himself for the impact, waiting for the bang. Then came the sound of crumpled metal as he careered into the rear left-side wing of the other car. Their car skidded along for what seemed like an age but it was probably only seconds before they slid into a ditch and next thing he saw was a grass verge outside his windscreen.

Paul sat in the seat, too stunned to move, his whole body shaking uncontrollably. His chattering teeth felt as though they were banging off his brain.

"Jesus Christ. *Jesus Christ!*" Aido kept repeating. "*Jesus fucking Christ!*"

"*Shut up!*" Paul shouted back at him. "*Just shut up!*"

Automatically he put the car into reverse, a savage pain shooting up his left leg as he did so, but it wasn't moving. *C'mon.*

He tried again with heavy revs but he was wedged up onto the bank and the wheels were just spinning, going nowhere. *C'mon the fuck!* He knew they only had minutes before the police would be here.

"*Get out and push!*" he roared at Aido who did as he was told and hopped out of the car.

As Aido used all his strength to push the car down off the ditch, he revved the engine. In the distance they could hear sirens. Paul revved the engine harder, battling against the pain in his left leg. The sirens were getting closer but his car wasn't moving.

"*C'mon, Aido!*"

He watched as Aido's face turned purple from exertion until at last the car started to budge. Aido jumped back in as Paul put his foot to the floor and they screeched out of there. His car was rattling and pulling to the left as he drove. He glanced back in his mirror to where the crash had happened but he couldn't see the other car, just the road blackened with curved tyre tracks.

40

Jean tossed and turned all that night. She tried to justify her decision, she tried to tell herself that it was the right thing to do, but it still didn't sit easy with her conscience. She told herself that she was doing what any mother would do but why then did she feel so physically torn apart? She wished she could just be morally weak like so many people on earth and look after her own first and let everyone else sort themselves out but then an image of the dead baby would come into her head, just staring at her, and she would start to sweat and her resolution didn't seem so right any more.

She thought back to when Paul was born and wondered, if she had known then what she knew now and how he would break her heart, would she do it all again? How does an innocent bundle who snuggles in your arms, depending on you to answer its every need and filling you with pure joy, grow up into a person that you still love and adore but do not necessarily like? How does that happen? It was hard to believe that an innocent newborn would ever be capable of any wrongdoing; could it be that a life of hardship was already mapped out for them? How she wished that he could have just stayed that tiny sleeping bundle in her arms, never having to grow up and face the big bad world. The sad thing was that he was still only a child; he was only seventeen years of age with his whole life ahead of him.

She thought of Paul at the same age that the baby had been, six months old, laughing and clapping and starting to express his personality with new high-pitched gurgles. She had to get out of bed and run to the bathroom to be sick. The cool tiles were a welcome relief as she sat on them, her back resting against the bath-tub, the room illuminated in silver moonlight. She stayed there all night sobbing. She knew that in the morning she would have to do the most difficult thing she had ever done.

* * *

At first light the next morning she rang the Chief Superintendent in Newtown Garda station and told him everything she knew. As it all spilled out, her heart felt as though it was being twisted and wrung out with guilt. She knew she had a few minutes before their world was to be shattered apart. She opened the door to Paul's bedroom and watched him breathing. She walked over and sat down on the side of the mattress and stroked his hair, the skin on his cheek smooth under her fingertips. His eyelids flickered momentarily, registering her touch, but then relaxed back to sleep again. It had been so long since she had touched him; she wanted to remember every piece of him. She could hear the rain pounding on the roof outside, hopping off it in staccato beats. She sat stroking his face until the doorbell sounded and it was time. She took a deep breath and left the room, racked with painful guilt for what she was about to do to her own son.

Her greetings to the Gardaí were monosyllabic. They went into the kitchen and they took her statement. She told them the whole story from the beginning, what she knew of it anyway.

They asked her for his car keys and she watched as they drove the car up onto a pick-up truck to take it away as evidence.

They asked her where he was and she wanted to scream to him to run and make a break for it, to run away from it all, but she gestured to his bedroom before breaking down, convulsed in grief, knowing their lives were forever going to be different from this moment onwards. She heard his startled wakening from the hallway, she heard them read his rights, she heard the click of handcuffs and bedroom door belonging to her two younger children opening and their sleepy heads appearing, wondering what on earth was going on. She hadn't known what to expect, maybe some resistance or that he would put up a fight, but she watched her son crying as he was brought out of his bedroom in handcuffs. He looked smaller, as the inches of his macho bravado had gone. An image of him on his first day of school flashed into her head. *Her son*. She walked up to him and squeezed his hand and whispered, "I'm sorry. I love you." She could see the tears in his eyes and there was unmistakable fear within their depths. He looked like the boy that he was. She watched as they pushed his head down into the back of the squad car and then drove slowly out through the estate. She felt her legs get weak and somehow she found her way to the floor. The confused faces of Chloe and Kyle, her own despair. They huddled together heaving in grief. Her heart felt as though it had been knifed in two, split down the middle and left exposed. This was the ultimate betrayal.

41

The first time Jean had been to visit Paul was one of the most difficult and emotionally draining days of her life. To see her son behind prison walls was devastating. He was allowed visitors for half an hour every Saturday.

On her first visit, she was shocked by the security procedures and searches she had to go through just to see him. She had only ever seen this sort of thing on TV. She watched as other people went through the screening rituals, like it was so normal to them. It seemed like water off a duck's back to some of them, but it dawned on her that maybe they had been coming here for years. Once she was led inside, it was like another world entirely. Life, albeit of a different kind, still carried on behind the old stone walls.

She had been shown to a small table where she waited for him to appear. As she looked around the room, she saw women with small children running around their feet, there were older people visiting adult children, people of all ages and all types. One particularly well-dressed lady caught her eye. She was dressed immaculately in a full-length fur coat and jewels that you just knew cost obscene money. A man of a similar age was led in to meet her and she wondered what their story might be.

Eventually she saw Paul being led into the room by an officer. Her heart lurched and yet again she wondered how had she let everything go so wrong that her son had ended up here? She felt the tears filling her eyes but she forced them back. She needed to be strong for him. After all, he was the one having to spend his time locked up here; she could still go home to her comforts, to freedom. The case had yet to go before the court so they still didn't know how long his sentence would be but she knew that the judge would look upon it severely, a hit-and-run would never be shown any leniency.

"Hi there," she said, her voice shaky as she forced herself to act as normally as she could for Paul's sake.

"Hi, Mam." He looked up at her with those large blue eyes that made her melt when he was a baby. For the first time in years there was no anger in them.

"So how are you getting on?"

"I'm having a real laugh." Although he was sarcastic, he was smiling at her.

"Are they feeding you okay, looking after you okay?"

"It's all grand – except obviously I can't leave, but there are a few lads the same age, so we hang out together."

"Well, that's good, love." Jean tried to hide her doubt and anxiety. Of course she wanted him to have friends but not the same sort of friends that he had on the outside. How would he ever break the cycle if he kept on meeting the same sorts?

"Look – I'm sorry, I really am," she said.

"I know, but what could you do? I'm not angry."

He was being civil, acting like an adult, and it felt strange to her. Strange and good.

They chatted until a guard came up and told them they had only five minutes left so it was time to start wrapping it up. Jean couldn't believe the visit was nearly over already.

"Chloe and Kyle said hi. And Nana, Granddad and Auntie Louise."

She didn't want to bring the twins to visit him, she didn't want them to see the bleak inside of a prison, she wanted them to stay as carefree and innocent as they could be in the circumstances.

He said nothing.

They chatted generally until a guard came up again and told them their time was up.

"Okay, well I'll see you next week, yeah?" Her voice quivered. "Thanks, Mam."

She could see tears in his eyes. He wasn't the big macho man full of bravado that he pretended to be, he looked vulnerable instead. She leant forward and wrapped him in her arms, his head pulled in tight against her chest. She wished she could keep him there. Soon though he was being pulled away from her.

"I'd better go, Mam."

"I love you," she mouthed at him, before convulsing into tears.

She had gone home and fallen to pieces. She knew she had no right to grieve in comparison to the family that had lost their baby but in some ways she couldn't help but think that she had lost her son too. Yes, he was physically present in the world, but thirty minutes a week across a table supervised by guards for God only knew how many years was hardly a great way to see your son. And he was still so young; it was all such a waste. What if she had done things differently? If she had acted sooner or stood up to him earlier, might things have been different? She knew he would never be the same again, how could he be after spending time in a place like this? She knew he would emerge, with that exterior people seemed to have when they came out of prison, as if they were now hardened to the world.

Her family had rallied around ever since she had phoned

them to say that Paul had been arrested for his involvement in the hit-and-run. They had been stunned and equally devastated by the news. Although he had been out of control over the last few years, they knew the real Paul underneath: the smiling baby, the good-natured child. They also found it hard to accept that this was his fate and they couldn't do anything to help him now. They blamed themselves for not acting sooner. Louise had said that if she had known that Jean was saving up to move out of the council estate, she would have just given her the money. But there were so many 'if onlys'. Jean tormented herself with them, but they had to accept that hindsight wouldn't help any of them.

They had insisted there and then in giving her the money to rent a house in the town and to get the hell out of the estate. They knew it wasn't the solution to Jean's problems but, if it prevented the twins from going down the same route as Paul, it would be worth it.

Jean was relieved to finally be able to leave behind the estate so full of bad memories. Every time she looked out the window at the graffiti, the gangs of teenagers younger than Paul, starting out on the same road that he had gone down, she feared that might happen to Chloe and Kyle too. They were at an impressionable age and she knew she had just a year or two before they would want to be hanging out with their peers.

She was looking forward to the fresh start in their new home; they all needed it after everything they had been through.

It was emotional boxing up all of Paul's clothes and belongings and wondering when he would get to use them again. She would come across family photos of him that she hadn't seen in years and his smiling innocent face would tear her apart. There were a few from his eighth birthday party with big gappy teeth and freckled cheeks as he blew out the candles on his cake. She was glad she had happy memories though; glad she didn't know then all the pain that lay ahead for them.

On the day of the move Rita from next door had come over with a small present and some sweets for the twins, saying that she'd miss seeing them both about the place. Jean promised her she would keep in touch and that they would call in to see her frequently and take her to see their new home. Rita had been so good to her over the years.

The new house was a world away from the house with the leaking windows that were always full of condensation running down the insides. It had all the mod-cons like a dishwasher and a tumble-dryer, luxuries she could only have dreamed about before, but Louise had insisted that they pay the bit extra and have somewhere decent for her and the twins to live. The twins each had their own bedroom for the first time in their lives and she even had an en-suite bathroom with an electric shower. She had to swallow back when she thought about Paul and that he didn't have a room here. The house was closer too to the twins' school; they would now be able to walk every day instead of having to get the bus. There was also a good secondary school nearby.

Although Jean was grateful to her family for all they had done for her, she still wanted to be able to pay her own way so she was back looking for a job. She was lucky that she had a lot of experience from her last job, plus they had given her a good reference, which she supposed she ought to be grateful for under the circumstances. She had a few interviews lined up, all with local firms so she prayed she would get one of them. She knew she had to keep busy, it was the best thing she could do. Although the last couple of months had definitely been the toughest of her life so far and her heart had been broken in two, she could see a glimmer of light again.

Part III

Part III

42

Emma had been out Christmas shopping with Zoe when she got the call that would forever change her life. Ironically, it was her first day to leave Fionn since he had been born six months before. She hadn't wanted to leave him and had hummed and hawed about whether or not to go but, with less than two weeks left before Christmas, she needed to make a start on her shopping. She knew that by having a baby in tow she would get nothing done, between trying to manoeuvre a buggy around shops that were thronged with people and stopping for bottles and nappy-changes, so reluctantly she had left him at home. Adam had practically pushed her out the door, telling her that he'd be fine and he was looking forward to having his son to himself for the day. So with trepidation and a long to-do list, she had kissed Fionn goodbye on the top of his silky head and pecked Adam on the cheek, making him promise to call her if he wasn't sure of anything. *Anything at all,* she had reiterated and Adam had laughed at her and gently propelled her out onto the doorstep.

Sitting on the bus into town, she had stared at her phone,

waiting for Adam to ring. After half an hour of that, she rang to check things were okay. He had told her to stop worrying, that things were fine, all under control and to enjoy the day of shopping.

She had met Zoe then and relaxed into it. They had strolled down Grafton Street where a crowd had gathered around a group of carol singers collecting for charity. They stopped to listen to the spectacular voices as they lifted upwards for the soprano notes of 'Oh, Holy Night'. The street lights were switched on and swags of ivy adorned with red bows hung from the buildings on either side. Even the lampposts had garlands wrapped around them so they looked like giant candy-canes. The shop windows were all embellished with festive sparkles of red, gold, silver and green, some with traditional snow scenes with slow-moving Santas and elves busy at work. It was hard not to get caught up in the atmosphere.

They trailed around a few shops, trying on clothes, which was a novelty for Emma who hadn't had much opportunity to buy clothes since she was pregnant. She couldn't walk past a baby boutique with a washing-line of miniature outfits hanging in its window. When she came across a ridiculous plum-pudding outfit, complete with a hat that had a holly leaf on top, she couldn't resist buying it for Fionn.

As they strolled along side streets, peering in through the windows of the antique jewellery shops, her eye was taken with a vintage chronograph watch with a silver face. It had a manual wind and a brown leather strap. Knowing it would be perfect as her Christmas present to Adam, she had gone inside to look at it. She ran her fingers over the leather strap, softened by years of wear, and when she turned it over she saw it was engraved with the initial 'A'. *An 'A' from times gone by,* she thought sadly. She took it as a sign. She waited while the shop assistant wrapped it for her. She couldn't wait to give it to Adam.

When the shops started to get crowded they decided to treat themselves to a glass of wine over a leisurely lunch. They took seats in the noisy bistro, the floor around their feet covered with their shopping bags. Emma had ordered a goat's cheese salad and Zoe had gone for a panini. They were sitting back, satisfied with their purchases and sipping their Pinot Grigio, when her phone rang.

It was her mother. She mentioned something about a car accident. And Adam. And Fionn. Emma couldn't process all those words together. Her world stopped, she could hear her mother still talking to her at the end of the phone but she couldn't answer. Nothing would come out of her mouth. She zoned out from the chatter in the bistro, still going on around her. Zoe had grabbed the phone from Emma's hand and, when she hung up, her face was ashen. She hopped up and steered Emma out of the restaurant, hailing a passing taxi to bring them to St Mary's Children's Hospital telling the driver it was an emergency and to hurry on.

Zoe using the word 'emergency' had startled Emma. *Was it an emergency?* She felt she was watching all of this from above. Only for Zoe, Emma didn't know what she would have done.

The taxi had overtaken slow drivers and broken red lights so that only minutes later he was dropping them off outside the hospital. Emma's dad met them in the entrance foyer and Emma realised that he had been waiting for her. He wouldn't make eye contact with her but she could tell instantly from his red-rimmed eyes that he had been crying. She remembered thinking how strange it was because she had never seen her dad cry before. He pushed open a door and guided her into a small room with just a laminate-topped desk, a chair and a trolley. Emma had wondered how he had known the room was there or even how there was no one in it.

Then he said the words that shattered her from within, piece by piece: *Fionn was dead.*

Her chest had tightened until her lungs wouldn't allow her take in any more air. The voices around her became loud and jumbled and her sight became a blurry vision of thick yellow and black stripes. She felt herself sliding away. Her mind left her body, floating upwards, and her feet deserted her until next thing she knew she was falling to the floor.

When she came around they were still in the room and she was lying on the trolley. They asked her if she wanted to see him. She nodded her head. It was an automatic response but what she meant was that she wanted to see him as she had seen him that morning, smiling and pudgy and happy, but she couldn't get the words out and they had guided her into a darkened room and placed the delicate body of her baby in her arms. Then they had backed out of the room, closing the door behind them, leaving her alone. It was all wrong. She just stood there for a while, not sure what she was meant to do or even what was happening. She hoped that maybe they had made a mistake and that he really was just sleeping. She stroked the smooth head of her baby. He looked like he was just sleeping.

After a while she sat back into a rocking chair that was in the room, just staring at him. He was perfect; the only mark on his delicate skin was a small purple bruise over his left temple. *Was he really dead? Were they sure? Didn't doctors sometimes get these things wrong?* She stroked his face, which was soft like a peach; it was still warm to the touch but she knew it was not warm enough.

She whispered into his ear the stories she used to make up about farm animals, while she brushed his downy hair back and forth, using her fingers. She sang the lullabies that had soothed him and she told him how dearly she loved him.

The doctors had come in after some time and told her it was time. It had taken a while to register. Time for what? Then they explained that it was time to say goodbye. *How was she meant to say goodbye to her son?* She didn't want to leave him go, her baby boy. She was overcome and had heard herself screaming. She didn't remember much after this. She assumed they had sedated her.

* * *

The next few days were a blur of heavy medication, awakening and remembering the awful truth, being overcome with grief and then more tablets. The days blurred into night and back into day again but the change in light didn't register with Emma. She felt black permanently. It was too awful a thing for a person to take in, so she couldn't, and instead stayed within her own world inside her head. Concerned faces came and went from her bedside. She had been plied with sleeping tablets by the familiar face of her childhood doctor and these allowed her to retreat back into her place of deep sleep, away from all the worried faces and the horrible physical pain in her chest. Each time she woke she had a blissful few seconds before she remembered what had happened and then her world crashed down all around her and she would relive the horror again.

It was like a cruel trick every time. And then someone would give her a tablet and she would sleep once again.

43

It had taken them nearly three years to get pregnant. Emma had been broody for a long time before she got married. She had wanted a honeymoon baby and had naïvely thought it would be that easy. She had assumed that she would decide the time and a baby would duly oblige her.

She had done all the preparation. She had done research on what were the best days to conceive, she had started taking her prenatal vitamins and folic acid several months before the wedding. She was ready.

When they first started trying to conceive, she had assumed that after giving her body a month or two to adjust to coming off the pill it would simply be a case of 'wham, bang, thank-you, ma'am' but she soon learnt it wasn't that easy for everyone.

After the first year of trying went by and nothing happened, she began to despair. Emma had never for one second envisaged that she would be in this situation. She had spent most of her teenage years, and her twenties too, praying she wouldn't get pregnant and it had all been a waste because here she was in her thirties, desperate for a baby, and couldn't get one.

It was made worse by people forever asking when they were going to start a family like it was something that they had control over. They would say things like they had been married now for quite a while and surely they would be hearing the pitter-patter of tiny feet soon – or that they shouldn't leave it too long, time was ticking and all that. Or the worst were the women who already had children who intimated that women like Emma were selfish for putting their careers first by waiting so long to have kids. Their insensitive comments cut to the bone and would leave Emma biting her tongue in rage.

She had bought sticks that pin-pointed when she was ovulating and her whole bookshelf was stuffed full of fertility books. But it still wasn't happening for them. So she researched some more and clung to any new nugget of information that she heard would improve their chances of conception. She had changed both their diets: leafy greens were in, alcohol was out. She examined her discharge with a new level of interest. She had become a pregnancy-test addict; instead of shopping for new face creams like she used to, now when she was in a pharmacy she would wander straight to the shelves that had the pregnancy tests to see if there were any new products on the market since she had checked there last month. She knew every brand there was and could even rank them in order of their level of detection. Before she got out of bed every morning, she would reach out to the bedside locker to feel for her thermometer so that she could track any temperature shifts which might indicate when she was ovulating. Days were counted down each month until they reached the all-important ovulation days and then sex was almost timed to the hour. Then the days were counted afterwards to see how early she could do a test. She could divide every month in two: there were the days before ovulation and the days of waiting after. No matter how many times she warned herself not to get her hopes up, she couldn't help it, and whenever her period arrived she would feel wretched, as a black cloud descended over her. She would spend the next few days in a deep depression until she pulled herself together with the hope of another month. She had become obsessed with trying to conceive.

It was made worse by the fact that all around her people seemed to be getting pregnant by just mentioning the word 'baby'. Women who she worked with, relatives and friends, the lady who worked in the deli beside the office – it seemed like everyone was pregnant except her and if she heard one more throwaway remark about how "it happened first time" she thought she might either hurl herself at the person in a fit of rage or dissolve on the ground crying – she wasn't sure which. She constantly found herself asking why them? Why were they having such difficulty conceiving a child when every schoolgirl just had to look at a sperm and could get pregnant? Or she would see mothers who sat around drinking in the pub all day and letting their kids entertain themselves and she would have to stop herself from walking up to them and telling them they didn't deserve to be parents. She felt as though she was going round the bend from the whole ordeal. She had always been in control of every aspect of her life and she felt panicked by the fact that this was the one area she had no control over, no matter what she did.

Adam had been terrific throughout; he was her rock even though she knew that some months it must have been like living with a time-bomb. He never complained, although he must have been feeling a bit taken for granted in his role as a sperm-donor. Whenever she was feeling low, he encouraged her to keep going.

It was Adam who had suggested that after two years of trying with no success they should go to their doctor. He had finally said the words she had been dreading. For so long she had managed to convince herself that they were okay, that they didn't have a problem. She had felt defeated. She was always able to sort out her own problems; she didn't like having to resort to anyone for help. But she'd been in denial for too long and she knew he was right. So, despondently she had agreed with him that it was time to hand control over to someone else.

The first doctor they had gone to see was from a different generation. He was reluctant to refer them for tests, fobbing them off with the line that they were "still young" and "had only been trying for a few months". *Only a few months?* She had shown him her ovulation charts and he had taken them in hand and peered at them over the rim of his glasses like she had just handed him some new-aged mumbo-jumbo that he had no time for.

They came out deflated. It had taken a lot of courage to get to the point of telling someone about their problems but they were just back to square one again. So Adam had suggested that they should go to a different doctor. They had chosen a female GP this time and, in contrast to the first doctor, she listened intently to what they were saying, taking notes all the while. She took them seriously and had immediately referred them for tests at a fertility clinic but warned them that the clinic was located in Dublin Maternity Hospital. Emma had to smile at the irony of this – talk about rubbing it in.

A month later, as Emma walked down the corridors to her appointment, she couldn't help staring at the massive bumps on the women all around her. She was fascinated by them all. Some were perfectly rounded like basketballs that were somehow attached prosthetically onto the women's abdomens, while some were just massive. It was amazing how big they actually got. She watched as one heavily pregnant woman struggled to get off a chair until her partner eventually gave her a hand up; she hoped that she and Adam would be in that situation some day. Another woman sat stroking her bump absent-mindedly while flicking through a magazine, oblivious to the strange woman who had fixated her gaze on her. She wouldn't allow herself to get upset; she told herself that she would be back here soon with a bump big enough to hold a baby elephant.

Once inside the clinic, she was greeted by a very cold-looking female doctor and Emma couldn't help wondering how someone with the bedside manner of a fridge ended up in a job like this. After she had poked and prodded Emma and performed a battery of tests on her, she sat her back down and informed her that everything looked perfectly healthy. She actually seemed like she was peeved that Emma was wasting her time and when she told Emma to "relax" and that "she was still very young", Emma could have screamed. Two years was a long time to keep having your hopes torn apart each month. She had expected more understanding from a fertility clinic.

Adam's sperm analysis had come back fine. His 'swimmers' were deemed healthy and his sperm count was actually above average. The clinic had termed it 'unexplained infertility'. But instead of feeling relieved that physically everything was all right with the two of them, she didn't, because she still was none the wiser as to why they hadn't conceived yet. It was beyond frustrating. At least if there was a problem with one or even both of them they could pin-point it and then hopefully solve it, but now they were on their own again ploughing on through the dark, wondering if they were casting a net into a pool that didn't have any fish in it or even if they were casting a net at all.

And then in September she had felt the familiar cramping before her period was due and, utterly deflated, she prepared herself for yet another month of coming to terms with the fact that she wasn't pregnant. That was it, she had thought, she couldn't go through any more of this. She felt exhausted and worn out by the whole ordeal. When she realised that her period was two days late, her hopes had started to rise but she cautioned herself to stop with the false hopes. She had reluctantly done a pregnancy test but nothing showed up. She felt like kicking herself for being that stupid. Why did she keep on putting herself through it? Would she never learn? She picked up the stick, ready to throw it into the bin, but then she noticed something that wasn't there a few seconds earlier. A very faint trace of a pink line had appeared beside the control. The more she stared at it the more she wasn't sure if it was her eyes playing tricks on her or if there were actually two lines there. She wanted this so badly, was she starting to imagine things now? She looked at the stick again and there definitely was a second line. She immediately unfolded the information leaflet that came with the packet, even though she already knew it word for word anyway and, yes, according to it she was finally pregnant. She was pregnant. She clutched her tummy as tears of relief and joy fell down her face. It was so hard to take in; she was going to have a baby! *They were going to have a baby.*

She waited for Adam to get home from work. She didn't want to tell him over the phone but the excitement was killing her. When she finally heard him coming in the door, she tore down the stairs and thrust the stick into his hands. He had taken it from her, trying to comprehend what was going on, and then he looked at it.

He stared at it, his eyes wide with hope. "So does this mean we're . . . *pregnant?*"

"*Adam White, we are having a baby!*" she had screamed.

He had picked her off the ground and swung her around in circles like a child before gently putting her down again.

"Sorry! I probably shouldn't have done that. I just can't believe I'm going to be a father!" He had said it over and over in shock and disbelief. "I'm going to be a dad! I'm going to be a dad!"

"No, no, rephrase that, you're going to be a *great* dad!"

"God, I hope so." The weight of the responsibilities that came with being a parent suddenly dawned on him. He felt daunted but excited at the same time.

"Don't worry, you'll be fine, we'll be fine," she said. "This baby is going to be so loved!"

"Do you feel any different?"

"No, not really, just a bit tired but I thought that was just because of work and the pitch for the Freeman campaign. I thought when you were pregnant, you would feel it, y'know? But I feel exactly the same!"

"Well, that's a good thing. God, I just want to run out and tell the world!"

"We can't tell people yet!" she said quickly. "You know what they say about the first twelve weeks . . ." Emma's stomach did a somersault. She felt anxious even just thinking about it, as if by having bad thoughts she would automatically bring that fate on herself. "We should wait. I don't want to jinx it."

"Okay then, I won't breathe a word." He laughed at her before hugging her close again.

It was supremely difficult to keep it secret from their families and friends, especially from Zoe. Emma felt so guilty; she normally told Zoe everything. She was so afraid of tempting fate that she didn't want to risk it, but she was rapidly running out of excuses as to why she wasn't drinking or why she was too tired to go shopping after work like they normally did.

The first twelve weeks were a nightmare. Morning sickness had kicked in the week after the test and the novelty of being pregnant had quickly worn off. From the moment she woke up in the morning she could feel her stomach churning and she would have to run out of bed to be sick. She spent a good bit of time in the toilets in work and even had to dash out of a client meeting. It only took something small like the smell of pesto or an overpowering perfume and she would feel nauseous. Her boobs felt as though they were on fire and her nipples permanently stood to attention. Plus she was utterly exhausted; she was asleep on the sofa before nine every night.

It felt as though the weeks were dragging on and on. As she

anxiously counted them down, she crossed them off the calendar, longing just to get to week twelve. Week twelve was the magical week where she could finally relax, but she wondered if her worries would stop there or if there would be a whole new set of worries to replace them.

When the twelfth week of Emma's pregnancy finally arrived, they made their way nervously to the hospital for their first scan. That morning before their appointment, Emma couldn't stop imagining all kinds of awful scenarios. No matter how many times she tried to force them from her mind, they would pop back in again. *What if there was no heartbeat? What if the baby had stopped growing?* Or the most ludicrous was: *What if she had just imagined the whole being-pregnant thing in the first place?*

The doctor had tucked some tissue into Emma's waistband and then spread the cool gel on her tummy. They didn't dare breathe as they watched the grainy image appear on the screen beside them. They looked anxiously at the doctor's face and back again to make sure everything was as it should be. As he moved the probe across her abdomen they saw a dark outline appear on the screen. It was their *baby*. It had quite a large head, a long bony spine and little arms and legs that moved in rapid jerky movements. It was tumbling around the place in its own little world, oblivious to the people watching in from the outside in amazement. She couldn't believe how much it was moving and yet she couldn't feel a thing. He let them listen to the heartbeat, which was rapid like the sound of horses galloping over arid land.

"Congratulations, guys, everything looks perfect. Your baby has a very strong and healthy heartbeat." He zoomed in on the heart and they watched the tiny organ pulsing away with life. Emma felt a tear roll down her cheek in awe of the moment.

"Would you like to know the sex?" the doctor asked.

"No!" Emma said. "We want it to be a surprise," she added quickly.

"Okay, well then you'd better look away for a minute while I check the leg measurements."

They laughed as they turned their heads to the side while the sonographer had a detailed look at that area.

Coming out of the clinic they had both been overjoyed and so proud of their baby for growing so well and for being strong. Adam had squeezed her hand tight and they had laughed at themselves – if they were this proud already, imagine what they would be like when the baby was born? They were relieved that they could now start to relax and enjoy the pregnancy.

Emma had said that they were finally able to start telling people. They had made the trip around to the houses of their parents to announce the news. As expected they had all been overjoyed, Emma's parents having long suspected that they had been having difficulties because they knew how set on having a baby Emma had always been.

Then they had driven over to tell Zoe and she had cried, which set Emma off again too.

"I can't believe I'm going to be an aunt!" she had said over and over.

Emma didn't bother pointing out the obvious that, technically, she wasn't but she would be as good as an aunt to the baby.

* * *

The pregnancy had seemed to stretch on forever. Emma, an impatient person by nature, wanted to hold her baby now. Now! She reckoned nature was flawed. Why did it need to take forty weeks? Surely the process could be speeded up into four weeks? She watched what she ate – lots of fruit and vegetables and red meat to keep her iron levels up – she did yoga twice a week and tried to walk most days. She looked forward to every scan and getting a glimpse of the wonderment that was taking place inside her, like a child waiting for

Christmas. She had felt the first movements, like little flickers of a taut elastic band being stretched, and then those movements getting stronger until they were full-blown kicks.

Once she reached the twenty-week mark, she consoled herself that she was halfway there, but if the second half was as slow as the first half then she was in trouble. And if she had thought her worries would ease after the first trimester, she soon learnt that they were only just beginning. *Was the baby moving enough? Why was he or she gone so quiet? Had she felt kicks yet this morning?*

As she got bigger and her baby's space became more confined, she could feel the head move underneath her hand if she pressed into her side and sometimes when she was lying in bed at night they would watch as her bump raised itself into a point as their baby stretched out its elbows or knees, they weren't sure which.

Like all eager first-timers they had everything bought and ready to go – the buggy, a cream wicker Moses basket – and her hospital bag was packed. Drawers already overflowed with cream, white and yellow Babygros. Tiny knitted cardigans and bootees hung waiting in the wardrobe and although it would be a while yet before the baby would sleep in his or her own room, a polished mahogany cot stood in the centre of the decorated nursery. Adam had attended all the antenatal classes with Emma. She'd had a list of questions about what to expect in labour and Adam had taken notes when the midwife giving the classes told them about the main signs of labour and how far apart the contractions should be before they should go to hospital. Eager for information, they had read all the pregnancy books and researched the parenting forums to try to learn what lay ahead of them in the coming months.

She counted down the days until she was due to go on maternity leave. She was big and awkward, the size of a small house as she kept telling people, and her bump sagged down from its weight. She wasn't sleeping well at night either. A combination of her sheer size and a mixture of excited nervousness made her tired. Her brain didn't fire as quickly as she was used to and she wasn't able for the fast-paced environment of A1 Adverts, the endless standing up presenting pitches and pandering to their clients' needs. She had other things on her mind now. So it was with relief when her last day in work finally came around. Emma packed up her desk, accepted a small presentation from Maureen and her colleagues, and ran out the door as fast as her swollen legs would carry her.

Adam had been waiting for her outside in his car as he had done every day for the last few weeks as she began to get too big for the rush-hour squash on public transport where people would avoid making eye contact with her so they wouldn't have to offer her their seat. She threw her handbag into the back seat of his car because there was no room for both her and it in the front.

She had lowered herself into the car when she suddenly felt tightness all across her bump.

"*Oooooooh!*"

"What's wrong?" Adam had looked at her worriedly. Every twinge he greeted with concern these days.

"Nothing, nothing. I think I just pulled something getting in the car there."

"Jesus, don't do that to me! I'm a bag of nerves as it is."

They drove along and she chatted about how much she had planned to do to pass the time for the next two weeks until her baby was due. She was convinced that she would go overdue, first-timers usually did she was reliably told by her doctor. Her to-do list included giving the house a good clean from top to bottom, going to get waxed so that her lady-bits were looking good for everyone that would be seeing them in the hospital and meeting some friends for lunch – plus she had a stack of books on her bedside table that she wanted to get through.

"What about relaxing like you're supposed to be doing?" Adam asked.

"I'll have loads –" She felt her whole bump tighten again and she took a sharp intake of breath. "*Oooh!*"

"What is it?" Adam looked at her in panic.

"Jesus, I don't know but it's bloody sore. I thought Braxton Hicks contractions were meant to be painless?"

"You don't reckon it's the baby, do you?"

"But I'm not due for two weeks yet!"

"Yeah but maybe it's coming early?"

"Nah –" But before she could finish, she was gripped with pain again. "Fuck, Adam, I think maybe you're right."

"What will I do?"

"I don't know. Start timing them or something!" she snapped.

Almost immediately the contractions had started getting longer and the time between them shorter.

"Emma, the last two were six minutes apart."

"Jesus, I thought they were meant to start off slow!" she said through gritted teeth. She was just getting over one before another would rise through her again.

Adam felt utterly useless. He was driving around in circles, not concentrating on where they were meant to be going. "Remember your breathing," was all he could think to say but Emma's glare told him she didn't find it helpful. They pulled over to the side of the road and, as the contractions started coming closer together, she would grab the dashboard with a white-knuckly grip until it passed. He desperately tried to remember what they had told him in the antenatal classes about when they should go to the hospital – was it when there were ten minutes or five minutes between each contraction?

"*I think we need to get to the hospital!*" Emma said through clenched teeth before she grabbed hold of the dashboard again as she got caught up in another wave of pain.

"Okay, okay." He tried to pull himself together. He got his bearings, took a deep breath and made for the maternity hospital on the other side of the city. The rush-hour traffic inched forward before coming to a frustrated stop once again. When Adam looked over at Emma he realised he didn't have the luxury of time so he cut into a bus lane and zipped up one-way streets. It was the kind of driving the ten-year-old boy in him had always fantasised about but now that he was doing it for real, in these circumstances, it wasn't fun. He felt powerless and scared.

Outside the hospital Emma tried to walk out of the car but she had to double over in agony. A porter spotted what was happening and rushed over with a wheelchair and they sped off in the direction of the labour ward, leaving Adam frantically running behind.

"I forgot my overnight bag!" she wailed at no one in particular when they reached the labour ward.

"Don't worry about that, we have everything you'll need here," a kindly midwife called Jenny told her. "Now I need to examine you, Emma, okay?"

Emma grimaced as the midwife did an internal examination and prayed she would remove her hand in time for the next contraction or she didn't think she could cope.

"*I need an epidural!*" She looked at Jenny desperately. For the first time Emma understood the power that drug lords held over their addicts. She was totally at the mercy of this woman: she had the drugs and Emma needed them. Her fate was in her hands.

Jenny removed her hand. "Emma, love, you're almost fully dilated. I'm afraid it's too late for that."

Emma felt her world had ended and she zoned out on what Jenny was saying as the realisation hit her that she was going to feel every inch of her vagina stretch to allow her baby to pass through. She didn't know if she could do it. She couldn't handle any more of this, she was afraid the pain might actually kill her.

But almost as if she could read her thoughts, Jenny said, "Now don't worry, women the world over do this day in day out and most do it more than once, so you can do it and you will be okay. Do you hear me?"

Emma nodded vigorously at Jenny. She had no choice but to put her trust in her. She felt the pressure of her baby bearing down on her and she knew she couldn't hold it back.

"Now what I want you to do is listen carefully to everything I say," said Jenny. "When I say push, I want you to push with all your strength, right down into your bottom. If you feel like you're going to do a poo, that's good because it means you're pushing properly. When the head is crowning I will instruct you to take short pants. If you keep your eyes on me and listen, we'll be fine. Yeah?"

Emma was nodding.

"Now then, Adam, I want you to grab hold of one of Emma's legs here and I will take the other."

Adam looked like he was almost about to faint. The blood had drained from his head. He wasn't expecting it today – even though he'd had eight and a half months to get used to the idea, it was still a shock that it was happening now.

"Okay, everyone ready? Now on the next contraction I want you to push, Emma. *Push*!"

Emma summoned up all her strength into pushing; she just wanted it over with at this stage.

"*Grrrrr-ahhggggh!*" She breathed out.

"And again, come on, Emma, come on, Emma, come on, Emma!"

"*Grrrrrrrr-ahhgggggggggggh!*"

"And again, one big push, Emma!"

For fuck sake, would they not allow her catch her breath at least?

"Grrrrrrrr-ahhhhhhhh!"

"Good girl, Emma, that's it. Keep it coming."

"Aaahhggggggggggggggggh!"

"Good girl, well done. I can see the head. Do you want to touch it?"

She shook her head emphatically and Adam thought he might get sick.

"Okay, now just pant for a few moments like this . . ." She blew gentle little streams of air.

Emma let her body recover for a few seconds before Jenny was back at her again.

"Now one more really big one this time and the head should be out."

"Grrrrr-aaaaaaaaaaaaaahhhhhhhhh!"

"That's it, that's it. There you go, well done."

Adam looked down at what looked like anything but a baby. It was covered in blood and vernix with a scrunched-up red face. Only the matted hair gave away the fact that it was a baby.

Emma caught her breath.

"Now for one final big push and you should be holding your baby, okay?"

"Grrrrrrrrr-aaaaaahhhhh!"

She felt the baby slither out of her body. And when she opened her eyes, miraculously there was small, wrinkly bundle on her chest, his skin red from his entrance into the world. Of course she knew that she was having a baby but it was still a shock to see one actually lying on her chest.

"It's a boy!" Jenny announced and then their baby stretched his lungs and gave a good hearty cry. "Oh, that's a good cry! Well, little man, you were in a hurry, weren't you?" Jenny cooed as she took him over to be weighed. "We don't normally see first babies come this fast!"

A boy! Shock was being heaped upon shock. Emma had been sure that she was carrying a girl. Everyone had commented on her neat bump and she was sure it was a girl.

She tried to get her head around the fact that three hours ago she had been packing up her desk in work and here she was now holding her baby in her arms. She was stunned by the speed of it all. It was almost like he was saying 'Okay, you've done that job, now it's time to have me'. She looked at his dark tufts of hair and a face so familiar, just like Adam's.

They had listened in amazement to the strength of his cry, a primitive animal sound roaring through an O-shaped mouth and watched as his pink hands furled and unfurled like a peony rose, in complaint about having been disturbed from the comforts of what had been his home for almost the last nine months. They named him Fionn.

* * *

When Adam had gone home later that night, Emma had pulled the curtain across her cubicle to give her privacy from the rest of the ward. It was the first time that she was alone with her baby. She had found herself staring in wonderment at the contented little face sleeping peacefully beside her, almost forgetting about the pain of the delivery. Already his face was less mushed and had opened up more, to reveal long eyelashes and pouty lips.

He was feeding like a dream. He was a hungry baby so she found it hard to keep up with his suckling demands, but she knew she should be grateful that he was like this when she listened to other women in her ward as they struggled to get their babies to latch on. She looked down at him when he fed from her breast, his rosebud lips attached to her and his blue eyes open wide, staring up at her contentedly. It was an indescribable closeness that she had never experienced before. He was so utterly small, so totally dependent on her.

In the days that followed Emma was detached from the tedious reality of everyday life and existed only in her own bubble of bliss with Fionn. When she had been pregnant everyone had told her how her life would be changed forever but nothing could have prepared her for the intensity of this feeling. She was buoyed up high on a wave of euphoria. She felt there was a beam radiating from her heart, directed into the cot of her infant son beside her. She would just breathe in his warm milky scent and, if she was a comfort to him, he was as much to her. Hours flew past just staring at him and then she would wonder where the time had gone to. The sound of his cry made her milk leak and tore at her gut, making her physically upset too so that she had to react immediately and do everything in her power to attend to his needs. She was convinced too that he was smiling up at her and even though the books said it was just wind, she liked to think that he was.

* * *

Adam had missed them both dreadfully while they were in the hospital and he couldn't wait to take his baby son home so he could get to know him too. The day he came to collect them, he was beaming with pride and excitement. He ensured the car-seat had been fitted correctly and they drove the slowest journey of their lives that day with Emma sitting in the back with their precious cargo.

He'd had flowers and balloons waiting when she walked into their hallway and told her to go upstairs to their bed for a much-needed few hours' sleep while he minded Fionn. He had sat in their living room as his three-day-old son lay sleeping in his arms, too afraid to move in case he woke him.

So he just sat there, staring at him, thinking about how much lay ahead for them. He swore he would be the best father he could be. His love for him was almost physical and he knew from that point on he would lay his life down for this baby even though he had been in his life only for a few days now. He also knew that forever more he was vulnerable as a person; how would he ever cope if anything should happen to his son? It was as if his Achilles' heel had been exposed for the world to see. He would do anything to protect this little person that he had been entrusted with. It was exhilarating but breathlessly terrifying at the same time.

44

It was days after the accident before the numbness began to subside and the awful aching took over her whole body. Emma ached so much to hold her baby that it felt like an elephant was compressing her chest. Sometimes the weight of her longing made it difficult even to catch her breath.

The fogginess of the drugs was beginning to clear and her mind was starting to process thoughts. She had so many questions that she needed answered. What had happened for a start? They had tried to explain it to her. They said something about a driver not stopping at a junction and hitting Adam's car on the rear left wing where Fionn had been strapped into his car seat. Adam's car had tumbled off the road and landed in the back garden of a nearby house. But to her it didn't explain anything, instead it just threw up more questions.

She had asked if the other driver had died. She had wanted to hear that he was dead too, tit for tat, a life for a life. He had wiped out her family with his carelessness and he should have to pay. But he hadn't even stopped at the scene. They were still

266

trying to track him down. She was so angry, like a force had gripped hold of her body and wouldn't let go.

Someone had asked her if she wanted to go and see Adam. He was in Dublin County Hospital. And it was only then that she remembered Adam. *Adam had been in the crash too.* They had tried to persuade her, especially her in-laws, saying that it would do him good to hear her voice but she didn't want to go. They persisted with asking her daily if maybe she felt up to visiting that day and she would shake her head. There was only so much her mind could deal with. She couldn't even contemplate what had happened and she wasn't able to process the demands being made of her.

She missed everything about Fionn, every part of his perfect babyness. His satiny hair, his plump newborn skin, his scent. His fingernails, his long toes, his rounded tummy. His neck folds that began to smell when milk got trapped within them. The way his joints were swallowed up with baby-fat. His defined chin. His sticky-out ears. She couldn't believe all of those parts of him that she had loved so dearly were gone. *He was gone.* She couldn't accept that she would never again hear his gurgling high-pitched squeals coming over the monitor in the mornings. She had been able to identify each syllable and, when he uttered a new one, she instantly recognised it as that, as if all his sounds were automatically programmed into her brain.

Sometimes the anguish and pain felt so sharp and over-whelming that she felt she might die too.

All she had been left with was a bag containing his "effects" as they had termed it. She didn't like that word; it seemed so clinical, so impersonal. The bag had the Babygro that she had dressed him in that morning, his white cotton vest and his soother. All those inanimate articles survived without a mark but Fionn didn't. She had slept with the Babygro placed under her cheek every night since; it was damp from her tears. She would bring it up close to her nose and breathe him in. She couldn't bear to wash it and wash away the scent of her baby. They had asked if she wanted a lock of his hair in the hospital and initially she had said no. She couldn't accept that this was all she would be left with and somehow felt by accepting this piece of hair she was accepting what had happened. She hadn't wanted them to touch him, not even a hair on his head, but her mother had told her that she might regret it so they had kept a piece anyway for her and now she was glad she had that small piece of him because as the reality dawned that he wasn't coming back, it was all she had left.

Sometimes she woke in a panic because she could not remember his face, exactly how it was. It was as if her brain wanted to torment her and purposely block out the very pictures she wanted to remember. She would beg: *Please let me remember his face. Don't take that away from me too*. Some parts of him would be wrong, the smile wasn't quite right or the eyes were different and she would look at the photo again to be sure but even that didn't capture him whole. It was missing his essence. She couldn't breathe when this happened and became filled with fear and panic. All she had left were the memories and if they were gone too then she would have nothing.

The room which had once been a sunny nursery, decorated with cream walls and white billowing curtains, now had an empty and dark feel to it even when the sun shone in through the window. His teddies sat in an orderly row on the shelf. She would go in there just to sit and remember, desperately trying to smell the sheets in his cot or anything that might still have some trace of him but as the weeks went on, his smell became less and she desperately clutched for something else. Babygros and vests stayed folded in the drawer, bibs and muslin cloths too. Tiny socks would no longer fall off tiny feet. Blankets with no one to wrap still lay in the cot along with a comforter that comforted no one.

45

The voices surrounding him had finally gone quiet. Sometimes they just kept talking – talking to him, talking about him, talking to each other, always talking and not allowing him to rest. Between the voices and the machines that bleeped all day long and the rumble of trolleys being pushed along the corridor, he felt like shouting at them all to shut up and leave him in peace. The fragments flickered past his eyes. He tried to summon the will to force them open. He felt his muscles twitch from the exertion. *Almost there.* He tried harder still. He felt pain. A deep pain that couldn't be isolated to a particular region because it was all over. It was as if every nerve ending and synapse was on a heightened state of alert, rapidly transmitting the pain until it radiated throughout his body. He didn't know what was going on. He forced his eyelids open even though they stung as he did so. The room was too bright, sunlight reflecting off whiteness. He saw a woman rush towards him. *Don't touch me.* He wasn't sure he would be able to cope with the pain if she touched him. He closed his eyes again and braced himself.

"Adam, Adam, can you hear me?" the woman asked softly but there was an urgency in her voice. "Adam, come on, love, I know you can hear me. *Adam.*" She wasn't giving up.

He opened his eyes again.

"Adam!" Her face lit up. "Oh Adam, you're awake! Thank God! Thank God!"

He looked around and took in the cream-painted steel bed frame, the equipment and wires and bandages, the white plaster cast on his left hand and the woman. The woman he knew, he tried to place her. He looked around to see a circle of familiar anxious faces. He searched for the people that he wanted to see but couldn't find them. The faces began crowding in on him and he wanted to back away but he couldn't go anywhere with the amount of tubes, wires and bandages that were tying his body to the bed. The woman reached out to grab his hand. *Ouch.* The pain radiated throughout his body. She bent her head into his arm and started crying and for the first time he noticed they were all crying. He was confused and bewildered by their actions.

"Adam, it's me – your mam. Dad's here too and Rob. You're in Dublin County Hospital. You probably don't remember, Adam, but you were in a bad accident. That's why we're so relieved to see you awake."

"Where's Emma?" His voice was weak and it took all his strength to get the words out. "Where's Emma?" he repeated, wondering if he was making sense.

No one answered.

"Where are Emma and Fionn?"

"She's not up to it, Adam, she's not feeling too great herself."

Oh shit, was she in the accident too?

"Is she in the hospital?"

Maybe they would let him go see her.

"No, Adam, no, she wasn't involved in the accident thankfully."

"Is she minding Fionn?"

"Well, now that you're awake, I'm sure she'll be here later." His mother had tears in her eyes and she was stroking his hand.

At least she knew who Emma was; that was something. He felt rushes of thoughts pound his brain, making everything confused.

"And Fionn, where is he?" he demanded but the tone he was using in his head didn't match up to the feeble croak that came out instead.

He saw her eyes dart manically towards his father.

"Do you think he remembers?"

"I don't know, I just don't know."

I can hear you, you know!

Joe White took a deep breath. "There was a bad accident, son." He paused. "Now Emma is okay, she wasn't involved and she's at home, she's . . . fine . . . but Fionn . . ." He took a deep breath before continuing. For Joe White this was the worst thing he had ever had to go through in his life. He had just lost his grandson, almost lost his son, and now he had to deliver this devastating news and watch him fall to pieces.

"I'm afraid, Adam, Fionn didn't make it . . . he . . ." his voice broke, "he died at the scene." His dad lowered his gaze. "I'm so, so sorry. Truly I am."

Fionn didn't make it. Didn't make what? He tried to process the information as it was presented to him. He looked at his mother for answers but she had dissolved into big heaving sobs, rocking her whole body and shaking her head.

Adam instantly felt the most acute physical pain right in centre of his gut. It was different to the other pain, it went much deeper. It was all starting to make sense to him now. The hospital, the tears, the worry on everyone's face, the tubes, the wires and the pain all over his body. He felt his chest tighten and instantly an alarm was triggered. Hysteria broke out in the room; he could hear his mother screaming, his father shouting for help. Doctors came piling in from nowhere, pushing his family back. They flicked switches, changed settings until the alarm stopped again. They gave him some tablets to help him sleep and he drifted off on a high-up cloud.

The next time he woke he had a few seconds to process everything before he remembered what had happened. They had said his baby son was dead but he had been in the crash too and he was still alive. Surely they had got things wrong? He forced himself to try and remember the exact sequence of events but he could only recall bits of it. He racked his head to recollect what had happened, anything at all that would give him some answers but he could only remember driving along in his car. That was it. He couldn't remember more after that. He needed to talk to Emma; she would know what was going on.

"Where is Emma?"

"She's not doing too well, love, she's at home at the moment. I'm sure she'll be in when she's up to it," his mother reassured him, rubbing his hand.

Jesus Christ. Did they not understand? *He needed to see her.* He wanted answers.

"I have to see her. I need to talk to her!" He tried to sit upright in the bed but the tubes kept him pinned down.

"You can't go anywhere, Adam – you're still in a serious condition. You shouldn't go upsetting yourself, love, it's not doing you any good."

"I need to see him." He couldn't believe all of this until he saw with his own two eyes.

"Who, Adam?"

"Fionn, of course."

"You can't, Adam."

"Why not?"

"Because, well . . ."

"Why not?" He was becoming agitated.

At this stage his dad had interjected, "Because, Adam, Fionn has already been laid to rest. I'm sorry, son."

His mother started dabbing at her eyes with a tissue.

They had already buried Fionn. *Without him?* He didn't even get to say goodbye. That couldn't be right surely? He closed his eyes shut again to allow his head to think straight. Was he just imagining all of this? He thought he would wake up now any minute and breathe a sigh of relief about all of this but when he opened his eyes they were all still there and the room was full of brightness with sharp edges and vivid colours and he knew it was too real to be a dream.

"Was Emma there?"

"No, love, I'm sorry, she wasn't up to it at the time."

The frustration of the situation overpowered him and he started to cry big heaving sobs.

"Why did it have to be Fionn? *Why?*"

His mother sat holding his hand, crying with him. He was blistered with grief; it pained him no matter how he moved or what he did. It was everywhere.

"I don't know, love. I don't have any answers for that one. Life isn't fair. He was too good for this world."

'Too good for this world' – what a ridiculous thing to say, Adam thought. His heart ached for Fionn. Their poor baby had been lowered into the cold ground without his parents at his side. It was wrong. He needed to see Emma. He had so much to ask her, so many questions. *Why wasn't she here? How was she coping? Was she going through her own personal hell like he was? Why didn't she want to see him? Did she blame him?*

He drifted in and out of consciousness and every time he woke he remembered the awful news that his son was dead. It all came back to him, the grief flooding down over him, no matter how much he tried to digest it, more pain washed down until he felt as though he was drowning. Sometimes it was easier to stay asleep than deal with the pain and the worry etched on the faces of his family watching him from his bedside.

46

Every day when Emma woke, she had a few seconds of bliss before the nightmare was remembered again. The tablets she had been prescribed helped her sleep a deep sleep where dreams couldn't find her but there was no tablet to ward off the reality of morning.

The reality of her loss. The reality of having to bury her little son. The same priest who had christened Fionn only three months earlier had called to the house to discuss the funeral arrangements. He had gone upstairs and tried to console Emma but he had left her soon after, knowing nothing he could say would offer comfort to this particular mother faced with burying her baby. So he had gone downstairs and spoken to her parents instead.

Emma hadn't been able to face the funeral. How was she supposed to do something like that – a mother, bury her own child? The baby that she had carried for almost nine months and had then lived for only six? Her mother had begged her to go, telling her she would regret it, that it might even help her deal with events. And Emma had wondered if her mother was really on the same planet as her at all, did she even know what had happened to her grandson only days earlier? Sitting in a church and watching her son's coffin being lowered into the ground was not going to help her grief. So she had stayed in her bed and the faces emptied out of her house until it was just Zoe left sitting with her and her son had been buried without either of his parents present.

Then the day came when Emma heard the phone ringing and people shouting, loud happy shouts. She heard someone say that Adam had come round. *Adam*. Her husband. They quickly bounded up to her bedroom and relayed what she had already heard. Adam had just woken up from his coma. They asked her if she wanted to visit him, they were all heading to the hospital straight away. He was asking for her, they had told her, but she had said 'No' and turned over onto her side so that her back was to them.

She had heard they had tracked down the driver of the white car. A seventeen-year-old male off his head after an all-night drink and drugs bender. It just made Emma angrier – his actions had ruined her life, she would never get her baby back. His mother had called over to apologise in person for her son's actions but Emma didn't want to see her. She was too afraid of what she might do or say. So she had stayed in her room and her parents had spoken with the mother downstairs. They had relayed it back to her that she was so sorry for what her son had done and that she was devastated beyond words that he was to blame for something so tragic. But, for Emma, no matter what words of comfort the woman offered, she still had her son. She'd had seventeen years with him, Emma had only had six months. She knew it would go through the courts and they would serve an appropriate punishment, but that would never be enough. It just served to heighten the sense of injustice that she felt.

* * *

They said when you lose a child that a part of you dies too. But Adam wished he had died instead of being in the half-limbo state he now existed in. He was in a numbed trance, with all his senses muted except for the awful feeling of loss that he had to bear. To outlive your own child was the cruellest blow a parent can suffer; it was a reversal of the natural order and he was left flailing in despair.

The hospital had sent a bereavement counsellor to his bedside to talk it through with him but he had pretended to be asleep and ignored further efforts at contact.

Everyone said how lucky he was to still be alive – he had been "minutes away from death" they told him. His crushed pelvis had perforated the surrounding blood vessels causing massive internal bleeding and his body had gone into shock. They'd had to perform major surgery on him, piecing his shattered pelvis back together but he wished they hadn't bothered. He had broken his arm and his collarbone too and his skin was sewn together in a patchwork of coarse black thread. His mother in her Catholic zeal kept on saying that it was his Guardian Angel that had been watching over him: "Blessed he was, blessed." But he didn't feel blessed, how could he? On the contrary, life hadn't done him any favours. His son was now dead. That wasn't very "blessed", was it?

He had so many questions to which there were no answers. Why their car? There were literally hundreds of cars driving up and down that road all day every day – why couldn't it have been someone else's car? Or why couldn't it have been him instead of Fionn? If he had died instead, he knew that Emma would do a good job of raising their son on her own. What if they hadn't gone? He was only calling to visit his parents, hardly something he needed to do. He shouldn't have gone anywhere. If he had left a little later or earlier or if he had driven fractionally slower or faster, the other car wouldn't have met his at that instant in time. What if Fionn's seat had been on the opposite side of the car? Why couldn't the car have hit them from the other side? What if he'd had an SUV – nothing would have touched him in that. What if the council had gritted the road? What if the sun wasn't glaring? *What if? What if? What if?* The words tortured his every thought until he couldn't bear them any more and his brain would shut down again.

He had gone over the journey that morning so many times before. He knew the Gardaí had arrested some little seventeen-year-old boy racer, but was some of it his own fault too? The post mortem had said that Fionn had died from trauma to the head, most likely caused by the impact from the car crumpling around him, but Adam was starting to doubt himself and wonder if he could have done something more to prevent his death. When Emma had been pregnant he had spent so much time researching the technical specifications for infant car-seats; which one had the best safety record and which was ranked highest by the experts and he thought he had followed the instructions on how to install the seat carefully, but maybe he hadn't? He had heard the statistic that eighty per cent of all car-seats are fitted incorrectly. Maybe theirs was too? Did he have the car-seat mounted into the iso-fix system properly? Had the straps been tight enough?

He couldn't believe that he would never see Fionn again. He had loved every hair on his head, his Buddha-like tummy, his long toes with their jagged toe-nails because they had been too afraid to cut them. How he giggled infectiously if you swung him in your arms or bounced him on the bed. How he opened his mouth for more spoonfuls of baby rice. How he had started rolling over a few weeks before or how he had found his voice and now shrieked at everyone all day. He had bored the lads to tears with tales about his toxic nappies that always managed to leak out the sides. Fionn had sat up on his own for the first time only that week, his muscles finally strong enough to hold him. Adam had been so proud – as if Fionn was the first baby to sit up – because his son was another step closer to his independence. The unjustness of the situation made him so angry that he wanted to hit out at something or someone.

Things were made worse by the fact that he still hadn't seen Emma; she was the one person he really needed to see. His heart had risen when he saw her family coming through the door of his room but, when she hadn't been with them, it had sunk back down lower than before. Every day he hoped he would see her face coming through the door. He knew she wasn't coping too well from what her parents had intimated. It was the not knowing that was the hardest. If he could just see her, they would get each other through. He needed to see her.

The next few weeks were spent in a blur of painkillers, physiotherapy and strengthening exercises. He faced a daily endurance test with the pain. The doctors were stingy with their doses of morphine so that he wouldn't become addicted.

It was six weeks after the accident before he took his first tentative steps on a Zimmer frame. The exertion wore him out after only travelling a few metres. It was gruelling but he was determined to get back on his feet properly so he persisted in his daily exercises until his face was bathed with perspiration. At his check-ups the doctors had said that the physical breaks were healing well but he was tormented with re-occurring flashbacks as he desperately tried to remember what had happened. Random scenes that he could put no order on constantly flitted through his head.

The weeks went on and Emma never came to see him no matter how much he asked after her. No matter how many people he told to pass on the message to her that he needed to see her, she still didn't come. He had tried phoning her a few times but she never answered. All anyone ever said was that she "wasn't up to it". He was beyond worried about her at this stage. So he persevered with getting back on his feet again so he could be well enough to get out of there and go home and be with Emma.

47

Emma still couldn't bring herself to wash the Babygros that had been in the laundry basket since the day Fionn died or the blankets from his cot. Her mother had packed away things like the buggy, the steriliser, monitors, bottles and toys but the absence of these reminders wasn't going to help her forget what had happened. Not being able to hold Fionn caused her to physically ache. It would overcome her whole body and on these days all she could do was stay in bed because she couldn't face the world.

Life still went on around her; the days rolled into night, Christmas passed unmarked, people went to work, children went to school, cars still went up and down the road, the post came through the letterbox and visits from concerned friends and relatives became less frequent. She felt like screaming at the world to stop. How could everyone just carry on as normal after all that had happened? But her grief was hers alone and, although people sympathised, they could never begin to imagine the pain she was feeling.

Then the seasons moved along too, the snowdrops had

braved the January frost to be pushed out by the daffodils in late February. The evenings got longer and brighter and then one day Adam came home. He just walked in through the door of their house and appeared in front of her in their living room as casually as if he had only popped out to the shops for milk. Seeing him there had startled her. She had felt the room close in around her as if she was a character painted onto the side of a spinning top. She reached forward and held onto the edge of the fireplace to steady herself. She just stood staring at the man, holding himself up on crutches. He was like a complete stranger to her; a memory from a different life. Looking at him was like looking at a living memory of Fionn, it was more than just the similarities in their look, their dark hair and pointed features; he was living proof that there had been an accident. While he stood in front of her the evidence was there in his repairing body. You couldn't shut it out or deny it. He had been the last person to see her son alive, he had been driving the car when he had died and when she looked at him this was all she could see.

"Emma, it's okay, I'm here now."

Adam was shocked by his wife's appearance. She was a shadow of her former self. Her usually slight frame was now gaunt and her eyes were hollow with blue-black circles underneath. They were vacant, as if nothing existed behind them. Her hair looked as though it hadn't been brushed in weeks; her soft curls now were matted and frizzy.

"I'm so, so sorry, for everything . . ." He trailed off. "Look, we need to talk. I've been worried sick about you."

He took a deep breath and took a step towards her on his crutches. He wanted to wrap her in his arms and look after her. He wanted to tell her that he was here for her now and that they would get through it together, but she stepped back away from him and slid wordlessly out past him. She went upstairs to their bedroom, leaving him standing in his own living room staring after her. He wondered whether he should follow her up or just stay where he was. He hadn't known what to expect from Emma but it certainly hadn't been a reaction like that. He realised that things were much worse than he had thought. He now understood what his family had tried to tell him in so few words. It was as if the old Emma had departed when Fionn had died. He had been waiting for so long, working so hard at getting better so that he could come home and be there for her, but it was like she didn't even know who he was and what was worse was that she didn't seem to care who he was. He had built it up so much in his head, imagining the scene. He had thought that as soon as she had seen him he would be able to lift her out from beneath the mountain of despair that she had been sinking under and they would get through it together. Over the last few months, all his energies were focused on getting strong enough so that he could help Emma; it was all that had helped get him through and kept him going. It had become his mission.

He tried not to feel disappointed; this was her way of dealing with her grief, he reminded himself. Why had he expected that once she saw him everything would be the same as before? How could he have expected her to still be that same person? He needed to be the strong one here. He knew it wasn't going to be easy but at least he was here now and he was going to do everything in his power to help her through.

He glanced around the strange but familiar room, unsure as to whether he should sit down on his own sofa that still had his shape moulded into its cushions. There were books belonging to him on the shelves and his CDs were stacked in the rack, there were even photos of his graduation and of him in his morning suit on their wedding day on the mantelpiece. Everything in this room was recognisable so why did he feel he was a visitor in his own home?

He walked out through the hallway and into the kitchen.

Normally you had to squeeze past the buggy to get to the kitchen but there was an empty space where the buggy used to be. He had to swallow back hard.

His eyes took in the kitchen which looked different since he had last been here. It looked barer somehow and then Adam realised that all the baby paraphernalia that had been sitting cluttering the worktops was now missing. The high chair was also gone from the end of the table. He noticed the pots growing herbs on the kitchen windowsill had all died, their shrivelled brown leaves now clinging desperately to the stalks. Everywhere he looked a different memory lay in store. He could feel his chest tighten, the familiarity was painful. In the hospital he had been spared the constant reminders of life when Fionn was in it but here they were everywhere.

As he looked around the kitchen, he could recall the morning of the crash with clarity. He had strapped Fionn into his high seat to give him his breakfast. Fionn had smiled and screeched at him and kept his mouth open constantly for more cereal. He had slapped his two palms down on the tray, causing his cup to fall off, and then he had leaned over the side looking at it on the floor. When Adam had picked it up for him, he had giggled. He saw it as a game and continued slapping the tray so that Adam would have to pick the cup up for him again.

After breakfast he had cleaned him up and got him dressed and decided they would call over to see his parents. They loved having any opportunity to spend some time with their grandson. He had packed up Fionn's bag with a spare set of clothes, nappies, wipes, barrier cream, bottles; he had hoped he wasn't forgetting anything. He dressed Fionn in his snowsuit to protect him from the chilly winter morning and strapped him into the car. The white sunlight flooded in through the car windows. He had driven slowly, leaving the city behind and within minutes was out in the countryside amongst frost-tinged trees and ditches. He passed by a farmhouse with red sash windows and wrought-iron gates marking the start of a narrow path leading to the front door. He hugged the bend of the road as his body pulled softly to the left with the car. Right ahead was a crossroads and a car shot through it at speed, startling him. He reached the crossroads as a second car tore out from the left.

And then Fionn died.

48

As soon as Adam came home, the faces disappeared just as
instantly as they had arrived. Emma's mother, who had more
or less moved in to take care of her in the aftermath of the
crash, said that they needed their own space and so she had
gone home to her own house. She gently told Emma that she
and Adam had to get on with things themselves as a couple.
But Emma didn't feel like part of a couple; she barely knew the
man who was now back in her house claiming to be her
husband.

She stayed holed up in her room because she couldn't bear
to look at the constant reminder that was Adam. Looking at
him alive was just too raw; she knew it was wrong but she
wished it was him instead of Fionn. The unjustness of it all
made her so angry. She couldn't talk to him; she couldn't find
words because her head was spinning with grief. He had been
the last one to see him alive, he had been driving the car for
Christ's sake, and she resented that. He kept persisting with
her, sitting by her bedside, trying to talk to her about Fionn,
trying to get her to open up, telling her he was worried about

her or asking if he should he get someone to come and talk to her. She never responded. When that didn't work he would switch to mundane topics and have a running monologue with himself trying to fill the silence with words. He would ramble on about the weather or about some news story about fraudulent bankers or whatever project he was involved in at work. His chatter grated on her. How dare he just come back here and try to act like things went on as normal! She couldn't bear to say Fionn's name, she feared that if she said it she might choke on the word like a lump stuck in her throat. Every time Adam mentioned his name she wanted to scream at him to stop, it was too painful to hear it out loud, a name that still existed but the person gone. How can a name exist for a person no longer there? The hollowness of hearing his name was too awful and it just tore at her chest, like a knife darting against her flesh.

* * *

The painkillers that Adam had been prescribed were no match for the morphine that he had been given in hospital. Every day was a daily battle against the pain. Nevertheless, there was something he had to do. His stomach was knotted together and he broke out in a sweat with dread whenever he even thought about it. But he still found it hard to believe or accept what he was being told; he needed to see it for himself.

He went through the turnstile of Primrose Cemetery and felt ashamed that he didn't even know what direction to go in. He didn't know where his own son was buried. He staggered along the twisting path on his crutches. Some graves were decorated with coloured pebbles; others were neatly sown with grass. Some were carefully maintained, more lay weedy, with cracked yellowing plastic crosses that once contained vinyl flowers. There were large, leaning headstones from days gone by. As he scanned the names and ages on the headstones, all belonging to people who had lived good long lives, it was another painful reminder that Fionn was taken away too early.

Birds could be heard tweeting their morning song on the crisp, sunny air and that almost seemed to be a mockery of how he was feeling inside. He made his way towards the newer plots at the back of the cemetery and suddenly he was faced with a small white marble headstone which had Fionn's name on it.

He moved forward and read the inscription:

Here lies Baby Fionn White
Born on June 6th 2009
Died tragically on December 14th 2009
Always remembered by his loving mammy, daddy,
grandparents, aunt and uncles.
Rest In Peace, Angel.

He wondered who had organised the headstone. Weeks of holding himself together made it suddenly hit home. *Fionn was gone.* He was lying here underneath this cold earth – his baby, his baby son. It was all he could do not to put his crutches aside and start scraping at the earth to dig him out and hold him again in his arms. His arms ached to feel his full weight. He'd had such a short time in this world.

He fell down onto his knees and hammered the gravestone with his fist repeatedly until it began to hurt. He stood back up and kicked a wreath that lay on the grass so that it flew up into the air over his head with the flowers falling off before it landed back down again. How dare this happen! What the fuck had he ever done to deserve this? It wasn't fair! If there was a God in this world – and he strongly doubted it – how could he let such a cruel thing happen? Someone had said to him that it was the circle of life, but how could it be when Fionn didn't even get past his first year?

"I'm so sorry, son," he sobbed over the grave. "I'm so sorry I couldn't do more for you. I'm sorry I even brought you out, we didn't need to go, we could have just stayed at home and then you would still be here with us today." His whole body heaved with the force of his tears, his shoulders jerking up and down. "If I could turn back the clock, just to hold you for five more minutes, that's all, just to hold you in my arms again and tell you I love you, I would. I'll always love you, Fionn."

When the tears finally stopped, he sat back, worn out, and rested against the headstone. Had he really done his best? Could he have acted faster? Could he have pulled them out of that spin? Had the impact of the crash killed Fionn or had he died when they tumbled into the garden? There they were again, the 'what ifs' tormenting him.

He pulled himself up and stood breathing in the chilly air in the lonely graveyard before hobbling on his crutches up to the top of the cemetery.

* * *

As the weeks went on, Adam soon realised things were not good with Emma at all and they didn't show any sign of getting any better. She stayed in her room whenever he was in the house and when he tried to talk to her, she didn't talk back. It was as if she was looking straight through him, like he was opaque and she couldn't see him standing there in front of her. He felt like shaking her by the shoulders to tell her it was him, Adam – her husband was back. *Did she not remember?* She went around like a zombie, oblivious to life around her. He felt like he was in her way and maybe she needed some space so, not knowing what else to do with himself, he decided to return to work.

After being off for four months, the office had seemed very different even in that short period of time. Firstly, there was a new receptionist, a mad little thing called Jo who seemed to have the entire male workforce in the company wrapped around her finger. Then everyone was busy working on a new project; the project he had last worked on had long since been completed.

His first day was awkward for everyone. People didn't know what to say to him when they saw him first. He still limped slightly but every day his muscles were getting stronger. He covered up his scars by wearing long-sleeved shirts and jumpers. His colleagues had taken it in awkward turns to come up to him with a mumbled "Sorry for your trouble" before quickly running away in case he fell apart in front of them. He almost wanted to tell them that their words didn't cause the memories to resurface because he constantly thought about what had happened. He knew they were wary about what they said in front of him. They carefully chose topics of conversation and those who had kids didn't talk about them. It had taken a while for people to relax around him but, after a few weeks, they gradually began to treat him like they always did. They included him in their chats and jokes or they asked him if he wanted to go out for drinks which he never did because he would always hurry home to Emma. Though he didn't always find her there.

He was surprised to find that work was actually a welcome distraction; it was a relief to be able to go in there and escape his house every day. He was distraught with worry about Emma's state of mind. He didn't know what was going on inside her head. He desperately wished she would just talk to him. He had tried everything. He didn't want to worry his family by telling them what was going on – they were already devastated after what had happened, they had been through so much as well. So he said nothing, and as far as everyone was concerned they were working through their grief together.

The nightmares tormented him on an almost nightly basis; they were becoming more and more frequent. He was finding it hard to go to sleep at night out of fear for what lay in store for him but inevitably he would drift off at some godforsaken hour only to wake in a sweat moments later with fragments of what had happened spinning around inside his head.

49

A few months after Fionn died, Emma had received a phone call from some poor intern in the Human Resources department of A1 Adverts who had been tasked with giving her a call. Emma could tell that the girl on the other end of the phone, who sounded young, and who stuttered and stammered as she spoke, was obviously embarrassed at having to make the call that no one else had wanted to make. She tried her best to delicately ascertain when, if ever, Emma might be planning on returning to work. Emma had completely forgotten about work. It just hadn't even entered her head that they might be wondering what her plans were now that a few months had passed since the accident. No matter how much she wished it wouldn't, everything still moved on.

At first she had been horrified at the thought of getting up and carrying on as if her life was normal when it wasn't. She felt as though Fionn would think she was already moving on, that she had already forgotten about him. Everyone was telling her the best thing that she could do was to keep busy and get some routine back into her life but she knew in her heart and soul that it still wouldn't stop her thinking about him every minute of the day. However, the more she thought it over, the more she realised that no matter how many times she relived what had happened, it wouldn't change anything – it wouldn't bring him back – so with an overwhelming feeling of guilt, she reluctantly had phoned the intern back and told her she would be back the following Monday.

When Emma had gone in the door on her first day back, she couldn't help but notice that people didn't make eye contact with her. When she spoke they would start shifting nervously and would lower their gaze to the floor. As she walked down the corridors she could feel eyes on her back and whispers crept around the office that she was back. She had met with Maureen in her office. She started by telling Emma that she was truly sorry for everything that had happened. Emma was used to hearing these words from people so she put on her strong face which seemed to make Maureen more relaxed. She told Emma to take her time and if there were days that she just wasn't feeling up to it not to worry about coming in, but Emma could see she was more than a bit relieved to see her. She briefed Emma on which campaigns they were preparing pitches for, which had recently been won and were now in the production stage and those that were starting on further phases. Emma could see there was a lot on.

Although everyone had warned her to ease herself into it gradually, Emma threw herself straight in. Instead of dodging the new client enquiries like the rest of the overworked campaign managers, she was now glad to take on more than her fair share of work. Whenever Maureen tried to suggest that maybe it was a bit too much for one person and that she would divide it up amongst the rest of her colleagues, Emma would shake her head, so reluctantly Maureen left her alone. She threw herself into preparing the pitches and winning business for A1.

The funny thing was that when Fionn was born, she had lost all interest in her job, she hadn't wanted to return to work, she had considered being a stay-at-home mum but they had a large mortgage as a result of buying their home at the height of Ireland's property market and she'd had no choice but to return to work. Now here she was a few months later, broken emotionally and using work as a crutch to escape the sadness of her life.

She stayed later than everyone in the evenings, even Maureen, and she worked through lunch most days but although people had said that the best thing she could do was to keep busy, it didn't help her to forget. Of course getting up in the mornings and leaving the house every day helped lift some of the blackness, but she thought about Fionn constantly.

Looking at Adam now was like looking in a mirror of the grief she was trying to hide from. She knew she needed to face him sooner or later but she couldn't look at him without it dredging up all the hurt and upset and resentment that he was just getting on with his life. That wasn't right. She was living day to day, not daring to think ahead about their future, but she couldn't ignore the tell-tale signs that life was running on all around her; winter changed to spring and spring to summer.

Emotionally she had been through her very worst nightmare, everything else was secondary. Her mind had shut itself off, and made her immune to anything which would hurt her, in order to protect her, like a ship seals off compartments to stop it sinking. Her senses had shut down. She was a shell of a person going through the motions, unable to make a decision, living from day to day, drifting along in the ebb of life because if she thought too far into the future, the thought of living an entire life without her son was overwhelming. So she lived from day to day; then days turned into weeks, and weeks to months and somehow that got her through.

* * *

Adam still bore the physical scars from the accident. He had a long lumpy keloid scar running down the front of his left shin from where he had broken the bone quite badly and one on the inside of his wrist which if he didn't wear long sleeves tended to draw people's eyes, but he was limping less now and his daily cycle to and from work was helping the muscles regain strength. It was the mental scars that were proving the most difficult to heal.

The dream was re-occurring on a nightly basis, hunting him down during the small hours of the morning. The ordeal was played out over and over in his head, night after night. Even when he was in an alcohol-induced sleep it still managed to find him, he had no escape. He could see the silhouette of trees shining in through his car window as he drove along on a crisp sunny morning. There were the trees, the branches covered in frost, the white sunlight cutting through the sky, the farmhouse with its red windows and wrought-iron gates. There was the bend in the road. The crossroads. Adam would wake up in a panic, soaked with sweat. He felt empty, alone and fearful. Things were bad enough without nightly reminders too. He was becoming too scared to sleep and he was exhausted. He would drink endless amounts of coffee in work, just to get through the day but it gave him a nervous energy, he felt jittery and restless. His foot or fingers were always tapping. Tell-tale bags had formed under his red-puffy eyelids, his skin was ashen and he couldn't keep the weight on him.

For some reason Adam didn't feel entitled to grieve. Although he had lost his child too, so much focus was on Emma as the mother that people expected him to be the strong one. They assumed he should be the one helping her through her grief and supporting her. It was as if she had a monopoly on the grief. He was expected to be a man, to be stoic and strong. He wasn't allowed go to pieces. But it wasn't easy.

He had no doubt but that Emma attached some of the

blame to him and he could understand it. Who knows, he might have done the same himself if the roles were reversed? He knew it wasn't her fault; she needed to blame something, to lash out at someone. When she looked at him, he knew that was what she was thinking; he could see it in her eyes. What if he had been driving slower? What if he had left the house a minute later or didn't decide to go to see his parents that day? He constantly wondered the same thing himself. And so the weight of his own guilt and Emma's blame, while never actually voiced, stood between them, growing by the day until the wedge grew so wide that they were where they were today. He couldn't help getting more and more frustrated by her behaviour. It wasn't his fault, he wanted to shout.

And then one day, Emma had come into the kitchen in her work suit. He had been amazed to see her properly dressed and not in her pyjamas. Her hair was done, she still looked pale and tired but he could see pieces of the old Emma that had been missing for months now. She didn't look at him, she had just grabbed her bag and walked out the door, but it was a start. He stood watching after her in disbelief and hoped that she might finally be starting to heal but his hopes had been short-lived. She worked all the hours possible so she was never at home. He barely saw her and when he did see her, she still wouldn't talk to him and continued to act like he wasn't there.

Recently things had gone from bad to worse between them; he hadn't even seen her this week. He knew he should be helping her; he was trying to be understanding of what she was going through but instead he just felt angry. He was rapidly losing patience and he didn't know how much more of this he could take. He was tormented too – why couldn't she see that? She needed to stop blaming him and accept that nothing would ever bring Fionn back.

* * *

When Fionn's first birthday came around, she didn't know quite how she was going to get through it. It should have been a happy occasion: a party, a cake, new toys, maybe his first taste of chocolate, he might have been walking or he might not. She felt robbed and cheated and so angry for losing out on all of this. Her mother had tentatively suggested that it might be a good time for her to visit the graveyard but she had never been able to get the courage up to go there. She couldn't bear the thought of him lying there cold and alone, her baby. Her mother felt it would do her good but she wasn't able to face it. So on Fionn's birthday she had tearfully written him a card, filling it with words trying to express just how much she loved him and missed him and was sorry for everything that had happened. She held onto it for him, she would take it to the grave someday, just not yet.

Part IV

50

January, 2011

From the kitchen Emma heard the doorbell sound. She opened the door to see the postman standing there. The long evenings had started to come in and dusk was falling. A rush of leaves swirled up at her feet. He had a parcel that she had to sign for and a letter. She thanked him and closed the door. The parcel was for Adam so she left it on the hall table for him. She looked at the address on the letter through the cellophane pane of the envelope. *To the parents of Fionn White*. She felt a lump in her throat. Emma opened the white envelope – normally these letters were reminders about his vaccines or from a PR company trying to sell her something for the milestone that he should be at now if he were still alive. She knew she should probably throw these things into the bin but for some reason she never could. She still hadn't been able to summon up the strength yet to ask them to take his name off their databases. But this letter had the red ink of the state harp on it. The gummed seal tore in parts so she stuck her finger inside and pulled it along to open it. She unfolded the white paper and read down through the letter.

The text began to dance before her eyes. It was Fionn's death certificate. There it was in black and white on paper. She looked at the shortness of his life written in front of her: *Date of birth June 6th 2009; Deceased December 14th 2009*. Six months old. Just six months. There it was in black and white in front of her – he was no longer considered to be a person of this world. The finality was overbearing.

She felt her knees buckle beneath her and she reached out to grab onto the post of the staircase. She used it to guide herself downwards so that she was sitting on the bottom step. Just as she thought she might be starting to heal, taking tentative steps forward, this had come and knocked her off balance again. She wasn't expecting it; it was like a below-the-belt punch coming at her, leaving her reeling in its wake. She needed to see his face as if somehow by looking at him it would confirm that he had been a real person. She ran upstairs and into her bedroom. Pulling out the drawer of her bedside table, she reached for his photo. The smiling baby staring back at her, so happy and full of life, was so at odds with what had happened. Sometimes she still couldn't believe this had happened to him, that he was gone and never coming back. The pain tore at her chest. The unjustness caught her again as it always did and she felt the sting of tears building up behind her eyes before spilling down her face. Would she ever get over how unfair the whole thing was? If only she had control, could turn back the clock. It was unfair that they didn't get a second chance. She screwed the lid off her tablets, swallowed two back and waited for the heavy sensation to come and numb the pain.

* * *

When Emma woke again everything seemed blacker. The room was still cloaked in early-morning darkness but nothing was as dark as how she was feeling inside. Today was one of those days that felt as though someone had turned out all the lights.

It had been a while since the blackness had descended upon her with such strength but now it felt like it was smothering her until she could no longer breathe. She knew Maureen would understand if she didn't go into work today.

She fell back asleep and managed to sleep right through the day and was only woken by the doorbell ringing. She opened her eyes and remembered where she was. The clock on her locker told her it was after six in the evening. She lay there hoping that whoever it was would go away but they were persistent so she dragged herself out of bed and trod downstairs to answer it.

"Hi there," Zoe said softly as she opened the door. "I rang you in work and they said you hadn't come in today, so I thought I'd stop by and see how you're doing?" She took in Emma's red-rimmed eyes and stained face. "Aw pet, today's a tough one, isn't it?"

Emma let her in silently and Zoe followed her into the living room. She sat on the couch beside Emma and encircled her in her arms.

"His death cert arrived today." The tears built up inside and spilled down Emma's face again.

"Oh Emma!" Zoe hugged her tight. She felt a bit puzzled. How could the certificate have taken a year to come, she wondered. "There, there, pet. It's okay, it's okay."

Emma's whole body shook with tears until her cheeks stung and her nose was running, streaming with watery mucous.

Zoe felt wretched watching her friend in this state. She was useless to her; nothing she could do or say would change anything.

"I just miss him so much, Zoe. It never gets easier. People keep telling me that time is a great healer but it isn't – the pain never goes away. It's always there, constantly, and I'm so tired of crying. I'm just so tired."

"Oh God, Emma – I'm so sorry."

"It's just . . . so . . . so . . . final."

Zoe rubbed her back while Emma cried hard.

A while after, Emma said she was exhausted and wanted to go back to bed.

Zoe helped Emma into bed and watched as she fell asleep instantly, worn out from all her tears. She stayed there stroking Emma's hair softly. It was painful watching her friend fall apart and knowing there was nothing she could do for her. So much time had passed but it was all still so fresh. While Emma snored gently, Zoe tiptoed quietly out of the room.

* * *

Just as Adam was dismounting his bike, he saw Zoe letting herself out their front door.

"Hi, Zoe."

"Hi, Adam," she said somewhat awkwardly. "I just called in to check on Emma."

"How is she?"

"She's not too good actually. You see, Fionn's death cert arrived in the post today. She's taken it pretty badly."

He took a sharp breath. "Jesus!" His eyes widened in horror. "Oh God, Zoe, I wanted to spare her that. I asked them to address it to me."

"Why did it take so long to come, Adam?"

"It was just a copy, Zoe. Em's parents mislaid the original in the months after his death and I only recently steeled myself to send for another."

His eyes began to brim with tears and he had to do everything in his power to keep it together.

"I'm sorry, Adam, I really am. I can't imagine what you're both going through." The man standing before her, the man who used to be tall and strong, now was broken.

"Is she in her room?"

She nodded. "I'm worried about her, Adam. She's in a bad way up there."

"Well, she won't talk to me. It's still as if she can't bear to look at me or she blames me or something. When she looks at me all I can see is contempt in her eyes."

"It's not easy for her."

It's not easy for me either.

"I know but she just keeps pushing me away. I just want to get inside her head to understand exactly what is going through her mind about me. Surely by now she should be coping better."

"I really don't know what to say, Adam. I know you don't want to hear it but be patient with her, it's still quite soon. And today is bound to be another setback."

"Yeah, I suppose you're right." He let out a heavy sigh.

She nodded and turned away. He watched her walk off into the dusky evening.

Adam let himself into the house and picked up the white letter that Emma had left on the hall table. He unfolded it. *To the parents of Fionn White.* That's why she had opened it. He had asked them to address it to him. He stared at the text. That was it: Fionn was gone. A piece of paper was all they were left with. He stood and broke into sobs as the grief flooded down upon him. He longed to hold Emma and to have her hold him back. He missed the closeness of his wife.

He climbed the stairs and stood outside her door. He had long since given up calling into her but he needed her right now. The lights were off and he could hear from her slow and heavy breathing that she was sleeping. He tiptoed across the floorboards. In the darkness, he looked down at her. Her hair was fanned out on the pillow around her. He reached out to touch her skin; his fingertips stroked its softness while he brushed the strands of hair back off her face but she didn't wake.

Adam slept fitfully that night. When he finally drifted off, the dream was back again with terrifying force, menacing him in the darkness, looming over him like a spectre waiting until he went to sleep to appear. It was all disjointed. Driving along.

The sun. The blinding sun. The frost-tipped hedgerows. Trees. The house. The gate. The bend. The crossroads.

His body bolted upright as beads of sweat ran down his bare chest. He tried to catch his breath as he sat trembling in his own bed.

He saw every hour change on the clock. His mind was whirring with activity. His world had been thrown upside down and it never got any easier. Today was another hurdle, another painful reminder when he had hoped things might be starting to get easier for them. He was free-falling and life felt out of his control. And he had lost his wife too. The one person he should have been able to count on kept pushing him away. He felt so powerless. Where could they go from here? He was slowly going around the twist from her torturous ignoring of him. She didn't want him around her. She didn't want him any more. Months of anxious worry were climaxing to realise his worst fears.

51

Zoe went home and poured herself a large glass of wine. She needed it. It had been awful seeing her friend and knowing there was nothing that she could do or say to help her. She had thought Emma was finally starting to take baby steps forward but the arrival of the death cert had been a major setback. Then there was Adam too, he had seemed devastated when she had told him. She phoned Steve and he insisted that he and Dave would come straight over to her. When he came into her apartment, he wordlessly wrapped her in his strong arms as she sobbed into his shoulder.

It felt like Zoe had known Steve for years. Of course she knew it was a time-old cliché but since the day she had met him he had felt like an old friend. They never had any of that awkward conversation-making or running out of things to say to each other – they had always chatted openly and easily. She was amazed at how quickly they had fallen into a routine. He would call into her a few evenings during the week and then she would join the thousands of others making the mass exodus out of the city on a Friday evening where they would spend the weekend together holed up inside Steve's seaside cottage. He would have a huge feast waiting for her when she'd get in the door. Rack of lamb, chunky vegetable soup or steak and homemade chips – always followed by a delicious homemade pudding. She joked to him that he was having a detrimental effect on her waistline but he loved cooking things and getting her to try them out.

Steve was good and steady, dependable. In his own way he was romantic too; he would pick wild flowers for her or if he spotted something quirky at a market, he would buy it for her as a surprise. She and Dave often went along to markets with him where she watched him at work in his stripy canvas apron, strolling around offering people samples. She was amazed to see he had a lot of repeat customers that came to the market on the same day every week just to stock up on his produce. He would be selling a loaf of bread and then he would suggest they try some of his relishes or jams, and because of his friendly nature no one seemed to refuse; he was a natural people person. And what was great was that he was in his element, there in the outdoors with people, doing what he loved. It made Zoe think twice about all the years of being stifled by her own job. Steve had balls, he had followed his dream, and there was an awful lot to be said for that.

Dave was doing well too. He was growing into a wiry young dog, always leaping up and running wild around the place. They would usually go for a long walk along the beach on Saturday morning with Dave running off ahead of them chasing the sticks they threw, before sprinting back again with the stick firmly gripped in between his teeth. They would try to prise it from his mouth but he wouldn't let it go so they would have to find another one to throw for him. Then he would act brave and chase the waves as they lapped the shoreline, but when they broke and washed out across the sand towards him, he would run back scared. Steve and Zoe would be helpless with laughter. It was still hard to believe that it was all down to Dave that they were together. It definitely was fate.

After a long walk on the beach, they would come back up to the cottage, Dave shaking sand everywhere while Steve would feed her some more of his treats. He would light the fire and the two of them would cosy up on the couch, reading or watching a film, sometimes sipping a glass of red wine. They felt as comfortable in silence as they did talking. She hadn't felt this relaxed since she didn't know when. She felt as though she belonged there and it had been a long time since she had felt like that. Even as a child she had never felt as though she truly belonged because she had been passed around so much. If you had asked her a year back if she could have ever envisioned being contented by such a lifestyle she would have laughed. She had always loved the hustle and bustle of city life, but she was surprised to find she enjoyed the quiet contentment of spending time with Steve in his remote cottage.

She had even worked herself up to tell Steve about her childhood and her mam but instead of being horrified like some of her exes had been, he took it all on board and listened. He didn't offer platitudes or sympathy and she had found it much easier to open up to him than she had anyone else before. When she had told boyfriends in the past about her upbringing they would start with the 'poor you' routine and, inevitably, even if they didn't mean to, they would start treating her differently. It would make her feel guilty then about the fuss they were making and she would wonder if they were with her because they felt sorry for her or because they genuinely liked her? But it wasn't like that with Steve.

When they went to bed together that night Zoe, worn out from her tears and worry about Emma, fell asleep as soon as her head hit the pillow. Steve wrapped her close in his arms and spooned her from behind as Dave snored gently on a rug on the floor beside them.

52

After hours of tossing and turning, Adam got out of the bed and walked over to the wardrobe. Reaching up to the top shelf, he pulled down his holdall. He packed it with most of his clothes and threw in some toiletries. He reached into the wardrobe and took out a pair of trainers and the shoes he wore to work and took some suits and put them into a bag. He looked at a photo of himself and Emma and Fionn that hung on the wall. He took it off the hook and held it in his hands. He stared at it briefly before packing it in with the rest of his belongings.

He knocked on the bedroom door where Emma was. As usual there was no greeting. She was lying in the darkness. He wasn't sure if she was asleep or awake. He switched on the light and saw she was awake but she didn't look at him, instead her two eyes stared straight ahead.

"I saw the death cert."

She said nothing.

"Emma, I'm sorry – I don't want to cause you any more pain but I'm at my wits' end. I can't take it any more." He took a deep breath. "I think it's for the best if I moved out for a while. Maybe just give you some space?"

Her expression remained impassive, giving no sign of how she was feeling or even if she was listening to him.

"Right. Well, I'll be in Rob's if you need me."

He lifted the holdall over his shoulder and closed the door behind him.

* * *

Emma listened to Adam's footsteps as they made their way down the stairs, across the floorboards in the hall and then the sound of the swooshing of their heavy front door closing. She wanted to react somehow but felt paralysed by her grief. She couldn't move. She listened to the stillness of the house; it was still dark out. She shook out a couple more of her tablets, swallowed them down and fell into a deep sleep.

When she woke again, she still felt exhausted. She had slept too deeply and it took a while for the tablets to wear off so she felt like a zombie detached from the world going on around her. And then she remembered Adam was gone. She felt numb. She couldn't even get out of bed. She just wanted the pain to go, just to leave her in peace even for a few moments.

She couldn't compete any more with the fight and struggle to live her daily life. She just wanted to be asleep again and not wake up to her horrible reality. She swallowed back some more tablets, but they weren't working any more – sleep didn't come so easily now. She opened up her drawer and took out the photo and stared at the familiar face of her baby boy. She tipped more tablets into the palm of her hand, looking at them momentarily before stuffing the fistful into her mouth and washing them back.

She lay back down and waited, but they still weren't working. She dragged herself out of bed, went down to the kitchen and pulled open the press above the fridge where they kept their alcohol. She reached up for the bottle of vodka that had been there for years, probably left over from some house party. She unscrewed the cap and watched the liquid slosh into a glass. She put it up to her lips but the alcohol stung her gums and made her grimace. She opened the fridge and found a carton of orange juice. She poured it on top of the vodka before knocking the whole mixture back. Within minutes she began to feel relaxed and subdued. She brought the bottle back up to the room with her.

She tipped out another few tablets and washed them down with the vodka. She was able to drink it neat this time; it didn't taste as bad now. She felt the familiar deadening of all her senses, the sounds from outside the house got further away. It was harder to see. She didn't want to move, she just wanted to lie there. She gulped back some more vodka and closed her eyes, enjoying the sensation of peace and deep relaxation until she was far away from all the heartache that was her life.

53

When Rob had heard his doorbell go in the early hours of the morning, he knew it was something serious. He had been dumbstruck to see Adam standing on his doorstep with his holdall on the ground at his feet. Seeing the dishevelled state that his brother was in was frightening. Adam was a shadow of his former self. His gaunt face was now creased and lined and the dark circles under his eyes showed a frightening depth. He ushered him in but Adam was barely able to speak.

Rob could make a good guess at what had happened, but he could hardly believe it. He had known things were bad between them but he had never thought that Adam would actually *leave* her. His brother adored Emma, he always had from the day he met her – they were the couple he always looked up to, his benchmark for an ideal relationship. They were the one couple he would never have imagined splitting up. They were good together, each still an individual but complementing the other.

He hoped that his brother just needed some headspace for a couple of days but he wasn't so sure and Adam didn't seem to know himself.

Adam sat in stunned silence on Rob's settee. He had been in denial for so long and he still couldn't believe it had actually happened. He had just got up and left her. He hadn't planned it. It hadn't been premeditated; he just literally had had enough. Seeing Emma's lack of expression had hurt. Deep down if he was honest some part of him had hoped it would have been enough to snap her out of the despair and to bring her back to him but nothing was giving. He had hoped that she might have sat up and asked him to stay, that she would say that she did still need him but instead her face had shown no reaction, as if she really couldn't care less or wasn't even registering what he was saying to her. As if he was a complete stranger to her.

He didn't know how long he was going to stay with Rob – it could be a few days, it could be months or maybe they would never work it out. All he knew was that he couldn't stay there any more.

54

Zoe dialled Emma's mobile number yet again but it just rang out and went to her voicemail. She had been phoning her and leaving messages for hours now and for some reason it made her feel uneasy. When she told Steve that she was worried, he said he would drive her over there. Emma had been very low over the last few days. She couldn't explain why but something told her she should just go and check on her friend. She had tried ringing Adam to make sure that everything was okay but she hadn't managed to get hold of him either.

When they arrived outside Emma's house on Cherry Tree Road, Steve stayed in the car while Zoe walked up the path and pressed the bell. She noticed Adam's bike wasn't there. Normally it was chained to the railings whenever he was at home. She waited for a while before ringing the bell again but no one was answering. She began to feel stupid then. Emma had probably just gone out. Or she might be asleep, in which case Zoe really didn't want to wake her. She rang Emma's mobile again but there was no answer.

She turned around and got back into Steve's car, cursing

herself for overreacting as usual. Steve was just reversing out the driveway when Zoe noticed that the bedroom light upstairs was on. Surely if Emma was asleep she wouldn't leave the light on? She asked Steve to stop the car again. She jumped out and ran back to the front door. She started ringing the bell again and pounding on the knocker but there was no answer. She couldn't explain it but she knew something wasn't right.

Steve joined her and they both went around to the side of the house and scaled the locked wooden gate before hopping down onto the patio. They tried the back patio door but that was locked too.

Zoe knew that Emma sometimes left a spare key in the shed. She swung back the creaky wooden door and went into the cobweb-covered shed. She went over to a frame of shelves and looked under the usual flowerpot but there was nothing there. She began to search under and inside other flowerpots and containers but she couldn't find it anywhere. Steve was just about to pick up a hammer and use it to break the glass door, when Zoe found the key wedged behind a box of tools.

They hurried to the back door. Zoe fumbled with the key in the lock for a few seconds before it clicked open. They let themselves in.

"Emma?" Zoe shouted. "Are you here, Emma? Emma, are you okay?"

She bounded up the stairs and pushed back the door to Emma's bedroom. She saw her friend lying there on top of the duvet cover, white froth coming from the side of her mouth.

Steve came into the room behind her. "Oh, *shit!*"

Zoe ran over to her and instinctively lifted her head in her hands before remembering hearing that you shouldn't move the person, or was that for people that had a physical injury? She couldn't remember, so she removed her hands and watched as Emma's head flopped backwards onto the pillow again. She observed the bottle of vodka and a brown plastic vial with a pharmacist's label.

"Emma, what have you done to yourself?" she whispered.

Steve put his head down onto Emma's chest. "She's breathing but it's very shallow."

Zoe jerked into action immediately and frantically tried to dial 999, her fingers clumsy and awkward on the vinyl buttons. An engaged tone.

"Shit, Steve, what's the emergency number from mobiles?" Her mind was blank and wouldn't allow her remember what she needed to.

"112."

This time a voice answered, "Hello, Emergency services, how may I direct your call?"

"It's my friend, I think she may have overdosed on some tablets, she's comatose here, she's – she's frothing at the mouth."

"Is she breathing?"

"Yes – but it's very faint."

"Okay, now give me your address and I'll send an ambulance over there immediately."

"59 Cherry Tree Road, Rathmines, Dublin 6. Please hurry."

She looked at Emma where she was lying splayed on the bed. She didn't know whether they should be shaking her or doing chest compressions like they did on medical shows or if they should just leave her alone altogether. All the medical advice she had ever heard was jumbled around inside her head, none of it helpful or any use in this situation. She willed the ambulance to hurry up. Every minute felt like an eternity.

Eventually they heard a siren blaring in the distance so Steve ran down the stairs and out the front door onto the road so that he could flag the ambulance down and hopefully save time.

The paramedics stormed up the stairs and within seconds they had lifted Emma gently off the bed and placed her still body onto a stretcher. They carried her downstairs and put her into the back of the ambulance. They allowed Zoe to come in the back with them and Steve said he'd follow behind in his jeep. One of the paramedics hooked Emma up to some machines and then they sped off.

On the journey to the hospital, they worked on trying to stabilise Emma. They asked Zoe questions such as "What's her name?" and "What medication was she on?" and "Has there been anything out of the ordinary with her behaviour in recent times?" Zoe wasn't sure where to start with this one. Should she go over everything that had happened in the last year – the accident and losing her son? As the ambulance whizzed down the road she could only see bits of the journey through the small portholes with an orange tint so people couldn't see in. She knew people were probably looking at the ambulance wondering who was behind its doors – she did it herself all the time to pass the time in traffic – and now that it was her best friend she wished she could swap with them and be the ones sitting at the traffic lights with the idle thoughts.

As soon as they arrived at the hospital, the back doors were thrown open and they flew off through double doors with Emma's stretcher. Zoe followed them but was told she had to wait outside the A&E.

Even though she had given up smoking years ago, Zoe desperately needed one now. She went outside and found herself asking an old man for a cigarette. It was a short, stubby green Major but beggars couldn't be choosers. She inhaled deeply, feeling the smoke catch the back of her throat; she had forgotten how strong they were.

Steve came up beside her moments later and put his jacket over her shoulders. "Here, put this on – you'll catch your death."

Zoe remembered Adam. She needed to tell him. She took out her mobile out and dialled his number.

"Adam – it's Zoe."

"What is it, Zoe?" He sounded apprehensive.

"I'm at the hospital, Adam. It's Emma – I found her – look, Adam, it seems she's taken an overdose."

He didn't respond.

"Are you there, Adam?" she asked urgently.

"Jesus Christ – an overdose of what?"

"Vodka and some sleeping tablets, I think. She's in Dublin County Hospital."

"I'm on my way."

While Zoe and Steve waited outside for Adam to arrive, she dialled Emma's parents' number.

She was relieved when Emma's dad picked up. She was afraid that news like this would break her mother altogether.

"Peter – it's Zoe."

"Zoe? Is everything okay?"

"No – it's Emma – she's in the A&E in Dublin County Hospital. It seems she's taken an overdose."

* * *

Emma parents, who lived only a short distance from the hospital, arrived first. Her mother had red-rimmed eyes and her father was ashen. They were back at the same hospital they had been in when they had lost their grandson. They weren't able for this. They had aged a shocking amount over the last year, more than they had in the last ten years; the rollercoaster of human emotion was too much at this stage of their lives. They were in their sixties, life was meant to be winding down for them now – instead they found themselves living through their hardest years.

"Do you know what happened?" Peter Fitzpatrick seemed to be the only one capable of coherent speech.

"I called over to her – and found her lying there. Her sleeping tablets and a bottle of vodka were beside the bed."

"Oh God – I – I –" Her mother broke down.

"She's going to be okay," Zoe tried to reassure her. Jesus Christ, she prayed she would be all right! "Emma is strong – she's a fighter."

"Can we see her?" Emma's dad asked as if she was the authority for the hospital.

"I don't think so, they told me to wait here. They're treating her at the moment."

"What about Adam? Where was he?"

"I'm not sure but I rang him too – he's on the way."

After a while they begged the hospital staff to tell them what was going on but were told only that she was being treated and they wouldn't know anything for a while.

They sat in anxious silence, praying that she would be okay.

55

The drive to the hospital in the darkness had seemed to take forever. Rob drove as fast as he could and luckily the roads were clear from traffic at that time of night. They sat in silence as the thoughts whirred around inside Adam's head. It was all his fault. He shouldn't have left her. It was stupid and selfish to walk out on her like that; he knew she was at a low ebb and he had just walked out on her. He would never forgive himself. Thank God Zoe had found her. What if she hadn't? Well, it didn't bear thinking about. What the fuck had he been thinking? She needed him more than ever and he had just walked out like that! He had pushed her over the edge. This whole mess was his fault. He could imagine her lying there barely breathing. What if she died? He couldn't do this again. He couldn't go through all of this again. He couldn't lose her too. He wasn't religious, but he prayed and begged God on that car journey to spare her.

As they pulled into the car park, the sight of the hospital brought it all back again. The awful ache in his chest, the feeling of life closing in around him; he could nearly feel the pain in his pelvis again as it had mended itself back together.

He sat in the car and wondered if he would even have the strength to get out of it but Rob, seeing him shrink back, held out his arm and pulled him out. As the two brothers walked towards the doors, Adam thought he might collapse. He wasn't able for this, but Rob gripped his arm tighter and pushed him on.

In the thronged waiting room, Emma's parents, Zoe and her boyfriend came to meet them. He didn't know what to say to them. Did they know that he had walked out on her that morning? Did they know it was all his fault?

"I'm sorry!" He broke down.

Emma's dad put an arm around him. "You're okay, it's not your fault!"

"It is – I left her this morning."

"What do you mean?"

"Adam, what happened?" his mother-in-law begged.

"I couldn't take it any more. I just couldn't do it. I don't know what came over me but I just walked out. I'm so sorry." His voice dissolved into a whisper.

It all started to make sense to everyone now.

"It's okay, Adam – it's not your fault. She was very fragile anyway." Peter Fitzpatrick patted him on the back.

"How is she?" Adam somehow managed to ask.

"We're not too sure," said Zoe. "We're just waiting to hear. Here, sit down." She cleared off an ancient copy of *Hello* magazine with a ripped cover and patted a seat for Adam.

They all sat down again.

"Adam, you haven't met Steve properly, have you?" said Zoe.

Adam vaguely recalled meeting him in his drunken state when Zoe and Steve had to put him in a taxi home.

They mumbled greetings to one another.

They all sat around, each transfixed by their own thoughts, oblivious to the hustle and bustle around them. No one spoke for long periods and then, when someone did open their mouth, it seemed too loud and incongruous so they just shut up again. Emma's father kept on clearing his throat as though preparing to break into song – then he would get up off his chair and pace nervously around the room before sitting back down again. Emma's mother looked as though she was saying a novena; her face was deep in pious concentration. Everyone else just sat still and either stared straight ahead or at the ground.

Adam sat and ran over the same internal monologue that had been running through his head since Zoe had first phoned him. He shouldn't have left her, he should have got her help – that was what she had needed, why hadn't he been able to see that? He would give anything to be able to turn back the clock to this morning. He needed to talk to her and tell her that he still cared, he was sorry, he loved her. He hoped it wasn't too late, because he couldn't bear that again, he could not lose another person in his life. He wasn't tough enough to withstand that. He wished someone would tell him how she was doing.

Peter eventually approached a passing nurse.

"I'm Emma Fitzpatrick's father – do you have any news on her?"

"I'm afraid I can't discuss that with you but the doctor will be with you shortly."

Peter had to use all his inner restraint to keep from shouting at her just to tell him what was happening.

He went back to the others.

"Bloody won't tell me anything, she's my daughter for Christ's sake!" he bellowed at no one in particular. He sat down momentarily before getting up just as quick. "I'm going out for some air."

He left and the others sat waiting again.

Eventually a man in a white coat came through the door to the A&E and approached them.

"Are you the family of Emma Fitzpatrick?" He looked around at the grave faces. They all nodded their heads at him, each too afraid to speak, each feeling their hearts lurching in their chest.

What was he going to say? What was he going to tell them? Please let her be okay, please!

The doctor went to sit down.

Dear God, no, this wasn't a good sign. Adam thought he was going to be sick; he had broken out in a sweat and his mouth was watering.

Emma's father arrived back at that instant.

"Well, can you tell us how she is?" he demanded.

"I'm Dr Jacobs. The good news is Emma will be okay."

They each internally said prayers of gratitude, some to God, some to no one except in a dialogue with themselves.

"She is still quite heavily sedated but we would expect her to come round later this evening," the doctor went on. "We've given her flumazenil which is an antidote for the diazepams she overdosed on. She is on a ventilator to help with her breathing and appears to be responding well. Normally diazepams on their own don't cause unconsciousness but in Emma's case she combined the tablets with alcohol, which can prove fatal. There was quite a high level of alcohol in her bloodstream – she is very lucky. We're hoping that she may be off the ventilator by this evening. We'll try to move her to a ward as soon as possible but, in the meantime, you're welcome to go and sit with her in A&E if you'd like. Only two people at a time though."

Adam went first, Emma's parents deciding to wait and go in together. He followed the doctor through the swing doors with round portholes and down a corridor lined with patients on trolleys. Doctor Jacobs pulled back some curtains around a cubicle and ushered him in, then left.

Emma was lying on a trolley hooked up to wires and machines. It was all too familiar. Adam sat down on the chair and took her hand in his and was surprised by the familiarity of her touch. Then the tears rolled down his face. They kept on coming, tears for Emma, tears for Fionn, tears for their marriage, tears for their loss, tears for the last few months of heartache and separation, tears for the fact that he had left Emma to handle her grief alone, tears because he wasn't there for her, tears because she had needed someone to blame and unfortunately that person had been him. How did it come to this? How did he let this happen? The tears would not stop spilling down his face.

"Emma, I'm so, so sorry," he mumbled. "So sorry. I love you, so, so, much, I really do. I need you – just you work on getting better and when you're ready to wake up I'm going to be here with you. Do you hear that? I'll be right here by your side. I won't leave you like that again. I know I've let you down but I'm going to make it up to you, just you wait and see. So I hope you're listening to me and getting stronger, do you hear me? I'm so sorry for everything you've had to go through for the last few months, I truly am. Just you work on getting better."

He stared at her as she slept. She seemed so peaceful, so far removed from the horror of the last year.

* * *

Later that evening they took her off the ventilator and were relieved to see her breathing well on her own. They then moved her to a private room where Adam sat with her all night, with Emma's parents relieving him for short spells.

Eventually, the next morning, he saw her eyelashes flicker and her eyes widen. She looked around the room before closing her eyes again.

"Emma, Emma, you're awake!"

She went to speak but couldn't get the words out.

"You're okay, don't worry," he said, "it's going to be okay. Do you hear me?"

"Where am I?" she finally croaked.

"You're in the hospital but it's okay, you're going to be fine, just fine. I love you, Emma, and I'm sorry, I really am, for everything."

She lay there, looking around the unfamiliar room and tried to straighten out her thoughts to make sense of what was going on. Her head was pounding and the bright room made the pain behind her eyes worse.

"How are you feeling?"

"I've been better," she whispered.

She drifted back to sleep and Adam quietly slipped out to tell the nurses and phone the Fitzpatricks. Then he went back to her bedside, brushing back her curls behind her ear soothingly, wondering if the worst was over and his wife had truly come back to him again.

56

The next morning Emma was feeling brighter. Her head still felt fuzzy and she was exhausted but the awful weight of sadness that she had been carrying around for the last few months didn't seem as heavy any more.

She had overdosed because she wanted to forget; she was in so much pain and torment that she had wanted to feel numb and the alcohol allowed her to do that and the tablets helped her sleep and the next thing she knew she was forcing them down her throat. She hadn't wanted to kill herself; she just wanted not to feel any more. She had hit rock bottom but it was as if a hole had been cut through the numbness that allowed a small chink of light to shine through. She felt embarrassed for all she had put Adam and her parents through; they had suffered so much without her adding to their woes. For the first time she noticed that her parents were starting to look old. Her mum seemed small and frail, she had let the colour grow out of her hair so it was now silvery grey and her dad looked smaller than she had remembered as a child. They had aged so much in the last year. God here she was at her age causing them all this trouble and worry, more than she had ever caused as a teenager.

Adam was still at her bedside when she woke and she felt content just having him present again, knowing he was beside her. For the first time since the accident, it was as if she could see him as her husband again, the way she used to see him. She could finally see past the fog and she might just be able to get through it.

* * *

While Emma slept peacefully, Zoe came in to visit that evening.

"Hi there," she whispered to Adam "How's she doing?"

"She's good, she's sleeping a lot but the doctors said that's to be expected – she's sleeping off the excess tablets. It'll be a few days before she'll be back to full strength but they reckon she should be able to come home tomorrow."

"Oh thank God!"

"I'm going to be there for her now – help her recover, be there for her properly this time. I've let her down. I'll never forgive myself for just thinking about myself and how I was feeling –"

"Don't be so hard on yourself – you've been through as much as she has, Adam! It was bound to take its toll on your relationship but at least you're going to work through it together."

"I know this might sound weird but it's as if she finally sees me again? Since the accident she just looked through me but now it's different."

When Emma woke later, she was surprised to see Zoe sitting there with Adam.

"How are you feeling, darling? Look who's come to see you!" Adam said.

"Hi, sweetheart. How are you feeling?" Zoe asked.

"Zoe," Emma said, smiling at her.

"I'm going to grab a coffee in the canteen, okay?" Adam wanted to leave the two of them alone. He knew they had some talking to do.

"Fine." Zoe smiled at him as he left. She turned back to her friend. "Emma, thank God you're okay – I – I got such a fright." Zoe's eyes welled up with tears just thinking about it.

"I'm sorry, Zoe – for letting you find me like that, for putting you through that – seeing me in that state. I'm so embarrassed."

"Don't be embarrassed for God's sake! Just promise me you will never, *ever* do anything like that again."

Emma shook her head. "I can promise you I will never touch the things again."

"So how are you feeling?"

"A bit better today, thanks, but still so sleepy – I just keep drifting off but at least the pounding headache has gone. But it's so strange – it's like I've finally came back to reality, y'know? For months I've just felt numb but it's like someone has shaken me by my shoulders now and said wake up. The last year has been a complete nightmare and it's only now I'm coming out of it. I think I might be okay – it doesn't seem so hopelessly bleak now."

"Oh Emma – thank God. And Adam, how are you finding things with Adam?"

"We're doing all right. We've talked – like, properly talked for the first time since it all happened. I think we're going to be okay."

"That's good. You and Adam need each other – you're good together."

"I think you're right." Emma smiled sleepily at Zoe as she drifted off again.

57

Zoe finally felt ready to bring Steve to meet her mother. It was the first time she had ever brought a man to meet her family. She had met his family only weeks after they had first met because he couldn't wait to introduce her to them. He was the second eldest of a family of seven children and his upbringing had been so different from hers. His family was very close – they were not just siblings, they were friends. It was a busy farmhouse full of energy and even though Steve said they argued constantly, you just knew at the same time that they all looked out for one another.

She had been so nervous before she went but she needn't have worried; they had welcomed her in with little fuss as she took a chair at the already full kitchen table while the TV blared some football match in the background. His mother had left pots of potatoes, bowls of carrots and peas, a roast chicken and a huge pile of knives and forks in the centre of the table and told them to "dig in and help themselves". Everyone dived in and it was then that the noise level went up a gear as every voice struggled to be heard and they all talked over one another. It was so strange for Zoe – as an only child she had never seen anything like it. It was the type of family that she had always yearned for.

She was surprised that she didn't feel nervous about bringing Steve home but she knew that he accepted her for who she was, he didn't judge, and if her mother was having a bad day he probably wouldn't think anything of it.

Zoe's mother could be one of two ways; on a good day she could be on a high, gushing and welcoming, running around making tea and apologising because she had "no cake but she did have biscuits, chocolate-covered Rich Tea in fact", but on a bad day she could literally let you in the door without any greeting and you would spend the next hour sitting in silent discomfort, which she seemed to be unaware of. You never knew what you were going to get when you knocked on the door and that was why Zoe didn't visit as much as she ought to. The worst moodswing though was when she was on one of her rants against men. She still hadn't moved on from Zoe's father walking out the door on her. She was blindsided by anger and hatred and felt that all males on the planet were like that. She didn't leave the house too often and had few visitors – mostly just the community nurse who checked on her daily, and her brother and sister-in-law who were good to her. She preferred it that way, she got angsty being around people for too long.

Zoe had rung her mother first to tell her that she would be calling and that she would be bringing someone too. The news wasn't greeted with a reaction either way.

* * *

Zoe opened back the rusty half-height gate with difficulty. The long grass obviously hadn't been cut since the last time she had got a gardener to come out and tidy up her mother's weedy overgrown front lawn. The lichen-covered concrete-slab footpath had weeds shooting up through the cracks. She made a mental note to give him a call again. The front garden wasn't that big, certainly not how Zoe had thought of it as a child, but her mother didn't bother with it.

She stood with Steve by her side and rapped the brass salmon-shaped knocker on the teak door.

Her small thin mother answered the door in a hairy bottle-green cardigan that Zoe could remember her wearing when she was a child. There was more grey in her hair now with just a bit of auburn left at the ends in the few months since she had last seen her. She had obviously decided to give up colouring it. From looking at old photos of her from her twenties and thirties Zoe knew her mother had once taken a pride in her appearance. Zoe felt guilty then. She knew she really should visit more often.

"Hi, Mam, this is Steve."

"Pleased to meet you," said Steve.

"Steve." She pondered the name abstractedly. "Well, come in, don't stand outside in the cold."

She showed them into the 'good' room, although it was a long time since it was 'good'. It was a dark room with net curtains hanging inside the bay window and gold-sheen wallpaper. They sat down on the blue floral-patterned settee that clashed wildly with the orange shagpile carpet.

"So, Zoe – how have you been?"

Her mother was being overly formal and polite but Zoe supposed it was better than shouting at Steve because he happened to be male.

"Good thanks, Mam, busy in work."

"Oh."

"I brought you a few bits." Zoe opened a bag full of groceries including a cake, biscuits and some essentials like milk, tea, butter, coffee and bread because it was hit-or-miss whether her mother would actually have these.

"Thank you, Zoe." She made no effort to take them from her daughter.

Zoe took the initiative and packed away the milk and butter in the fridge, throwing out some out-of-date cartons and butter. She put the kettle on and called Steve to give her a hand to make the tea and slice the cake.

The gold-plated clock on the mantelpiece chimed as they sat drinking their tea and eating an M&S sponge cake in silence.

"Will I put on the TV for the two of you?" her mother asked her as if they were ten years of age.

"Sure, go ahead."

She turned on an old episode of *Murder She Wrote* and they watched Jessica Fletcher solving the puzzle again.

"How's Uncle Ed and Aunt Lydia?" asked Zoe.

"Good."

"How is Ed enjoying retirement?"

Her mother didn't answer, her eyes fixed on the TV screen.

Zoe checked her watch. She knew that after an hour they could go but there still was a good twenty minutes left.

After some general chit-chat, mostly on Zoe's part, and a few polite questions from Steve which didn't elicit any response from her mother, Zoe stood up and excused herself with promises that she wouldn't leave it so long the next time and she would call in again soon.

"I think he's very nice," Zoe's mother said out of the blue as they walked out into the hallway.

Zoe was amazed to get this seal of approval from her mother. They kissed goodbye and Zoe hugged her mother tight before they went back out across the broken footpath and stiff gate and got into Steve's car, her mother waving at them from behind the net curtain.

"Well, go on, you can be honest. Was it awful?" Zoe asked as Steve pulled out onto the road.

"Don't be silly Zoe, she was fine."

"She's bats, isn't she?"

"Not bats. Well, maybe a little . . . *detached*."

"*Detached* – mmmh, I like that description. I must remember that one. At least she liked you."

"How did you come to that conclusion considering she never even spoke to me?"

"She does that to everyone. But she said you were nice – that's a ringing endorsement if I ever heard one."

"Maybe we should go over again in a few weeks?"

"Really? You wouldn't mind?"

"Of course not, I could even sort out her garden – I'd say the neighbours are going mad – she's ruining the manicured gardens of suburbia."

And then Zoe knew it. He was 'The One'. He accepted her for who she was, her baggage, her strange mother and all. He didn't bat an eyelid.

"Look, I don't know if now is the right time but, well . . . I was wondering if . . . you want to move in with me and Dave?"

Her face lit up. "Really?"

"Well, yeah. You stay over every weekend anyway and I know it would be a bit of a commute from my house into the city every day, but I love being with you, Zoe, and I want to wake up beside you every day."

"And you won't mind sharing your bed every night?" she teased him gently.

"Who said anything about sharing a bed? You'll be taking the spare room!" he mocked.

For the first time in her life, Zoe felt safe and secure.

58

The day flew past in a whir of different family members visiting and chatting and it was only when they were finally on their own that Adam dared broach the subject that each of them knew had to be talked about sooner or later. They couldn't avoid it forever.

"Why did you do it, Emma? I couldn't have coped if anything had happened to you."

"I was so tired, Adam. I couldn't sleep, the pain was awful. It just all got too much, you know – I didn't mean to, I just wanted to escape my own head. I was so low, I felt so alone, I had lost Fionn and then you, and I just felt so worthless and full of self-hatred. So I was taking my tablets but they weren't helping at all so I drank the vodka and then I woke up here . . . I'm sorry."

"I'm sorry too. I let you down – I just couldn't take it any more."

"I know, Adam. I understand now. I locked you out and left you alone when you needed me. I didn't see your suffering, only my own. I just want to say now that I love you, I always have. I know it may not have seemed like it, the way I've been treating you, but I just hope you will be able to find it within your heart to forgive me . . ." She trailed off.

"There's nothing to forgive." He leant his head down to rest upon her chest.

They lay like that for a while before Adam spoke again.

"Emma, I still miss him desperately. It hurts so bloody much."

"I know," she said in almost a whisper.

"I keep going over and over what happened and just wondering if I had done anything differently, would things be different now? If I had braked coming up to the crossroads after seeing the first car go through . . . or if I had gone through faster. It drives me mad, all the endless combinations and permutations of scenarios and wondering what might have been."

"Adam, love, it wasn't your fault – I keep thinking the same thoughts myself – what if I hadn't gone out that day, what if I had stayed at home – but all they do is send you doolally and drive you demented."

This was the first time she had ever said this and the weight of what she was saying was felt by Adam.

"I'll never know if I could have done more, Em. But it all happened in a moment. There was no time to react."

She remained quiet; it was hard to hear what happened. It felt like an open wound just discussing it, she had to take it slowly and let each piece of hurt settle in before she could discuss it some more.

"There was nothing you could have done," she said then. "It was just chance. We were just so, so, unlucky, weren't we?" The unjustness of it all hit her again, a wave of unfairness washed up her body and she felt the anger rising after it once again, until it caught in her throat and tears began to flow.

Adam rubbed her hand.

"Do you think we'll ever be the same again?" she asked.

"I can't say that, Em, I don't know. Probably not, if I'm honest. Sometimes I miss him so much it feels like a physical longing to hold him, or I can't breathe with grief if I think about him."

"Me too – some days I couldn't even get out of bed with the pain. That's why I was so distant from you, because when I looked at you I saw Fionn. You were a constant reminder of him and it was too painful to be around you. I'm so sorry, but he looked so like you, you know."

"I know."

* * *

The next morning a counsellor came around to speak with Emma. Adam left them alone and went to get a coffee. He sat in the coffee dock with a few other lonely souls flicking through magazines. He mulled over the events of the last few days which seemed light-years away from what went before. The grief that had pushed them apart had now drawn them together again.

The counsellor was satisfied that, after all Emma had been through, she had reached rock-bottom and with Adam by her side she would now start to heal. He had advised them to seek couples therapy or even go alone to get help with their bereavement.

Her doctor was happy with her recovery so he allowed her to be discharged. Together they went back to their home.

* * *

It felt strange being back in their house. Emma felt as though she was looking at it with fresh eyes, new eyes, almost like the first day that they had got the keys and moved in here.

They went to bed together that night and slept wrapped in each other's arms – once a familiar routine, they slotted easily back into it again. The touch of his skin was still the same and she was surprised at how much she had missed it.

Adam lay awake for a long time, while Emma still under the influence of her tablets, slept heavily beside him. It was a new beginning for them.

Epilogue

In a garden children ran and played, a mother brought out a homemade birthday cake with lemon buttercream icing in the shape of a butterfly. She bent down to light the four candles but had to do it a few times as the flame kept being extinguished by the gentle breeze. Then the children and adults all stood dutifully around the table while her four-year-old daughter beamed as everyone sang 'Happy Birthday'. When it was time for the little girl to blow out her candles, her brother barged in to do it for her.

"Let Ava do it herself, Jonathan!" the mother chided.

"She's not able to – I have to show her," her bossy older brother replied.

Ava let her brother show off to the crowd as he helped her blow out the four candles with over-exaggerated breaths. The cake was cut and served up to everyone. The children had to be harangued to pose for some photos and shouted 'cheese', revealing big toothy grins before running off again, weaving in and out through the other guests like a train as they chased each other with the younger children trying to keep up with the older ones. They zigzagged around sun chairs, prams, buggies and babies sleeping in their grandparents' arms and a long wooden table laden with treats, leafy salads and bowls heaped with ripened fruit, a jug of homemade lemonade and a cake stand stacked with pink and yellow cupcakes. White, willowy butterflies flitted through the hot air and honeybees could be heard buzzing about their work.

A man with a newborn in a sling was feeding some bits of burger to a chocolate-brown dog while chatting to the host who was turning sausages over on the barbecue, the smell of charred meat wafting in the summer air. Chinese paper lanterns hung from trees billowing in the breeze.

The mother returned inside to the welcome coolness of the house to get more food. She opened the fridge, took out a bag of salad and shook it into a bowl before tossing it around with some balsamic vinegar and olive-oil dressing. She grabbed a packet of ice-creams and a bottle of chilled white wine and put them onto a tray with the salad. Passing back out through the hallway, she glanced at a photo in a silver frame of a baby lying on his front, body raised up by his arms, his smile beaming at the camera. She stood momentarily just looking. She smiled wistfully at the photo of her baby. It was just like he was smiling back at her. At moments like this her heart literally ached with wishing she could hold him in her arms again and he could be included in the celebrations, running around with all the other children.

"Mammy, mammy, where are the ice-creams! We all want the ice-creams! We are soooo hot and hungry!" the birthday girl exclaimed dramatically from the doorstep. Her mother snapped back into the present, to where she was needed.

"Coming, love, I'll be there in a second."

Balancing the tray in one hand, she kissed the tip of her index finger and planted it firmly against the glass of the smiling baby before walking back out into the garden.

If you enjoyed
In a Moment by Caroline Finnerty
why not try exclusive chapters 1 and 2 from her
fourthcoming title
A Small Hand in Mine also published by Poolbeg?
Here's a sneak preview . . .

A Small Hand in Mine

Her decision would tear her family apart

CAROLINE
FINNERTY

1

"A mother is she who can take the place of all others but whose place no one else can take."
Cardinal Mermillod

I had always thought that she was selfish for doing what she did. I know that sounds harsh but, if she had done things differently, then everything could have been very different. I often wondered, if she had known the outcome, the way that it would all play out, would she still have made the same decision? It was on my mind a lot, at the time, the questions spinning around and around inside my head, especially when I was left alone with my idle thoughts. I suppose with everything going on, it was only natural. There was just no escaping it though, no matter how much I tried.

The Tube jerked to a stop and the doors slid apart. No one was getting off, yet more people managed to squash on. It never ceased to amaze me how, just when you thought it was impossibly packed, there was always room for one more person. The crowd moved back to make way for the new people, causing the crotch of the man standing in front of me to move even closer towards my face. I turned my head to the side and rested it against the scraped and graffitied plastic window. The rhythmic motion of the carriages snaking along through the tunnels made me feel sleepy. I closed my eyes and listened to the voice broadcast the stops as I did every morning. Finally it was Green Park and I stood up, feeling light-headed as I did. The man sitting beside me closed his book so that a grubby bookmark with a furry monkey's head stuck out over the top of the pages. It was at odds with his pinstripe suit and leather briefcase – like he had robbed it from his child in a hurry. He stood up to let me out before sitting back down again. I grabbed onto the pole to steady myself. Disgustingly, it was still sticky with sweat from the last person. I squeezed through the small gaps between bodies until I got to the doors. Some people hopped off to let me out before getting back on again. I stepped onto the platform and made my way to the escalator. A wall of warm air hit me full force in the face as I walked and I thought I might be sick. Beads of sweat broke out all across my forehead and I could feel my mouth beginning to water. *No way, not here.* I ascended on the escalator from deep down in the bowels of the city, gliding past posters advertising films, books and shampoos that claimed to reduce split ends by 52%.

When I finally emerged into the cool morning air, I breathed it deep into my lungs and felt better instantly as my body started to cool down again. The low sunlight was glinting off the shop windows on the street and burning a golden trail on the footpath in front of me. The gallery was only a five-minute walk from the Tube station. The London traffic inched forward on the road beside me, the roofs of the black cabs sticking out amongst the melée of cars like hard-shelled beetles. Some people hate this city – they hate its relentless pace, how it sucks you in and then when it's finished with you, after you've given it your all, you're broken, you're spent, and it just chews you up and spits you back out again – but I love everything about it. I feel alive here, the endless possibilities of things to do, the centuries of history fronting every pavement, the streets always full – you never feel alone here.

Soon I was at the gallery. I pushed the door open. Nat was already in.

"Morning."

"Hi, darling."

I walked over and lifted the strap of my yellow satchel over my head before putting it onto the white contemporary Formica desk. Our reception desk was the only piece of furniture in the gallery, which was all stark white walls with black-and-white photos inside black frames and honey-wood floors.

"Want a coffee – I've just boiled the kettle?" Nat asked.

"Nah – better not."

I turned on the computer and waited for it to boot itself up while she went into the kitchen and came back out a minute later with a mug of instant coffee clasped between her hands. I had brought the mug back for her from Majorca a few years back. It was one of those tacky ones with the caption *Someone I Know Went to Majorca and All They Brought Me Back Was This Mug*.

Nat and I practically ran the Jensen Photography Gallery ourselves. We displayed the work of several high-profile photographers – they paid us a small rent for the space and a commission for any work we sold. The owner, a lady called Tabitha Jensen, spent most of her time living *la dolce vita* in her villa in Tuscany. She only came to check up on us a handful of times a year. We emailed her a weekly report with sales figures and a summary of what was happening in the gallery and she was happy with that.

"What's wrong?" Nat said as she combed her fingers through her thick auburn hair before tying it up loosely with a bobbin so that the front of it stuck up bumpily like waves on a choppy sea.

"Nothing."

"C'mon, I know you too well."

"It's Ben," I sighed. "He's like a dog with a bone."

"Is he still harping on at you about going back to Ireland?"

She said 'Ireland' in the way that all English people said it. I have always liked the way their accent made it sound – like it was a place that you might *actually* want to go to.

She perched herself on the end of the desk with her two hands wrapped around her chipped mug.

"Uh-huh. He just won't let it go." It had been eight years since I was home – I hadn't been back since my younger brother Patrick's wedding. And I wouldn't have even gone to that except that I might as well have severed whatever thin ties with my family were left altogether if I hadn't. I had got a flight to Dublin that morning and flew straight back home to London first thing the following morning, less than the twenty-four hours later.

"He's never even met them, has he?"

"Nope."

"Well, maybe now would be a good time – you can't stay away forever."

"You sound just like Ben . . ."

"Well, he just wants to meet them – find out more about where you come from –"

"I've told him all he needs to know – why does he need to meet them?"

"Come on, Kate – stop being unreasonable."

"He knows what happened – I'm not keeping anything a secret from him."

"He's not asking for that much – he just wants to meet your family!"

"He reckons I have 'unresolved issues'." I sighed wearily at the phrase Ben was so fond of quoting at me.

"Well, you do!" She laughed, showing her teeth. She had good teeth, straight for the main part and just slightly overlapping on the bottom. Most people would probably get them straightened but I thought they suited her better like that.

I started to laugh then too.

Nat had known me a long time, longer than Ben even. We'd met when I first moved to London at seventeen years of age. I had finished my Leaving Cert and then the very next day I packed my rucksack and took the boat to Holyhead. I would have gone sooner but Dad wouldn't let me leave school without having done my Leaving. As soon as the ferry pulled out from Dun Laoghaire harbour, I felt nothing but relief. Not even a twinge of sadness or regret. From Holyhead I took a very long and slow bus down to London because I couldn't afford the train fare. We travelled through Welsh tunnels carved out of rock, chocolate-box villages and acres and acres of tumbledown country estates. For the first few nights after arriving in London, I stayed in a hostel full of American backpackers and students who were inter-railing around Europe. They would be comatose in the bunk beds every morning after only getting into bed a few hours previously, while I got up early to look for a job. I would try and make myself look somewhat presentable in the hostel's dimly lit, six-inch-square bathroom mirror before heading out onto the streets to start my hunt. I had a very limited amount of money to tide me over. I needed to get work quickly before the money I had saved from my part-time job in the local supermarket at home ran out. I didn't have a clue about what kind of job I wanted to do – I was just so glad to be away from home that I would have taken anything. I had dropped into a few of the large department stores on spec but they weren't currently hiring. So after a few days of not getting anywhere, I decided my best bet would be to register with a recruitment agency.

As I was walking down the street to the address that I'd been given, I walked past a gallery with a beautiful taupe-and-green-striped awning outside. I noticed a handwritten sign in the bay window, which read *Now Hiring*. Deciding that I had nothing to lose, I pushed back the door. It had one of those old-fashioned bells that gave a *trrrrrrring* when the door was opened.

A tall, muscular girl stood up from behind the counter. She looked to be about the same age as myself. She had the kind of build that women described as 'striking' often have. Her height was further emphasised by her hair, which was backcombed several inches off the top of her head. She was wearing a black scoop-necked bodysuit tucked into a tight stonewashed denim skirt which laced like a corset up the back. Her make-up was dramatic, with heavily kohl-rimmed eyes accentuating cool blue eyes with vivid flecks of green. My eyes travelled down her body and landed on a pair of scuffed Doc Martens. Her style was way beyond anything I had ever seen at home – suddenly I felt self-conscious in my baggy jeans and frumpy sweatshirt. My hair didn't have a style – it was just dead straight and hung down at both sides of my face like a pair of curtains framing a stage. I had only ever seen people dressed like her on TV. If I had worn those clothes back home in Ireland, let alone the hair, I would have been the talk of the town. I had felt intimidated by her. I wanted to turn around and run back out the door again.

She looked at me expectantly, waiting for me to speak.

"I'm here about the job?" I said timidly.

"You Irish?"

Her accent was pure London. I had only been there for a few days at that stage but already my ear was starting to distinguish the different accents. She looked at me quizzically with her head tilted to the side as she tried to assess me.

"Yeah."

"The owner's not 'ere at the minute – hang on and I'll give her a call . . ."

"Okay." I stood there, idly glancing around the gallery while I listened to her talk on the phone.

"Yeah, yeah, yeah okay. Got it. Byyyye!" She hung up the phone and turned back to me. "She says it's fine with her, once I'm happy with you. The name's Nat – what's yours?"

"Kate," I said.

"Well, Kate, looks like you've got yourself a job."

"What? Don't you want me to do an interview or something?" I had only been enquiring and it felt like the job had just been thrust upon me. And even though I was desperate for work, I wasn't sure I wanted to work with her. I didn't even know what kind of work I would be doing.

"Nah, no need!" She waved her hand.

"Okay, well . . . I suppose I should say thank you."

"Do you smoke?"

"No," I said, feeling instantly like a Goody Two-Shoes. "I gave up a few months back." Then I added, so she'd know I wasn't completely square: "Because I couldn't afford them."

"No worries – here, can you hold the fort while I run round to the shop and get some fags?"

"Em . . . okay," I said, looking around at the high gallery walls wondering what I had let myself in for.

"Listen, Kate, there's no need to look so scared – I'm not going to bite you, love." Then her face broke into a big grin and I started to relax.

I knew then that we were going to get along just fine together.

It was such an eye-opener for an Irish girl from Ballyrobin, coming to London. It was so depressing at home – both in my house and in the country in general. All I seem to remember when I think back on those years is grey. Grey weather. Grey classrooms. Grey people. There was a whole generation of people who left Ireland for London in the eighties and I was a decade late. Just as I was leaving, the economy was starting to pick up.

People were buying new cars and they weren't ashamed of it. There were jobs to be had now and for the first time in decades expats were starting to come back home to work. But I went in the opposite direction. My dad couldn't understand why I wanted to emigrate at a time when things were finally starting to go Ireland's way. In the eighties he had spent a lot of time worrying if his kids would have to leave the country like almost all young people at that time. So when it looked like things were on the up, he was relieved. For the first time since the eighties there were jobs to be had and not just in Dublin. But it wasn't about the work – it was never about the work.

I know Ireland is a different place now of course – I can see it's changed whenever I meet other Irish people or watch the news. But London felt like the place that I belonged in as soon as I arrived. Within days of coming over here, I felt more at home than I had in my seventeen years in Ireland. The anonymity was a revelation. People wore what they wanted to wear. People didn't whisper wherever you walked – they didn't talk in scandalized tones because the Gardaí had brought you home last night because they caught you necking back some snakebite up in the playground.

Nat turned out to be the best friend that I could have asked for. When she heard I was staying in a hostel to save money, she invited me to sleep on her mum's sofa until I found somewhere to live. She introduced me to all her friends so they quickly became my circle too. After a week in her mum's house, I found a poky two-roomed flat in Clapham. Although there was only one bedroom, Nat decided to move in with me. We shared a room with two single beds and not much space for anything else. The paint was peeling off the walls and there were black mildew spots in the corners of the ceiling. The seventies furniture was looked as though it was taken from the landlord's family home and he was just looking for somewhere to get rid of it. There was too much of it to be functional. A huge sideboard was squashed into the hallway so that you had to turn sideways to walk past it and, even though it was only a one-bed-roomed flat, the long rectangular table in the kitchen could sit eight people around it comfortably.

Yes, the flat was tiny, but we had so much fun there. I could go out when I wanted to and come home at whatever hour of the morning I chose. There was no-one banging on my door calling me for Mass on a Sunday morning. We would go home from work in the gallery and then we would usually head straight out to a party or a club or have friends over to ours. We were out almost every night of the week. For the first time in my life I had freedom. I didn't have the weight of home dragging me down. Leaving was, without doubt, the best decision I ever made.

London is where I belong now.

2

At six o'clock we turned out the lights in the gallery to head home. We said bye to one another and Nat put her bag into the basket on the front of her bike and cycled off while I walked in the other direction to the Tube. It was a warm summer's evening. Joggers overtook me on the pavement before cutting into the park. People spilled out of the pubs and onto the streets, keen to make the most of the evening sun. I weaved my way around where they stood on the path, beer bottles in one hand and taking long drags on cigarettes with the other. Their laughter carried on the summer air.

I arrived in the door to the smell of curry. Even though I had bought the ingredients for it myself the day before, now the smell of the coconut milk just made me want to hurl. I stood at the door into the kitchen, looking at Ben's broad back as he stood in front of the cooker. He was angling the chopping board and tossing green peppers into the frying pan. Our kitchen was so poky: a few small grey-painted presses, a sink, washing machine, cooker, fridge and a small table and chairs was it. We had a few pots of herbs growing on the windowsill – they were Ben's babies, not mine.

"*Euuuggggh!*"

He turned around and smiled at me from where he was stirring the pan.

"Don't tell me – the smell is making you sick?"

I pinched my nose and nodded my head. He left the pan and came over and wrapped me in a hug. This was without doubt my favourite part of the day – when I would come in wrecked from a long day and Ben would put his strong arms around me and all my worries and stresses would just fade away.

Ben was a primary school teacher so he was always the first one home. He loved his job. I knew most of the children in his class by name myself, just from listening to him talking about them. I was spoiled rotten because he usually had dinner ready and waiting for me when I got in every evening.

"How's Baby Pip doing?" he asked, nuzzling at my neck.

"I think I started to feel kicks today – it's so faint though, it's hard to know."

We called her Pip because when I had first found out that I was pregnant the book said at five weeks she was the size of a pip and somehow it had stuck even though it was a bit cheesy.

He placed his hand on my tummy. "I can't feel anything."

"Well, *duh* – the movements are only tiny at this stage plus she –"

"Or he," Ben interjected.

"Or he – isn't moving at the moment. It's a girl anyway."

"How do you know?" He started to laugh.

"I just do."

"Please can we find out the sex at our next scan?"

"No! I told you already, I don't want to find out – but I know I'm right."

He held me at arm's length and stared at my tummy.

"You're getting a distinct bump."

"Yeah, I know – I haven't got long left in these trousers. I had to open the top button this afternoon when I was sitting down behind the desk."

"Well, I'd say that looked well! Although you could pretend it's some new form of artistic expression."

Later that evening as I lay in bed on my own I could hear Ben laughing away on his own at the TV in the living room. The sounds were muffled as they travelled through the walls to our bedroom. We lived in what was all originally one house but in the eighties the owners had decided to convert their upstairs bedrooms into an apartment and rent it out. It was a red-bricked terraced Victorian house. We had two bedrooms, a galley kitchen-cum-living area and a small bathroom. The rent was typical of London – big money, small place. We were saving up to buy our own place but then I had found out that I was pregnant so we decided to put our plans on hold for a while until after Baby Pip arrived. There must have been something particularly funny on because Ben was howling with laughter below.

Ben was definitely the smiley one in our relationship. He was always in good form – he had what you might describe as 'a sunny disposition'. It wasn't that I was a grumpy person but I just wasn't constantly in good form like he was – nothing ever seemed to get him down or to send him into a rage like me. Everyone loved him as soon as they met him – he was just one of those people. And he always knew how to pull me out of a mood. I was fascinated whenever we were out together, watching how everyone automatically migrated towards him. I would hover somewhere on the periphery, staring, taking it all in. Ben saw the good in everyone whereas I was a lot more cynical. I tried not to be but I couldn't help it. I think that was why he wouldn't let the whole 'trip to Ireland' thing go – he wanted to make everyone happy just like him and he thought that a trip home would do that for me too. It was like the baby had put a deadline on it – he wanted it resolved before Pip came along. But it was never going to be that simple – eighteen years of anger and hurt can't just be reset with a quick visit home. I knew he meant well though.

I placed my two hands flat on my bare, swollen stomach. I could definitely feel Pip moving. I knew I wasn't just imagining it. It was such a surreal feeling to think that there was actually a baby in there, growing away, doing its thing, doing everything that it needed to do and knowing when to do it. The pregnancy was going well – except for the nausea, which still wasn't showing any signs of abating even though I was just at the halfway mark. I had been assured by all in the know that once I entered the second trimester the morning sickness would go and I'd get a new burst of energy but they were all liars because I still felt like shit.

The whole thing was making me think a lot though. I wasn't prepared for that side of it – it had brought a lot of old memories back to the surface. And Ben wasn't helping by constantly banging on about it. I had known this was what would happen and that was why it had taken me a while to come round to the idea of having a baby with him. Ben had been broody for a long time – he was the one who would stop a mother on the footpath to coo over her infant whereas I just saw sticky hands and runny noses. While I had always wanted children, it was more a case of 'one day' so it came as a bit of a shock when I had found out that I was pregnant. But when I saw the two pink lines on the test stick, I'd got really excited – the time was right, Ben loved me and I loved him.

Ben came up to bed soon after and spooned me from behind. He pushed up my pyjama top to put his two hands on the skin of my stomach and Baby Pip started up again just like she knew that her daddy was there. I turned over to face him and smiled.

"She knows you're here."

"Really?"

"Yeah, she's started kicking again."

"When will I be able to feel them?"

"Not for a few more weeks according to the books."

He propped his head up on his elbow. "So when are we going to Ireland?"

"Not tonight, Ben," I said testily.

"Come on, Kate!"

"Soon."

"You're nearly five months pregnant – your family don't even know. You need to tell them – I've never even met them for Christ's sake!"

"I will tell them."

"When?"

"I'll ring Dad."

"You can't keep on carrying this baggage with you. It's not good for you or the baby."

"Will you stop going on about it?"

"You can't keep running away from it."

"I'm not running away from anything!"

"Oh Kate – you're infuriating!"

"Please, can we leave it for tonight? I feel like crap – I'm exhausted."

"All right, all right, but you need to face up to your demons sooner or later." He sighed.

Blah, blah, blah. I turned away so my back faced towards him and I felt him do the same on the other side.